I0666952

MUD AND STARS
25 STORIES

DAX XENOS

American Visionary Artists
Lexington, Kentucky USA

MUD AND STARS

Copyright © 2018 by Dax Xenos

Published by:
American Multimedia Publishers
P.O. Box 365
Lexington, KY 40588
U. S. A.

"To A Lady I Once Knew," originally published International Library of Poetry, 2004.
"The Hunt," originally published in the Austin American-Statesman, October 31, 1996.
"Death of a Duke," originally published O. Henry Awards Stories 1989.
"Miami Beach Blow-Up," originally published in Easyriders, August 1985.
"An Irresponsible Reptile," originally published in Joint Endeavor, Winter 1984-85.
"A Moment at Home," originally published in Joint Endeavor, Fall 1983.
"Rare Sonnets Surface in Prison," originally published in Joint Endeavor, Fall 1983.

Cover and book design by Banning K. Lary.
Original drawings by: David Zeigler, Duffy Duggan, Frank Albertson.

Library of Congress Cataloging-in-Publication Data
Xenos, Dax 1955-, Lary, Banning Kent, 1949–
Mud and Stars / Dax Xenos, Trade Paperback Edition
An American Multimedia Publishers Book
ISBN No.: 978-1-885832-88-7 1. Fiction 2. Short Stories 3. Poetry
Registered U. S. Copyright Office, case 1-6666035101

Printed in the United States of America
By American Multimedia Publishers, Lexington, KY 40588
First printing June 2018

10 9 8 7 6 5 4 3 2 1

*"Two men looked out through the same prison bars,
one saw mud and one saw stars."*

**– Frederick Langbridge
(1849–1922)**

PERSPECTIVE

"...for there is nothing either good or bad but thinking makes it so."
— Shakespeare, *Hamlet*, Act II, Scene 2

Short stories are stories which can be told short and poems are those flashes of inspiration one cannot ignore. Spielberg has said God does not scream but whispers, and when one becomes attuned to the Voice, one must be loyal or lose it. My father once told me if you don't capture these gossamer visions, the source closes. This deprivation to those who thirst forces discipline and heightens awareness, as you never know when the ideas may come.

You recieve a captivating notion and stop whatever your are doing to apply words on any scrap of paper close by. If you are driving you pull over to the side of the road. If it wakes you out of a dead sleep, you get up and go to the computer. Absent paper, you scrawl on a cocktail napkin or your hand. You capture the plot, the essence of a character or the voice you will tell your story through. If you don't, these gifts will not come for a while. The source will punish you for disloyalty to your sworn resolve. Be patient and attentive and the brass ring of precious inspiration will come around again and you grab it the first time.

Man's intellect distinguishes him from other life forms, its origination still inexplicable from neuroscientists at the edge. The mind is not the brain, but biochemical impulses in our nervous system said to be responsible for thoughts. Over time and through constant practice, a writer hones his skills by translating these impulses into words, phrases, sentences and paragraphs in the attempt to render intelligible the ineffable. A lot of it depends upon one's chosen point of view and attitude. Does one look out through the barred window and focus on the mud, or elevate the eyes and glimpse the stars?

This anthology has been wrought over the past several decades while creating other books and educational documentaries. Some of these stories have been published in magazines, while most have lain fallow waiting to be included in this collection. They include: *Sam,* a story about a great dog. The title for *An Irresponsible Reptile* is a metaphor for a Latin Consul revenged by an unlikely source. In *A Moment at Home* a new inmate gets a lesson in prison etiquette. In *Ablution* a father says good-bye to his sons at their favorite fishing spot. *Miami Beach Blow-Out* is a parody of the hard guy novels. *Rare Sonnets Surface in Prison* is a satire about long lost poems of William Shakespeare. *Retribution Day* is a vengeance tale where a terrorist receives his just rewards in a public execution.

In *The Hunt* a junior professor evens the score

during Halloween in Austin. *Cyberdoc Squabble* derives from an actual discussion between "physicians" who argue semantics and professional acumen in a chat room. My PEN winning story, *Death of A Duke* describes how power struggles on the cell block once came to a violent conclusion. In *Me and Bob* the reader questions who is really in charge as the dog tells the story. In *Baggage* three captives are forced to carry contraband across the Rio Grande. A hack writer in *Baby Shoes Never Worn* reminiscences about Hemingway's prowess. *The Three Graces* is a priceless statue a jilted husband retrieves from his ex. *Wiznet* is a dancer at a Washington DC party who might be more than she appears. In *The Walk* a bigot learns a valuable lesson about himself during a stroll across the tracks.

In *Peripeteia* (a fancy word meaning reversal of fortune) greedy heirs get more than they planned for thanks to the perspicuity of the aging matriarch. *The Neighbor* is a mysterious stranger who has the neighbors talking when he arrives in an old hearse. In *Bledsoe*, Hangtown will never be the same once they try to string up the town Casanova. *Mariposa* is a strange girl with two hearts looking for a friend. *The Plan* is a winding humorous tale how things can go awry when a postman tries to kill his neighbor's pet alligator. Things get rough during the prison volleyball tournament in *The Championship*. In *The Boy with the Golden Shell* a young boy is aided through a difficult time at home. *Falala* is the story about a young girl in a foreign land coming of age and her generous benefactor. And, in *The Donor,* a loving father makes the ultimate sacrifice for his family.

I've thrown in a few poems too. Poems are tough to write, tougher to read. You can encapsulate a love relationship (p. 168), a dream sequence (p. 106) or even a person's whole life in a poem (page 144). William Faulker suggested to the *Paris Review* in 1956 that every novelist first wants to write poetry. But when he finds he can't, he "then tries the short story, which is the most demanding form after poetry. And, failing at that, only then does he take up novel writing."

I've written novels too and while I don't really agree with Faulkner on this, I appreciate where he is coming from and his noble nod to the poets. Poems to me are those flashes of inspiration which seize the mind until you write them down. It's hard to sit down with the intention of writing a poem and have it be any good, while hundreds of purposeful hours at the desk are exigent to crafting stories and novels.

Faulkner also said "there is no good writing, only rewriting," and with this I perfectly agree. And editing.

I do not expect everyone to love, or even like, every story. You may find some of these stories to be crass, profane or even ridiculous. Then again, you may find something that makes you think, moves you to tears or at least causes a chuckle or two.

Enough said, let's get to the stories.

Dax Xenos, June 2018
daxxenosbooks.com

*This book is dedicated to my family, my source
of joy, inspiration and discipline.*

THE STORIES

Gray Day

Took a jog

in the smog

walked my dog.

SAM

*"If you pick up a starving dog and make him prosperous
he will not bite you. This is the principal difference
between a dog and man."*
— Mark Twain

Had it not snowed that cold November day
almost a decade ago, I never would have seen the abandoned puppy some heartless fool had left to God's mercy off Route 55 outside of Lebanon, Kentucky. I was on
sabbatical to scrub civilization from my head and receive
therapy from the stars and fresh winds that have blown
since time immemorial ahead of a cold front running east.

Nothing is as soothing as whipping past endless
miles of land covered with pine and poplar, land unspoiled

by even the slightest notion of a developer. Cover the sun-bleached grays and luscious greens with a thin blanket of white snow and the scene is pure magic, like God had dropped a vast silken bed sheet to drape the landscape as evidence of His personal promise that worldly things would some how turn out for the good.

I stopped to water a fence post, having not seen so much as a taillight since sunset, when a black spot on the snow wiggled in the distance. Now larger as I walked closer, my instincts decided the spot was warm-blooded, perhaps a mammal. Two brown eyes caught my headlights and burned with a fire that ignited something deep inside me. Without a second thought, I slipped off my coat and wrapped it around the pup and carried him back to my car.

I found my classic 1976 El Dorado convertible the same way I found Sam, weather-worn and beat-up along a roadside. I was driving some little Jap import sheathed in steel so thin it would dent if you looked at it too hard and made sounds like a weed eater if you gave it too much gas. I swore I would ditch it at the first opportunity. When the bearded old codger ambled from his trailer, I knew we could cut a deal.

His name was Erasmus Miller and he had maintained his outpost for three decades as a protest against runaway technology he said was "designed to swallow a man in his own ignorance." He was a small man, wiry and flexible as pignut hickory. He sold varmint skulls decorated with pop rivets, snake skin belts, stuffed raccoons, fox tail vests, an assortment of oddities he had crafted out of an environment that gave up nothing without a fight.

Erasmus freely poured shots of Black Jack into jelly jars as I checked the points and plugs and tinkered with the carburetor. His interest in the "old gas-hog" that didn't run faded in direct proportion to the falling level of caramel liquid in the square bottle, as did his appreciation rise for the dependable vehicle that brought me by chance to his lonely backroad hideaway. I unclogged the jets with a generous dab of Jack on the corner of my shirt tail, freed the choke plate and adjusted the mixture. When it roared to life, Erasmus said the old Caddy and I were destined to be together and traded it even for my tinny foreign sedan.

He smiled widely when I drove away, like I had relieved him of a great burden, though I knew I had gotten the best of the bargain. In my mind it was like trading a pastured gelding for Secretariat.

My orphan pup was no thoroughbred. He was a black-and-white hound of dubious ancestry, shepherd mixed with American pit bull terrier and a dash of retriever that added silky curls to his ears. I called him Sam because he was a true American, a melting pot of the best of many bloodlines that combined to create a formidable package.

Sam slept at the foot of my bed in the modest house I maintain on a forty-acre farm outside of Paris. It's not a fancy place, but has big uncluttered rooms and a wide porch that runs around four walls made of native fieldstone. Thick rough-hewn tulip poplar beams span the ceiling under lengths of first cut tongue-and-groove pine. It's a simple solid house, built on a small rise that affords a panoramic view of the countryside, perfect for a man on his own who prefers thoughts to money and privacy to fast empty talk that never amounts to anything.

I found it pointless to do any landscaping and left the yard to the designs of nature. Abundant deer roam freely over the property, assuring any efforts spent planting bushes or raising vegetables came to naught. Deer have a predilection for soft cultivated leaves and tender shoots, and the day you wake up and find your garden shredded you learn a valuable lesson about how things operate and what things are best left alone.

Sam was a born guard dog with instincts of a desert reptile, yet with the kindred compassion of warm blood. He never hurt the deer but sure scared the hell out of them, dashing back and forth inside a herd, nipping front hooves or leaping up against their sides to push them away with his paws. Routing deer was good sport to Sam and provided me with solid evidence that he was my partner in managing our domain.

The spring after I found Sam I planted a garden out back within view of my kitchen window. I had been preparing the soil for years, tilling in vegetable scraps, lawn clippings and fire place ash in anticipation of one day mastering the deer problem. The plot was purposefully located over my drain field to reduce water needs. I elevated the garden into beds held in by weathered railroad ties and planted a Spartan mix of beefsteak tomatoes, yellow crook-necked squash, corn, radishes and a variety of herbs. A tomato plucked at the peak of flavor is well worth the trouble as is steamed fresh squash, or lamb chops seasoned with just pinched rosemary.

In the mornings Sam would clean up whatever was left of my breakfast, then trot off to take his constitutional. I kept a bowl of dry Purina next to his water on the back porch for him to snack on during the day, but at night Sam wanted to feast. Year round, bright summer sun or overcast February night, Sam knew when it was supper time. He would find me, wherever I was, in the den pounding away or off on the perimeter clearing brush, and would dog me relentlessly until I gave him his due for being a faithful servant and best friend.

And thank God he did.

I was removing some cockspur hawthorn with a chain saw one cool December evening about dark when Sam came from behind and grabbed my shirt in his jaws.

"Stop it, Sam," I said. But he didn't stop and kept pulling. "Fool dog. Let me finish this and I'll feed you. It won't be five minutes, I swear."

Sam persisted, his teeth notched into the flannel, his paws steadfast in the dirt and bluegrass. I turned off my chain saw bent upon delivering a severe reprimand when I heard the rattles. My efforts had uncovered an unseen nest of timber rattlesnakes, the mama curled and ready to strike. I backed away in the direction Sam was pulling me, lowering the long metal tongue of my chain saw like a shield. Mama uncoiled into a biting lance in a split second. I can still hear her fangs ringing against the steel blade.

I had been marinating a big Porterhouse and threw it over charcoal after pumping several shells through the breech of my trusty Winchester to eradicate the trouble. Sam looked surprised when he got the big T-bone with half the meat still attached. If he realized he had done something special that day, Sam didn't show it. He had just done what he was supposed to do. I had saved him once and he had saved me. We were even.

Sam also fished like an equal. I developed a pond out back from a natural topographical depression and lined the bottom with clay. I borrowed a neighbor's herd and spread hay a foot deep over the clay. When the hay was gone, the cattle had hard-packed the clay so well it held the spring rains year round. I stocked the pond with enough brim and crappie to balance my annual take with their procreation and have never since had to run into town for food when the cupboards got bare.

Sam thought it odd when I skewered a worm on a hook and dangled a line from the cane pole in the water at the end of my little wooden dock. But once he got the taste of beer-battered crappie, it all made sense. Sam noticed the crappie would surface for cornmeal scattered on the water. He would watch them feed, still as a stone, forepaws curled over the end of the pressure-treated fir. Sam would never take the first one. He waited for the big one. At the right instant, Sam would leap, catch the crappie in his mouth, swim it over to the shore and drop it up on the bank. If it tried to flap its way back to water, Sam would hold it with a paw, or flip it up higher, much like a cat would tease a mouse.

Sam was also an excellent bird dog, though unorthodox, as he would crouch rather than point, then spring forward and out dash the other men's dogs to retrieve felled game. If it was ducks, Sam would wait in the blind and leap when he saw one fall, dog paddling out through the reeds, his eyes keen on the floating bird past the decoys. We'd gather around a wood fire, swap stories and melt big blocks of paraffin in oil drums, then dip the limp ducks in the hot wax so their pin feathers would rip away in sheets after the wax cooled in the marsh water.

There's a lot to be said about the camaraderie of men on a hunt with their dogs, of the rough talk and tribal intelligence that reduces the most civilized of us to a primal common denominator. Nothing will recover a man to himself quicker than trading a corner office for a duck blind, or a Hickey-Freeman suit for jeans and a cotton flannel shirt. All the money in the world can't buy the sensation of that first drawn breath in a pine forest on a cool clear morning or that first tug on a fly rod when standing in a backwoods stream.

Sam knew all this without having to think about

it, and could explain it more eloquently with a low growl or a glance than any human could in a hundred pages of written words. Sam was aware of certain subtleties of the human condition that escape a lot of people. Things like waiting to eat until everyone is served, or allowing another person to go first, or being willing to sacrifice himself to save another. Sam practiced common courtesy to his fellow creatures and that, in my book, made him a first-rate soul despite the imperfections that finally did him in.

After the last mass of cold air stalled in its trek down from the Arctic and rains began to release wildflowers along the roadways, the big spring moon exerted its pull on warm-blooded creatures everywhere. Atop the rocky ridge outside Paris, Sam listened to the haunting melodies howled by every dog within earshot. He sat at attention emitting sympathetic groans, his head cocked side-to-side, until a particular voice made him take his feet. He'd go to the edge of the porch, add his rich baritone to the cacophony and wait.

About the third spring Sam began to ramble. The other dogs came for him in the night and where he went I'll never know for sure, though it must have been far and involved females in heat. One year Bill Grimes told me he saw Sam west of Lexington heading toward Versailles. Another year Eliza Elkins swore it was Sam in a pack of mixed breeds who rustled a chicken from her hen house in Mt. Sterling. Reports in later years placed Sam in Cynthiana, Carlisle, Clintonville, even over at the Blue Licks battlefield twenty-two miles away.

No matter where he went or what he did, Sam always came back. It might be days or weeks later when Sam would drag himself up the gravel road, drink his fill at the bowl and crash smooth out. He'd sleep for two or three days, rising only to gulp some more water or nibble at the dry food. He'd dream and twitch during the night and sometimes would howl at the top of his lungs in a trance, or moan laying on his side with his eyes closed. And sometimes Sam would come back hurt.

I learned to look him over real good while he slept. He'd receive nasty gashes around his neck and on his flanks and I'd clean them with peroxide and dress them with a healing salve. I often had to stitch the bigger wounds closed until they got a grip. One year Sam limped in so badly I took him to a vet for an x-ray. Little dots stood out around the bones of his back legs and were pronounced inoperable. The vet said to remove the buckshot might cause more trouble than he already had. Maybe it would slow him down some, the vet said. And it did until the next spring, until that last spring, when Sam didn't make it home.

That was over a year ago and I keep hoping to see him limp up the drive toward the house. I fill his bowl every morning with fresh water and set out dry food, but it stays there until rot sets in from moisture or mice carry the pellets away. The deer are back in my garden and I don't even bother to plant any more. I can't stomach the thought of getting another dog, though friends and neighbors have offered. Every once in a while I go to look over their litters, but none of the pups seems worthy. They just don't possess Sam's potential. I leave empty-handed, always hoping.

Sometimes late at night I'll be sitting on the porch and see Sam's silhouette running to catch the moon on a distant ridge across the valley. I'll call out at the top of my lungs: "Sam! Sam, come home!" And I'll wait up all night, only to find myself asleep in my chair, awakened by the rude dance of deer hooves on rocky ground. Or I'll be driving a back road and see Sam swimming a stream or chasing a fox in the cedar bush or running a coon up a tree. I'll pull a big Porterhouse out of the marinade and throw it on the grill and watch the smoke rise up to the heavens.

Sam is up there somewhere. Hunting with Orion or diving after Pisces, or roaming the back range of some galaxy trying to get home.

AN IRRESPONSIBLE
REPTILE

"In revenge and in love woman is more barbaric than a man."
– Friedrich Nietzsche

The Consul waited on the island. Parrots hawked above in the palms, rattling the corrugated fronds as they sprang off, beating the air with short choppy strokes.

"Damn this heat," the Consul muttered to himself, crushing another mosquito against his neck with a thick thumb. Sweat soaked his khaki clothing and dripped to the ground. He stood in an expanding pool, waiting.

The Consul froze as something touched his boot. His head still as a stone, he rolled his eyes downward, submerging brown irises to the pupils. A mottled green boa slithered past his boot, sporting a bulge that, an hour before, had been a languishing iguana, complacent in irresponsibility.

The Consul held his breath until the thick snake had passed, then gasped and jumped back, pulling his revolver, aiming. He hesitated... What if he missed or wounded the boa? It might come back for him and all his waiting would be ruined. He checked the breach for the hundredth time, saw it full of six clean shells, snapped it shut and filled his holster, watching the boa disappear in a rustle among the downed fronds and grass. A school of bonefish fed in the shallow water gently lapping on the sugary sand, their tails stirring abstract patterns into the bay's surface, a mirror undisturbed by the windless dawn.

Distinguishable from the incessant jungle din, the whine of a small outboard engine grew in intensity, magnified by the Consul's anticipation. First rays of sunlight were beginning to silver the trees as the Consul looked past the shore break to the point. A little dark speck was moving, coming closer. He checked his watch and stepped back behind a covering palm, bending down a dewy frond to peer out and watch the speck, retaining his concealment.

The day's first puff of breeze blew an instant of relief through the Consul's thinning hair as the small skiff chugged closer through the cove. A single figure stood in silhouette, hand on the engine's rudder, guiding it straight toward the beach. The skiff came in quickly, slicing through the suspension of his thoughts, to drive its neat prow into the soft sand, the aluminum ringing.

The Consul's hand tightened around the crumpled note in his pocket that had arranged this meeting. Who was this man? Of what scandal of his could the man possibly have knowledge? The Consul clenched his small even teeth as the man hopped from the skiff, pulled it up secure on the sand. The man was young, clad only in a thin shirt and shorts and barefooted. He wore a soft straw hat and a bandana with no visible weapon to match the Consul's revolver. The man appeared thin, effeminate, not much of a fighter.

How he had worried about this meeting! The Consul chuckled to himself. Better to err on the side of caution, he thought as he stepped from the palmettos.

"Over here," he announced with a deep voice.

The thin man whipped around toward the sound and tripped in the sand, losing the hat, unfurling a long mane of black hair.

"A girl!" The Consul laughed. He reached down to pick her up and she sank her teeth into his hand.

"Owwwww!" He yelled, tearing his hand free, then backhanding her down into the sand. She sprang up like a hyena and attacked his leg.

"Crazy bitch," he cried. "What's wrong with you?"

The girl holding onto his leg was sobbing. Waves of sorrow ascended his leg and softened his heart. He began to stroke her hair.

"Come on, now. It can't be that bad," he said, his voice full of crocodile compassion. "Let me help you."

The Consul bent down, loosened her arms from his leg and sat in the sand next to her. She slumped into him like a rag doll. He put his arm protectively around her as her sobbing waned.

"That's better," he said, pushing the hair off her eyes with his delicate fingers. "You are far too pretty to be crying on a lovely day like this."

The sun was rising over the ocean past the little cove, sending shimmering streamers toward them on the beach.

"Wait here. I'll be right back."

The Consul let her release onto the sand, disappeared in the jungle and returned in a moment with a large papaya. He drew a sheath knife from his belt and made perfect slices out of the ripe fruit. The girl accepted one and took an apprehensive bite. Then took another bite, consumed the slice greedily and looked up, her large doe eyes melting away the Consul's fear.

He smiled and fed her the rest, a slice at a time, until it all was gone. He watched her curiously until he came to admire her strange courage and innocence. She went to the water's edge, washed her hands and face and came back to the Consul and sat down. His eyes on her probed deep. A pretty young girl. A deserted stretch of beach. Who would ever know what passed between them? He pulled the crumpled note from his pocket and handed it to her.

"Did you write this?"

"Yes. I did."

"And now you have come to make your promise good."

"Yes. I did."

"But in your note you said you wanted to take my life, that I had taken the life of another. Someone close to you?"

"Yes."

The Consul eyed her curiously. This girl seemed no threat. He could have his way with her and be gone and that would be it. They sat for a long minute, alone in their silence. Then the girl looked up at him and spoke.

"Eighteen years ago today. You were crossing the Plaza Del Mar, drunk as a donkey with another man. On the corner was a girl such as I, selling carnations and melons from a pushcart."

"That was a long time ago," the Consul thought back. "It is possible."

"Her name was Rosalita. You wanted something more than carnations. You and your friend lured her to the gazebo. You did things to her."

The Consul furled his brow in thought.

" I don't know. I don't think so. I would not have

done such a thing!"

"But you did. First you took her and then your friend. But your friend was not able."

I... I do not know..."

He cowered in the light of misdeeds long forgotten, admonished by the possible truth of this young girl's recollection.

She rose and stood over him, brushing sand from her clothing, her feet planted firm, her hands framing ripe hips.

"I am your daughter, señor," she said, glaring down at him.

"My daughter? I have no daughter!"

"You have me, señor. By Rosalita, my mother, who passed away last week in a home for paupers."

"Passed away?"

"Yes. She worked day and night to take care of me until the day she died, never confessing the truth about my father."

"Oh? Of what did she die?" The Consul asked.

"She died of shame."

The Consul recovered himself. How could he permit such a little slip of a gal talk to him like this? Maybe it was true and maybe it was not. It didn't matter. What was done was done. He began to stand up.

"Okay. That's enough. You've have your fun. Now it's time we put and end to this –

His words stuck in his throat as the papaya knife

entered his chest just below the ribs and found his heart.

"Rosalita was her name," the girl said, pushing the knife upward until the blade could go no further. "Say it!"

"Rosalita," the Consul whispered, his punctured heart spilling blood down along steel shaft onto the sand as she withdrew the blade.

"Rosalita," said the girl. "On her deathbed she told me the story and made me swear I would find you and do this. Now it is done."

The Consul fell down against a coconut palm, the disturbance releasing a dozen green parrots that cawed their noisy departure. The girl wiped the knife handle on the Consul's shirt and placed it inside the fingers of his right hand.

"Suicide can take a long time for those of us who struggle," she said as life left the Consul's eyes. "But for some, it comes quicker."

She took the crumpled note from the Consul's other hand, smoothed out the folds and put it in her pocket. She walked across the sand toward her skiff, brushing her footprints away with a palm frond.

The Consul's final vision was of the daughter he had never known, growing smaller toward the sunrise, the light blinding as it reflected off the waves.

Ossifying

Resplendent

neolithic regalia flies

    brother reptile

    the pit swarms.

Sifting sands

perpetuating truth

    penetrating

    embalming.

A MOMENT AT HOME

*"A wise man can learn more from a foolish question than
a fool can learn from a wise answer."*
– Bruce Lee

Lester was a drive-up, a new boot, a fish. Right from the first I could tell he was headed for trouble. Not that coming to prison ain't trouble enough, but once you get inside there's a different kind of trouble free world folks know nothing about.

He was a smart-ass kid, twenty-three and thought he knew it all. Had a chip on his shoulder big as the Taj Mahal. Somebody had mistreated that youngster some-where along the line and it showed, in his face, his attitude, the way he treated other people. That ain't no excuse. We've all had more than our share of bad blows.

It started out on Wednesday. Lester cruised up to my cell in new whites, fresh from Diagnostics. I was resting up for the night shift in in the laundry, reading a book on my bunk.

"An old man. Ain't that my luck," he said when he saw me.

I looked up at him over the edge of my paperback, *Rich Man, Poor Man,* a wonderful novel about growing up in America by Irwin Shaw, a writer who could distill in a few words what others took days to explain without Shaw's brevity or eloquence.

"A bookworm too," the kid spat derisively, pointing to the stack of books, the last of my worldly possessions. "I hate to read."

Lester was short and trim with a wiry kind of strength I've seen in boxers. His disturbing blue eyes looked for a quarrel above splotches of whiskers. Blond hair cut short jutted out at odd angles from his face. The kid had failed to make friends with his first barber. He was an accident waiting to happen and wouldn't see it coming. Maybe I could help him. Coming to the penitentiary ain't like climbing aboard a pleasure cruise. Besides, I could afford to be generous. I was doing a life sentence. This was my home.

"Hello there, young fellow." I sat up and offered my hand through the bars. "Name's Joe Cobb. They call me Pop."

The kid looked at me like I was a bowl of spinach he had to eat before he could leave the table, then slid his hand into mine. It was soft and limp, like a dead mullet.

"Sanders. Lester Sanders. 5-4-3-2-1 or whatever they gave me." He withdrew his hand from mine and wiped it on his pants.

"Be good to actually know your number," I advised. "The guards don't take it lightly when you act flippant."

"Yeah yeah." He nodded toward the empty bunk in my cell. "What happened to the guy in there before?" I got the feeling if I said I had murdered him in his sleep the kid wouldn't have been surprised.

"Transferred to the Ellis Unit. They needed welders and Ted was once of the best."

"Welder, huh. They put me in the fucking hoe squad." He said it like it was beneath him, as if assistant warden was more what he had in mind. I tried to point out the bright side.

"That's not so bad this time of year. Fresh air, plenty of exercise. You'll lay in half the time due to the rains."

Down at the end of the run, the guard rolled the doors open. Lester, and his wrinkled brown paper bag of possessions, stepped inside.

"Top one's yours," I said trying to make him feel welcome. "Shelf is yours too. Since I'm on the bottom I use the floor."

"I can see that," he said, tossing his bag on the thin mattress. "You only got one leg."

He was right. I lost it a decade ago working as the dog boy. The dog boy takes care of the dogs and keeps them trained so they can chase down a runner. A runner is a convict who makes a break for it and thinks he can out run a dog. Training involves a dog boy playing escaped convict who gets head start. The dogs get released a few minutes later while sergeants, on horseback with rifles, monitor the action.

I was running when the dogs caught up to me. I tried to climb a tree, but fell and they tore into my leg. The damage exceeded the acumen of the prison doctor to fix it and there was no time or money to take me anywhere else. The carelessness of the training exercise would be an embarrassment to the warden, so they anesthetized me and removed the leg. Instead of apologizing, they spun it to make themselves look good. "Prison Doctor Heroically Saves Inmate's Life," the headline read in the local paper. I was advised to keep it quiet and, in compensation, was awarded an easy part-time shift in the laundry folding clothes. To fight it would have been futile. The word of a three-time loser wasn't worth squat next the sworn state-ment of a prison employee with a clean record, the case adjudicated in a prison town. Plus, I got special treatment and got fitted right away for a fake leg. I felt like Captain Ahab.

The heavy steel door closed with an unsettling bang

and Lester winced as he looked around: two steel bunks welded to the wall, corner stainless steel sink commode combo with push buttons, a bare 40-watt bulb with a pull chain. He began to tuck the sheets in around the thin plastic covered mattress.

"So, where're you from?" I asked, hoping conversation might ease the pressure.

"Chicago. East side." He tied two corners of the sheet together and slipped one over the mattress end, then the other. He worked frantically, like a hurricane was coming and he was running out of time.

"What'd they give you?' I asked.

"What?"

"How much time?"

"Three years. For a couple ounces of pot. I never should have come to this fucking state." He said it like he had *my* time.

"That's not so bad. Ol' Jonesy is doing ten for a pound."

He snapped the blanket around the mattress, let it fall down. The kid could make a bed anyway.

"Yeah yeah. I've heard it all before. Three years seems like a long time to me."

"Keep your nose clean you can make trusty and be up for parole in nine months."

"Well," he put his foot on my bunk and climbed up top. "I can't wait that long." He stared up at the ceiling, starting to brood.

I wiped his footprint off my sheet and went back to reading, letting him stew in his own juices. The kid will come around, I said to myself. Culture shock. He just has to get adjusted.

Half an hour later and twenty pages further into my book, I felt a pair of eyes on me. The kid was leaning down over his bunk, smiling like a con man.

"Bum a smoke, Pops?"

"Sure. I've got some Bugler, but you have to roll it." I set my book down and passed him a can of tobacco with rolling papers inside.

"I can roll, old man. Rolled enough dope on the street."

"You'll need this." I handed him my Zippo. The kid didn't realize it, but having a cigarette lighter inside prison was a privilege afforded very few. Those who had them were trusted inmates, long-timers, deserving of respect.

"Thanks."

Ordinarily, when you let a guy use your lighter, or anything else for that matter, he gives it right back. This little punk set it on his shelf along with my can of tobacco. He had no manners.

"Why don't you pass that stuff back down here," I said, firm but gentle.

"Oh, yeah. Sorry," he said. But I could tell he didn't mean it. He was testing me.

He tossed the lighter on my bunk. The next thing I knew it was raining ashes.

"Hey, kid. Your ashes."

He peered over the side. "Didn't getcha, did I?"

"No. It's all right. Use this." I held up the end of an old Bugler can with little wedges cut into the rim. My ash tray.

"Okay." He snatched it from my hand like a school-boy took a necktie his mother made him wear to church.

Just then Jim Willis came to the door. He was about my age, early sixties. A nice taciturn fellow, Black, with silver around the temples ascending to a distinguished nappy pate.

"Hey, Pop."

"Hey the same."

"Whatcha got to read?"

Good books soften time and I served as a conduit for protecting solid titles for those with an appreciation. Willis liked westerns and an occasional spy thriller and I tried to always stay one ahead of him. I found the Louis L'Amour and pulled it from the stack.

"You read *Comstock Lode*?"

"Don't believe I have." He took it gently through the bars, turning it over like a priceless Ming vase in his hands.

"Thanks, Pop. I'll bring it back."

"Take your time."

"Thanks again." He walked away slowly, reading the jacket, caught up in the promise of the splendid hours he would spend with his new treasure.

"Who's the nigger?" barked the petulant voice from above.

If I had been twenty years younger I would have stood up, pulled that young clown off his bunk and beat the living tar out of him. But, patience and tolerance are lessons of age. I tried once again to take the high road and serve by example.

"His name is Jim Willis. He keeps the run clean and does a lot of little things that make life easier for all of us in here. And, I wouldn't refer to him as a 'nigger' if I were you."

The kid snickered. "He sure was acting funny. Like that book was made of gold or something."

"Let me tell you something, sport," I tried once again. "When that man came to this hell hole twelve years ago he could neither read nor write, but made up his mind he would get something positive out of his time in here. Day or night, whenever I saw him, Jim would always have a little pocket dictionary in his hands. When it got so worn he couldn't read it any more, I got him another one. Then another after that. It took him four years to earn his G. E. D. Next June he will graduate with an associates degree in English."

"Well, whoop-tee-fuckin'do."

"Jim has found meaning in life. Found a purpose. He'll probably make parole next year too on a forty-year sentence. He plans to spend the rest of his life teaching young Black children to read so they can get an education and avoid the problems he had growing up. Problems that led him to this place."

"Oh yeah? What did he get forty years for? Baby rapin'?"

I stood up and looked him square in the eye. He was laid back against the wall, smoking, glaring at me like a weasel.

"It's none of your business what a man did. But I'm going to tell you because you might learn something that will keep you from getting killed in here. Something that may incite a little maturity so you can work out whatever it is inside you that makes you such an obnoxious little punk."

"Yeah, what's that?"

"He was in a bar one night and a man pulled a gun on a woman. He was drunk, said she's been messing around on him and was going to kill her. Jim tried to stop it and went for the gun. The gun went off. The man didn't make it."

"It wasn't his fault. He should have got off. Self defense."

"You're an expert in the law now?"

"Why didn't he fight it? Must have had a shitty lawyer."

"Lawyers cost money and the law isn't always fair. Besides, he didn't have the heart to fight it."

"Then he's stupid. He deserves to be here."

"You don't get it, kid. Yet you run off at the mouth

like you got everything on God's green acre figured out."

"Yeah? What don't I get?"

"The man was his brother."

For a split second I thought a spotted a glimmer of humanity rising up from deep within him where it had been squashed long ago. Then it disappeared, as quick as it came, like an angel lit a match and the devil blew it out. I didn't understand this kid. He was too young to be so cold, so insensitive. We didn't talk again that night. He crashed out on his bunk and I did my late night shift in the laundry.

*   *   *

The next day was a real scorcher. Even with the fan on high, being in the cell was torture. I remembered what it was like outside in the fields. I worked the hoe squad when I drove up on my first offense, full of piss and vinegar like Lester. I was a drinker and a brawler and got five years for assault. If I stuck to my fists it would have been probation, but I carried a knife and had to use it. They wear you down in the fields, bleed off that extra testosterone so the cellblock is civil when everyone comes home. Chopping weeds all day with a five-pound broad blade blisters your hands and breaks your spirit.

My second time down was for robbery. Another stupid escapade on a drunken night. I can't say my pals talked me into it, I was willing and it just took a nudge.

A foolish shoot-out and I got twenty years, served nine. After two stretches in prison a man isn't worth much on the streets. With that X on your back, decent folk want nothing to do with you, and the only jobs you can get are menial so you have to start drinking or using to mask the shame and handle the pain. You start thinking about getting back inside where you know your place and everyone's the same.

I got my third case on purpose, just had to wait for the right opportunity. Find a sleazy bar and eventually some guy is going to start abusing some woman. You step in with a strong right hand and cold cock the sucker. The police will come and when they run your jacket, it's a ride downtown. Three strikes and you're out, or back in where you belong. Admittedly the lodging isn't great and the food's not gourmet, but a man can get adjusted to about anything given enough time. You get a job, a warm bed in the winter, marginal medical care, but you can survive without a lot of effort. And, with an endless supply of weathered paperbacks and a command of the English language, you're aboard the *Pequod* with Ishmael chasing the white whale, swashbuckling your way back into high society with Edmond Dantes in *Monte Cristo,* or trying to find your identity and bring down the Agency as Jason Bourne.

The hoe squads came in about three-fifteen and hit the showers. Half an hour later my new cellie came draggin' up to the bars. He took a quick look inside, then turned, sat down against the wall and waited for the doors to crank open. I glanced up at him over my book. His face was red from the sun and he was shaking a little. His eyes bore the glaze of repressed horror as he looked down at his hands. They were swollen and blistered, ready to fall off. His shiny new brogans looked like they been in the fields a month. They had worked the kid all right.

I didn't say a word, just kept on reading and minding my own business. The kid was a like a wild badger and needed breaking if he was going to be fit for human company. Time, and the institution, were on my side.

The doors opened after a while and Lester got up and hobbled over to the cell. He clomped to the sink, filled the bowl and tried to soothe his hands in the cold water. It didn't help. He patted his hands on his pants, sat on the commode and struggled with removing his shoes, wincing and groaning. I came to the end of a chapter, dog eared the page and closed my book.

"How did it go today?" I asked evenly.

He glared at me, like I should have already enquired about his misery and well-being.

"Horrible!" He exaggerated his discomfort by wildly pulling at the laces.

"Oh? Seemed like a pretty day."

"Are you crazy? Do you have any idea how hot it was out there? Three guys passed out before lunch, if that's what you want to call it. A baloney sandwich on white bread with too much mustard. The fucking sadistic guards worked me like a mule. Chopping dead grass all day with a dull hoe on hard ground. Run down, run back. Two minutes for water. I threw up twice. Look at these hands."

He held them up. They were a mess all right.

"Better take care of those. Looks like you might lose a nail."

"Lose a nail? I can't go out there again. It'll kill me."

I took a long look at the kid. A day in the fields was all it took to bring him around.

"What did you think it would be like? You're in prison, kid. This ain't the country club."

"A couple guys almost jumped me. Said I wasn't keeping up with the line." He was getting hysterical.

"You've got to pull your weight or everyone suffers. Can't expect another to do it for you."

It was too much for him. He was trembling like a leaf in a windstorm, couldn't untie the laces and the boot was stuck on his swollen foot.

"I can't take it any more," he shrieked, then burst into tears. He covered his face with his hands, but the salt hung in the cuts and he drew his hands away. His crusty veneer was gone. He'd made a mess, now he needed a little help cleaning it up.

"It's all right, son," I said. "It's going to be all right."

"No, it isn't," he moaned. Then he began his confession. "I'm locked up in prison after spending five months in the county jail. I've got no money. I haven't heard from my parents since the trial and they probably disowned me. My girlfriend hasn't written and I think she seeing my best friend. Now, my hands are worn out after the first day, I'm dead tired and can't keep any food down. It's going to kill me if I have to go out there tomorrow."

He looked up at me with puppy dog eyes and almost broke my heart.

"You don't suppose the captain will give me a lay-in, do you?"

"No, son. Not without a doctor's note. I've seen them a lot worse than yours and they send them right back out."

"What am I going to do?" He hung his head, broken and defeated.

A man is a funny creature. He'll keep it all tied up inside and let it build and build, like rain clouds sucking up the sea, his exterior all swelled with foolish pride. Then, all of sudden, when the time is right, it becomes too much and the bottom blows out. Some find release in drink, others in fighting, neither too wise in prison. Sex is out, if you want to remain a man. Crying is the safest route, a cleansing of the soul. This kid was ready for a friend and circumstances had decided it would be me.

I hopped over to the sink using a crutch, wet a hand towel and gave it to him.

"Here you go."

He took it gingerly without looking at me and wiped his face.

"Let me see those hands." I had some anesthetic salve the doctor gave me to accommodate the callouses forming where my stump met the prosthesis. I rubbed some gently into his palms. The effect was almost immediate. With a sigh, Lester returned from his self-immolating reverie.

"Better?"

He looked at me. His eyes were clear, free of the disdain and cockiness with a touch of gratitude and humility.

Just then the familiar tone of the mail sergeant came from the run.

"Cobb."

"Right here, boss."

He passed me a letter and a small package, torn open to reveal a book.

"You got a Sanders in there, Cobb?"

The kid's face brightened. "Right here, boss."

I took the mail and passed it to him. Two letters and a money slip. The pain in his hands was gone and he tore open the envelopes. His spine straightened as his eyes danced over the pages.

"Hey, Mr. Cobb. It's a letter from Mom and Dad. They don't hate me. They say they forgive me for the pot case and everybody makes mistakes and they will be there for me when I get out."

"That's great, kid."

He sniffed the other envelope, then held it out for me to smell. The perfume resurrected memories, which in my case, were best left buried. I nodded.

"Pretty sweet, hey." Lester opened this envelope delicately, like not wanting to disturb a sleeping baby. He breathed deeply as he read the letter, her words filling the emptiness, making life tolerable. When he finished, he looked at me again. This time the tears were of joy as he read the lines aloud.

... I've been so worried about you the past few months. All my letters have been returned. I called and they said you wouldn't get mail until you arrived on your unit, so I hope this letter finds you well. I miss you terribly and can't wait for the day when we can be together again. All my love always, Julie.

Things were looking up for the kid. I read somewhere that many fears are born from loneliness or fatigue, and when things seemed like they can't get any worse they suddenly take a turn for the better. Like God will only test you to your breaking point then brings you back to demonstrate His infinite compassion.

"What's this, Pop?" Lester waved the money slip.

"Your commissary account. Somebody deposited."

He looked at the slip again. "A hundred dollars! Cigarettes are on me next time, Pop. I'll buy some Marlboros. The hell with this roll-your-own Bugler bullshit."

"I like my Bugler, thank you. But I will have an ice cream."

"Yessir. Any flavor you like."

"That's very kind." I learned a long time ago to save your first impressions of a person. They didn't always hold true as time passes and the personality reveals itself.

Another voice at the bars. "Hey, Pop."

"Hey, Jim." Willis pushed a little parcel at me. Warm meat wrapped in bread protected by a tissue.

"Thought your new cellie might could use a little somethin', bein' his first day and all."

"Sure, Jim. Just what the doctor ordered."

I passed the sandwich to the kid. He stood up, came to the bars, offered his hand then pulled it back.

"I'm Lester Sanders, sir. Thanks for the sandwich. I'd like to shake your hand but it's a little sore right now."

"You're more than welcome. Time enough for that later."

"How's the book, Jim?" I asked.

"One of his best, just like you said."

Willis waved and ambled off. Lester tore into the sandwich like the Governor called and gave him one last meal.

Then, a loud noise outside, like a burst of gunshot fired to quell a ruckus in the yard. Lester stopped chewing and looked at me for an answer.

"Rains, kid. The fields will be flooded. No work tomorrow."

"You mean it?" He chortled around a huge last bite.

"Absolutely. Then the weekend. You got three days to heal up before you go out again."

Lester sat there grinning like a leprechaun.

Hardship has a way of introducing a man to himself and every once in a while you get an even break. The kid was going to be all right. I winked at him, picked up my book and found the dog-eared page. Soon I was off in another world a long way from home.

ABLUTION

"Anyone can be a fisherman in May."
–Ernest Hemingway

The path to the stream was overgrown and barely visible, but Walter knew the way. As a boy he had fished there for brown trout with his father, and later brought his sons with their fly rods and wicker baskets. Standing for hours in cool moving water, threading out the line, flicking the bamboo tip so the tied fly landed precisely, freed the mind and refreshed the spirit.

"Don't force it, Kevin. Make friends with it. Respect it. Take joy in the dance between man and fish."

"Yes, daddy."

Kevin was his younger child, always cheerful and eager. He listened well and learned from the mistakes Aaron made, three years older. Aaron had already mastered the fly rod when Kevin was six, and made perfect casts while his younger brother wrestled with a backlash.

"Need help, Kev?"

"No, I got it." His pocket knife cut away the kinked line and he retied the lure.

By the third year they were fishing as equals, standing in a swift eddy tossing their lines ahead of the ripples made by the fishes' tails. Once they snared two beauties at the same time and laughed, eyes sparkling in mutual respect.

Walter smiled from the camp, blowing on the fire that would cook their dinner. Kevin was adept with a sharp knife and would surround the filets with green onions, garlic and chestnuts in the iron skillet prepared with sunflower oil. After the bottoms browned, he would flip the filets and add a dash of Cholula hot sauce.

These memories occupied his mind as Walter made his way through the cedars toward the stream. A red fox darted across his path. An owl screeched overhead. Dank odor from the fecund carpet of leaves rose to meet his nostrils. He was at home, just another creature among many in the neighborhood.

A flash of color that did not belong. Walter bent down for the orange food wrapper, wadded it up and stuck it in his pocket. It appalled him others could disrespect Mother Nature, but he let the thought go.

Beyond the cedars the path opened into a lush

green meadow. He could hear the rush of the stream, the cool clear water sliding over the smooth rocks. It was just as he remembered it. Pristine and soothing. He went to one knee and cupped his hands. The water was a glorious, life sustaining fluid, and he drank deeply.

He slid off his rucksack and untied the leather cylinder fastened beneath, pulling the zipper around the crest. He extracted six pieces of bamboo and assembled them, slowly twisting the ends together, until they were snug. He flicked the rod and it cut through the air like a whip. He stood there in silence, visualizing the rod in Kevin's hand, that last time two years ago before the cancer.

Kevin's coordination had gone first. Aaron had kidded him about the hot sauce and dismissed his little brother's clumsiness as indigestion. Then came the seizures. Sporadic at first, then more frequent.

"Glioblastoma," the doctor had said. "Kevin has a large tumor in the right hemisphere of his brain."

"What can we do?" Walter and Tracie asked, feeling hopeless and afraid.

"We try radiation first. Then surgically remove what we can. Then the chemo."

"What are his chances?"

"His cancer is in stage 4. Not many survive."

The family abandoned their plans and moved to Memphis to be with Kevin for the radiation, staying in lodging provided at St. Jude's. The tumor continued to grow and they moved on to surgery at the Cleveland

Clinic. The incision was stitched like in a baseball, curving over Kevin's ear. The family remained close for daily rounds of examinations, treatments and physical therapy, leaving after visiting hours only when the nurses made them go.

"The MRI shows the tumor is growing back faster than before," the doctor said, recommending an experimental technique for producing a vaccine form his tumor's cells. But the tumor persisted and a second surgery removed the new growth to relieve the pressure inside his skull.

"We've done all we can for him," the doctor said, visibly shaken. "Perhaps you should take him home."

Kevin didn't want to die in the hospital, and passed in his own bed holding hands with those who loved him. His tumor was donated to the hospital for research.

Walter pulled out a second set of bamboo pieces and assembled them, laying the rod next to the first on the soft green grass. Aaron had died the month after Kevin. Despondent and drinking on a rainy night, he swerved to miss an oncoming car and crashed into a light pole. Two granite headstones in the tiny church cemetery in remembrance of his boys. There would be no graduations to celebrate, no weddings, no daughters-in-law, no grandsons.

Walter withdrew the third set of bamboo pieces from the sheaf and assembled his own rod. He thought of Tracie, how after their sons were gone could she not bear to look at him. She left for Illinois to live with her parents.

Donning rubber waders, Walter stepped waist high into the stream, carrying the three rods to the center where the current was the strongest.

"Good bye, sons." He laid the rods together on the surface and watched the current take them past the flat mossy rocks where the fish always waited. He then pulled a pistol from his vest, placed it against the spot where Kevin's tumor had been. He pulled the trigger an instant after a big trout hit his leg and caused him to slip.

Walter sputtered in the cold water, his feet finding purchase. Blood ran from the crease along his hairline.

He looked up. Two eagles were winging skyward. A third eagle stared down at him, unmoved by the gunshot.

A sense of peace swept over him.

He threw the handgun as far as he could into the stream, then crawled up onto the shore.

The Fox

Too slick for the noose
     he's always loose,
He can have chicken,
     he can have goose.

MIAMI BEACH BLOW-UP

The infamous hard guy, Mack Ballson, crusades
against hostile hotel inequities.

The .44 automag hungrily gulped another tight clip of 240-grain boat tail slugs as Mack Ballson sprang from the roof of the hotel in a perfect full gainer layout. As the hard man boomeranged through the air, the big bore bucked nine times, spewing forth a scythe of seething savagery.

The first to take a hit was the cabana boy. A molten missile traveling 1640 feet per second pinned him through the neck to a saffron chaise lounge. He flapped wildly, like a speared carp, his severed jugular climaxing crimson jism where once before, under a moonlit night, one dear to Ballson lost her precious flower.

Next, Ballson drew a bead on the bald meat-butcher known as Leo. Astrologically unfortunate this day, the lion died like a squirrel, upchucking a quarter pound of fancy walnuts onto eighteen ounces of inferior sirloin he sold as prime.

With 1455 foot-pounds of muzzle power, the next two blasts smashed into the maitre d' and sommelier like sledgehammers wielded by Arnold Schwarzenegger, collapsing the pair of puffed breastbones like hollow eggshells. Their blackened hearts seeped into pockets to taint undeserved and usurious gratuities.

The night manager spied Ballson as he was midway through his flight before the series C automag spat sullen fire. Guilt flooded the worm's face a nanosecond before his lying lips got pushed into a crude channel cut through his cerebellum, a mental organ that would never again forget a wake-up call.

The bell captain peered out the plate glass window at the carnage mounting around the pool. A pencil flame flash forecast his fast demise as glassine needles stitched him like a substitute substandard Louis Vuitton two-suiter.

A sea green Rolls Royce Silver Cloud screamed

around the hotel's horseshoe drive way, crashing into the oval fountain as Ballson squeezed out a front tire deflating dagger. Another round punched its way into the tank of high octane petrol. The Rolls exploded, jumped high in the air and flipped over, cooking the car boy in the last ride he ever contemplated stealing.

The bartender and two cocktail waitresses next received invitations to the promised land from the pulsating magazine. Spinning lead ripped down through bubbles of the outdoor Jacuzzi, nailing the philandering trio in a final sordid shudder. The corpses slipped down in the strawberry fizz, never again to delay a drink or dilute a tropical cocktail served under a tiny umbrella.

Mack Ballson's steel-toed jungle mesh boots touched down on the tip of the three-meter board and rode the spring up, converting his momentum into a double-somersault with a full twist. This gave him time to stash the stainless steel flesh-shredder in a hip holster and withdraw three incendiary grenades and two four-ounce packets of plastique.

The hard guy hit the flagstones running. A long mahogany bar ran along one side of the polygonal swimming pool. A good place for a little fireworks. He inserted triggered time fuses into the soft gray packets, slapped them up against the ice machine, then ran for the hotel lobby.

Someone on the balcony of the owner's penthouse screamed an alarm in guttural Spanish. Ballson responded by lobbing up the three pineapples, pulling pins with his teeth.

The scene exploded.

A thundercloud of smoke and debris billowed out from the blazing skeleton of the penthouse. Scraps of tropical print fabric fluttered down following chunks of PVC furniture. The air became tinted with a mist of blood and weak vodka tonic.

The daylight warrior reached the door to the spa to find the steel lever rigid in his hands. He took a step back and launched a karate kick into the lock. The hinges made a cry like a trapped wolf as they tore away from the wooden frame.

Ballson glared at the obsolete exercise equipment as he strode across the thick shag carpet toward the aerobics class. A dozen curvy ladies bent over at the waists, a bobbing bevy of bodacious buns. The hard guy smiled at the ladies and kept on moving. His quarrel was not with them.

At the front desk, an over-muscled attendant regressed to adolescence before the formidable stranger.

"Wake up! This gym is right out of the '60s," Ballson growled.

"But –," the dinosaur began.

"Shut up!" Ballson ordered, reinforcing his statement with a curled knuckle jab straight into his solar plexus. The brute gagged and dropped to his knees, dry-heaving into a stack of monogrammed towels.

"You need work on a Roman chair," said the

self-appointed equalizer. Ballson exited into a hallway that took him to a garish dining room. He looked around and decided to seek out the decorator just as the double-doors to the kitchen burst open. Two waiters, unctuous Latinos – unsympathetic to the purpose of his mission – entered carrying trays of iced melon.

They saw Ballson. Ballson saw them. Reactions on both sides were spontaneous.

The waiters hurled the trays of iced melon and reached for their uzis. But the big guy had already drawn his Glock. He went into a tight roll, aiming the bucking handful of plastic fire power. The first waiter's head exploded like an overripe casaba, torn to shreds by three rounds from the fifteen held in the Glock .357 SIG Model G31. The white ruffled shirt of the second lackey soaked up crimson released by four penetrating rounds spat from the well-oiled barrel.

The equalizer's nose detected the odor of broasting squab, a known clue to his quarry. He pulled out a pair of concussion grenades, extracted the pins and rolled them through the double doors. His own kind of insurance policy.

Sucking in huge lungfuls of air, the good guy sprinted through the Tiki Lounge into a wide hallway lined with mirrors. At the far end, a door opened. The hotel detective had been disturbed from an excellent Swedish massage. He wore a thick terry cloth towel, unable to conceal his corpulent center, and held a .38 Smith and Wesson snub nose that spoke flying lead.

Ballson dived into a recessed doorway. The mirrored wall behind him disintegrated into a shower of sharp silvery shards. This task demanded deployment of the Ingram machine pistol.

Ice-blue eyes squinted as a cold finger squeezed around the curved steel trigger and swept the compact harbinger of death in a neat arc. The 30-round magazine emptied in 1.45 seconds, silenced by the MAC suppressor to sub-sonic levels. This allowed the detective's final screams to be heard as the rounds thudded in and around the terry cloth towel, beating a massage he would remember for ninety-seven seconds, the time it took for exsanguination to separate the verminous thug from his consciousness.

The seasoned combat warrior took the first corridor left and followed it into a courtyard bordered with well-manicured azalea hedges.

El Gordo, the fat man, sat with the girl at a wrought iron table composed of little interlocking fleur-de-lis. They were sipping espresso from Wedgewood demitasse. A generous plate of coconut mini-cakes laced with dark chocolate was half gone, allowing a glimpse of three pink hibiscus floating in a clear bowl.

The hard guy paused, drawing on a sixth sense, a thick vein throbbing across his forehead. Gordo and the girl looked at Ballson. Ballson looked at them.

"You betrayed me, fat man." Ballson's voice was

granite.

"A simple misunderstanding, señor," the fat man retreated, dabbing a handkerchief to sop up the rivulet sprung about his double chin.

"I was promised a king-sized suite with an ocean view. You stuck me in a flat with a fold-out bed. My window looked down on a gravel roof with pigeons shitting on a rattling air conditioner."

"You may have my penthouse, señor."

"Ten minutes ago that might have been a solution. Now, it's too late."

"Whatever you wish, señor. Take the girl!"

The girl got huffy and smacked Gordo with what was left of her lobster thermidor.

"Your stone crabs are small, your drinks watered down, your service slow, your food has no flavor," accused Ballson, reciting his litany of grievances. "Your doorman steals luggage, your housekeepers steal socks, and there's too much chlorine in the pool."

"I will take care if it, señor Personally." The thermidor dripped from El Gordo's beard.

"You are ridiculous, Gordo, and overpriced."

The hotel owner winced, wishing he were back in Barranquilla, as the big man moved in and looped a garrote around the fleshy neck.

"Please! I will dismiss my staff."

"Fool! I took care of that myself."

The hard man crossed forearms built like two steel

rails, and snapped them back over each other. Gordo's head toppled like a pumpkin and rolled into the mango salsa.

"Ooooh!" said the girl. "Take me out of here!"

Mack Ballson measured her in a glance: twenty-six, about five-eight, hundred and twenty pounds, a firm disciplined build with dark shoulder length hair and blazing green eyes.

"He made me sit with him and eat those," she said, pointing to the coconut cakes. "450 calories each!"

She was his kind of woman.

"I recommend Nautilus equipment," the warrior replied. "I use the gym at the El Morroco."

The girl stepped close and threw her arms around his neck. "Kiss me, damnit."

He obliged her. Deeply. In perfect understanding.

Ballson led her through an opening in the hedge. In seconds the throaty roar of his twin V-pipes echoed loudly, not disturbing the eternally slumbering silence of the carnage he left behind.

RARE SONNETS SURFACE IN PRISON

"Poetry is an echo, asking a shadow to dance."
— Carl Sandburg

Dear Editor of the *New Yorker* magazine, I am excited to report what may be an extraordinary literary find. According to a man I met only once, and just recently, the manuscripts are authentic. While we kept a cell together for only seven days, he trusted me enough to pass on his legacy, his last possession, before he died.

Being a man of letters impassioned with love of language, my hands trembled. the bare bulb in the ceiling spewing a dim cast across the hand-scripted pages, so brittle and yellowed with age, they creaked as I opened the creases they had worn for untold decades. Then, the old man snatched them back and secreted them inside the tube he entrusted me to keep once he was gone. I sat on that thin worn mattress, drinking tea from a soup can and listened to the old man's tale. His pale blue eyes glistened as he croaked his epitaphic tale, his bony fingers tracing an arc through the air.

In the late fall of 1610, six years before his demise, William Shakespeare, bard of the Globe Theater, heavily plied with drink, stumbled to the farm of his cousin Theobald and scripted several sheets with his poetic fires, then fell fast asleep in the barn. A tremendous thunder storm rolled through valley in the wee hours, blowing open the shutters and scattering the master's just inked sheets akimbo, setting them to rest behind a woodpile. The next morning the poet woke with a terrible hangover, and without a word to anyone, went off in search of relief, impervious to his literary outpouring the night before.

The cold front demanded heat and when Theobald went to the woodpile he discovered the pages and recognized the hand of his cousin Will, whose level of fame outstripped filial loyalty. Miffed and jealous, Theobald saw a windfall in his discovery, but wisely decided not to reveal his treasure to anyone until after his cousin's passing. He thought it would occur soon enough, hastened by the master's intemperance and lasciviousness.

Theobald sat on those pages for six more years until the glorious event occurred. No more would he be chained to the drudgery and vile fragrances of the farm. He was the cousin of England's most famous poet and playwright and soon he would be rubbing noses with the literati and their coterie of buxom wenches.

Then Theobald got another idea. Why should he play second fiddle and ride on his cousin's fame when he could ride on his own? Securing the same style and size of paper on which Will had penned his sonnets, Theobald carefully wrote them over in his own hand and submitted them to the *Stratford-on-Avon Gazette.*

He became an instant celebrity!

Even the sceptics thought Will's cousin had a potential past the south end of a northbound plough. Soon Theobald was caught up in the fast company of actors and actresses at the Globe Theatre, his sonnets lavished with praise. Promises were made for production of a play he hinted was in the works. For a time, the wenches he had longed for were at his beck and call, much to the dismay of homely Edith, his wife. Six months later when his wages were spent and no words produced, Theobald was turned out as a fraud and charlatan. He limped home to his farm where he met his ignominious end by falling on his pitchfork.

Sorting through his things after the funeral, Edith found the original sonnets and gave one to each of their five sons with the stipulation they were not to be made public during her lifetime. The shame of poor Theobald being a one-hit-wonder would be nothing compared to that of a plagiarist, especially being a thief of the greatest writer the English language had ever produced. She burned Theobald's forgeries and made her sons take an oath, which they did and kept.

Shortly after her death, one of the sons, an Ignatius Meriwether, confided to a collector of rare antiquities he might have an original William Shakespeare manuscript and would he mind taking a look. The collector, Robert Thorogood, agreed and when he returned from London was bright-eyed with the possibility of securing all five manuscript pages from the five brothers. It took some waggling and chicanery, but Thorogood accomplished the task. He then took the pages back to London to seek a publisher.

When news got around town five unseen sonnets penned by the master were available, a bidding war ensued that reached as far as Paris and elevated to a sum in the high five figures. This was to be the crowning achievement in Thorogood's lackluster career that would enable him to live out his life on a sweet grass farm in Devonshire. A good plan, until someone came along who let the air out of his bloated haggis.

Charles Barton, eldest of Theobald and Edith's five

sons, had parted with his sonnet for a flagon of ale and a serving of shepherd's pie with the provision he could reclaim it at any time for twice the same when the drink wore off and he could find work. Appearing at Thorogood's shop on High Street with six shillings, the stipulated amount, he was turned away and told summarily a deal is a deal and that is that. To protect his interest until the sale closed, Thorogood hired a night watchman without performing a due diligence, only to find his charge asleep in his chair the next morning and his shop robbed. The strongbox containing his precious manuscripts was gone, and the sale to the French *L'Mode* forefeit.

The police questioned Charles Barton, but did not press the issue. Thorogood had the reputation of a cheat and a scoundrel and sympathy resided with the poor farm hand who scratched out a hardscrabble living. The matter, squashed as it was in public enquiry, sought settlement in the underworld and Thorogood spent his modest fortune in the hire of inept criminals without success. A year later, he went penniless to his grave without recovering the manuscripts.

Charles Barton did not keep the manuscripts as all those who possessed them had come upon bad luck. Instead, he traded them for a plot of land he could call his own, and lived out his days raising sheep and cutting peat out of the bog. The recipient was Lord Alexander Farrington, a nobleman, who deeded Barton a small corner of his estate. He was a private man and had no need to share his treasure with the world. Rumor was he would bring out the pages in front of the fire and read the sonnets to his sweetheart, his wife Galinda of fifty years. Will's sonnets were their little secret, until the missus joined her husband upstairs, around the year 1700.

Leading up to the American Revolution in 1776, the growing tension between England and Colonies resulted in many ships sailing back and forth across the Atlantic carrying soldiers, supplies and deported dissidents. One such rascal, a Montgomery Smythe, had been in the service of Lord Farrington's grandson, Claxton. Through the years Smythe had grown into friendship with the new lord and one night had been privy to the tale of the manuscripts with the aid of some highland malt whiskey. Smythe's mind churned until he had concocted his exit strategy.

Claxton Farrington was a piss of a man and a churlish braggart. Displeased with Smythe's cheeky back talk and lassitude, Claxton had Smythe arrested on false charges of buggery for which he was to be deported to the Colonies. It took all of Smythe's persuasiveness and savings to bribe a guard to take him the night before the ship left to have one last drink with his old friend Claxton. Inside for half an hour, Smythe returned to the constable's charge and acquiesced to his fate, the manuscript sewed into the lining of his jacket. Claxton was left drunk and unconscious, but unharmed.

In the Colonies, the life of an indentured servant was rough, working the fields from dawn to dusk seven days a week. But rumblings of revolution permeated the fields and dank quarters of the white slaves. One night Smythe and a dozen others broke from camp and joined the rebels, meeting the British soldiers at Lexington and Concord, armed only with pitchforks and hoes. After the battle, Smythe was able to disappear and become assimilated within the revolutionary forces, eventually becoming a free man with a land grant in Fincastle County, Virginia, the area that became the state of Kentucky on June first 1792.

Smythe worked hard, married the daughter of a colonel and achieved a measure of respectability in Bourbon County, Kentucky, siring six sons and four daughters. Working hard to make his way in the new world. Smythe forgot all about the old manuscripts still sewn within the linings of his jacket, buried in a chest in the basement where they remained as long as he lived.

Smythe's youngest daughter, Eleanor, cleaning through his things after his passing, came upon the jacket, felt the lumps, cut away the stitches and pulled out the Bard's pages, just before the start of the U. S. Civil War. A neutral state, Kentucky was sympathetic to both the North and the South, with Union and Confederate forces seeking lodging at the Symthe farm.

On one occasion, Eleanor brought out the pages to show Confederate Major Markham Pierce who dismissed them as fake, yet absconded with them the next morning as his troops rode off by way of Troublesome Creek to fight with General Morgan in the Battle of Mt. Sterling. On June 2, 1864, Morgan's superior forces overran the Union positions, capturing some 380 men along with a large amount of munitions and medical supplies. Celebrating their victory, the Confederates were unprepared the morning of June 9th when Union General Burbridge attacked the men sleeping in their tents. Major Pierce was one of the causalities.

Stripping the dead soldiers of their leather and weapons before burial, a sexton by the name of Hoodie McLeash came across the manuscripts tucked inside Major Pierce's tunic. Not being a literate man able to recognize their value, he tossed them into a box where they lay among other war documents retrieved from the Confederate encampment. When General Robert E. Lee surrendered to Lt. General Ulysses S. Grant at the Appomattox Court House on the morning of April 9, 1865, the Civil War was officially over. The box was taken by horse drawn lorry first to Winchester, then to Paris, Kentucky, where it was stored in the Bourbon County Courthouse basement for almost 100 years.

In the fall of 1963, a historian by the name of Amelia Cahill was hired under contract to sort through and organize documents in the many boxes stored in the courthouse basement. On November 22nd she opened the box containing the Shakespeare sonnets and was trying to ascertain their significance, when news came over the radio that President Kennedy has been assassinated in Dallas.

Confusion ensued and public buildings were closed and locked down across America. Wanting to study the aging hand scripted pages more closely, Cahill slipped them into her briefcase and carried them home.

The more she studied the pages, the more convinced she became of their authenticity and their value. They had nothing to do with Kentucky history and had evidently made their way to that box by mistake. No one would miss them. They were hers to exploit and no one would be the wiser. Still, she had to explain how they came into her possession and went about concocting a story that would not only be plausible, but historically accurate. Much of what I have just conveyed is the result of Ms. Cahill's research.

However, this is where the case takes an interesting twist. In order to establish absolute pedigree to Will's hand-penned pages, she had to travel to London and meet with the archivist at the Globe Theatre. Untrusting of air travel, Cahill withdrew her life savings and booked passage on the last transoceanic voyage of the Queen Mary in September 1967. Her plan was to get the manuscripts authenticated, sell them through Sothebys in London, return home to Kentucky, and buy a horse farm near Clintonville.

Three days out of New York, a terrible squall sprang up on the North Atlantic, inciting seasickness in most of the passengers. Amelia Cahill was no exception. Dining with a new gentlemen friend when the storm created uneasy rolling of the large vessel, he offered to provide her with dramamine tablets and she followed him to his cabin. The gentleman remained so until the tablets took hold, rendering poor Ms. Cahill unconscious and quite vulnerable, confessing her quest with the manuscripts before she passed out. The gentleman, whose name remains a mystery, carried Cahill to her cabin, tucked her neatly in bed and relieved her of the pages, stashing them inside a waterproof cylinder in one of the lifeboats.

The next day when Cahill returned to her senses, she discovered the theft, went to the ship's captain, reported the man and insisted on a thorough search of his cabin. It was ordered and done. Nothing was found. The man took offense despite the numerous apologies, slugged the duty officer and was placed in the brig until the ship reached Southampton where he was summarily turned over to the police. Cahill, near penniless, stayed on the ship for the return voyage, went back to work and never breathed a word about her loss.

The city of Long Beach, California, outbid the scrap yards and bought the Queen Mary to use as a tourist attraction. A special mooring was created in the harbor near Howard Hughes' famous flying wooden boat, derisively nicknamed the "Spruce Goose" by a Senator on a special committee set up to investigate Hughes for war profiteering. The ship's boilers, propellers and other equipment were removed to make room for restaurants and exhibits. During the conversion, a carpenter by the name of Thaddeus Weeks happened to be working on the lifeboat and found the waterproof cylinder. He eyed the pages curiously, hid them in his lunch pail and showed them to his brother-in-law that weekend in Beverly Hills. He showed them to an art dealer and interest began to rise.

But greed set in, and not liking the way he was relegated to a subordinate role, Thaddeus stole away the pages. A bit of a rascal, Thaddeus thought he could handle the transaction himself and enlisted a couple of his mates from the shipyard. They met at a wharfside bar to plan out their scheme. One drink led to two, and two led to six, and before long they were all at odds with one another, got into a scuffle and the barman called the police. Thaddeus was taken into custody, booked for drunk, disorderly and resisting arrest. They ran his name and found he had an outstanding federal warrant in New York for smuggling cigarettes. A marshall was dispatched to pick him up so they could get the case off the books.

Sentenced to a year and a day, Thaddeus, was stripped of his clothing and possessions when he entered the Federal Correctional Unit in Otisville outside of Manhattan. By then the manuscript was nothing but a nuisance and he tossed it in the trash where the unit bookkeeper spotted it. He kept the pages until his last day, then passed them to me in the lonely cell, reciting what he knew of this tale I have just laboriously conveyed.

I transcribed the words so I could send them to you. The original manuscript rests in a vault in the Cayman Islands, placed there by a private investigator who verified the provenance of the manuscript as I have just described. Here are two of these inestimable works.

The Jolly Twins O'Toole
When passing chanced upon a golden lass,
  Riding deep within an autumn time wood,
I felt fine fortune rise and come to pass,
  The look she gave me was not of motherhood.
Imagine my joy when down from my steed,
  A double appears, quite supple and trim,
'Twas little trouble to compound my need,
  Mine for the taking away on a whim.
On through the evening, and on to the next,
  How many ways can there possibly be,
With two nubile maidens so oversexed,
  To save what was left I hastened to flee.
Listen, my friend, if you value your jewels,
Spend only one day with those jolly O'Tooles!

The Unsolvable Uncertainty
'Tis time again, she must find an answer,
  To the question for centuries has lain,
Can't ask a Duke or even a master,
  The problem is hers, quite simple and plain.
Will it be cotton? Or will it be lace?
  With ermine perhaps, a cape to the floor?
An utter monstrosity lacking in grace,
  Whatever, for sure, it won't be a bore!
And, oh now puff, how her face does redden,
  She seems a stranger, quite distant and far,
Her breathing comes quick, feet slide as leaden,
  As far as it goes, for her this is war!
Can she make it right? Select a winner?
Oh, what will the lady wear to dinner!

Surely now you are intrigued by the brilliance of
the meter, the dazzling display of intellect crafted by the
immortal bard in his own hand, some five centuries ago.

A Bed of Hay

Shall I compare thee to a bed of hay?
*   First, I might note, thou art far much softer,*
And, instead of lumps that cause me to say,
*   "I'll sleep elsewhere," 'tis hard to get off her.*
Stalks of straw are often golden like grain,
*   Silky brown's the patch between your thighs,*
When lit you cry, "Again and again!"
*   While the flax when wet can only draw flies.*
For a horse to be healthy, hay is a must,
*   Fair food for a stallion in stable or field,*
Fare of another sort, yours is of lust,
*   A hunger, a longing, must bend and yield.*
While hay is flat, quite two-dimensional,
*   Laying with you redefines sensational!*

End of the Road

A wayfaring bard, a rambler it's true,
*   My pleasure's a song, good wine my best friend,*
I stay where I like and take care to undo,
*   Any cares neither borrow or lend.*
'Twas once outside Kent, a lady in silk,
*   Came crashing through brambles, torn and in heat,*
The brute was outrageous, she was in bilk,
*   With a swing of stout cordwood he lay at my feet.*
As impassioned a mistress had never been seen,
*   Juices of gratitude flowed like a spring,*
Before it was over she called me "Dad!"
*   Was unable to convince her 'twas merely a fling.*
Now, ten years later, a father of four,
*   My pack gathers dust on a peg by the door.*

Oh How I Wish You Were A Bluebonnet

Oh how I wish you were a bluebonnet,
  So I could find you on a grassy hill,
And sing to you, perhaps write a sonnet,
  Sniff your bouquet until I drank my fill.
Why, I could bend and pluck thee from the ground,
  With a twist insert thee through my lapel,
Then walk about hearing nary a sound,
  But the music rising up from your well.
It would take a flower to understand,
  A caressing breeze touching so light,
The deep heat of the sun that feels so grand,
  Combined in spirit 'tis oh so right!
When dusk's death falls upon the purple plain,
I'll pick another you, do it all over again!

By now all doubt is surely removed and you must be convinced these sonnets are from no other than the great bard himself, lost treasures of literature which have traveled many miles and endured countless hardships to be presented to you at this time. I only ask that you treat these noble works with the honor they so rightly deserve and publish them prominently within your esteemed periodical.

So there is no mistake, I am offering you first publication rights only, after which all rights revert back to me. I intend to then find a suitable home for these sonnets, perhaps in the Archives of the United States in Washington, DC, or at the University of Texas, an institution widely know for its proclivity to obtain the finest original manuscripts regardless of cost.

Your speedy reply is requested as there are many others clamoring to get first glimpse of these words, unmistakably those of William Shakespeare, lost for centuries, now uncovered and available for the first time to the world.

You have until Monday to make up your mind or they will be sold to the highest bidder.

> Sincerely,
> Madey Burnhoff #10-98276
> Federal Correctional Institute
> Otisville, NY

Rekindled

Haunting perfume
still mists
from your difficult letter;

like a wolf
blood scent calling
that fragrance
ignites passion's rage
to far flung fantasy;

    I spring from
    coiled haunches into
    a Celsius defying
    pool;

    we drown together
    before
    I wake.

RETRIBUTION DAY

"Vengeance is mine; I will repay."
—Leo Tolstoy, *Anna Karenina*

In the ghastly predawn quiet, Dexter Windslow lay in bed thinking, waiting for the alarm. With the clarity of a sage, he reviewed the events of the past three years that would, today, culminate in the execution. Then he would be rid of it. Then he could go home.

He had been married once, but now lived alone. After Mary was gone, he let his possessions languish. One by one they wore into obsolescence or were stolen by vandals. His room was vacant save for the cot he slept on, a change of clothes, his alarm clock and his tools.

Dexter was a fix-it man, the last of a dying breed. Few things needed tool fixing any more. Possessions were disposable or, after electronic diagnosis, fixable by robot chip replacement. Bare wires, metal pipes, concrete, nuts and bolts were seldom seen. Everything was wireless, pre-cast, pre-assembled. Fix-it men were only needed to repair old things. It was clumsy boring work no one wanted to do, yet easy and well-paying for those who lived in the shadows and traveled at society's fringes.

His tools weren't anything fancy, just simple sturdy hand tools. A good eighteen-ounce framer's hammer, a pair of bolt cutters, a dozen screwdrivers, socket and pipe wrenches, clamps, rulers, vice-grips, needle-nose pliers. His two titanium lockboxes also held a pneumatic nail gun, which could drive a sixteen penny galvanized ring shank three and a half inches into solid pine with one squeeze of the trigger. Electricwise, Dexter carried a battery powered half-inch drill hammer, circular saw and saws-all capable of cutting through concrete and metal.

With this collection of tools and accompanying fasteners, he could fix about anything. He got his business by word of mouth and was expert enough to take only the jobs he wanted. Others had to wait months for his services and he might not get to them at all, no matter what the price. But starting today, his appointment book was conspicuously blank.

The phone rang and Dexter spoke into the air. "Dexter."

"Are you ready?"

"I'm ready."

"You sure you want to go through with this?"

"I'm sure."

"I can't talk you out of it?"

"No."

A pause, a mutually agreed silence. The caller, his best friend, Jimmy Reed, wanted to be the first to call, wanted Dexter to know he was there for him, no matter what happened.

"All right. I'll pick you up."

"Thanks. But I want to walk."

"I want to go with you."

"I know you do. And I appreciate it. This is something I have to do alone. I don't want to see anyone. I don't want to talk to anyone. I just want to go there and get it done."

"I just don't think it's healthy."

"I love you, brother, but I don't care what you think. What anyone thinks. This is closure for me. Then I'm out of this God-awful place."

"We'll talk tomorrow then."

"For sure."

"Good luck."

"Luck's got nothing to do with it. Only the bad luck that brought it on."

"Look at the bright side. Today you get even."

"There's no getting even, Jimmy. It's way past even

and never coming back."

"Later man."

"Bye Jimmy."

Dexter clapped his hands and the phone discon-
nected.

Then it rang again.

"Yes?"

"Mr. Windslow? This is Norton Grebbs with the
Daily Journal."

"Go away," Dexter spat with finality.

Then, "Disconnect. Cancel service. Deduct final
bill, return deposit." He clapped his hands once more and
cut his umbilical cord to the world.

                    *   *   *

Over at the state prison, Seston Thad was having
his last meal: anchovy omelet, rye toast, hot coffee and
a Benedictine chaser. Thad had gotten religion in prison
and, to his great surprise, discovered that Benedictine was
made by monks. He felt a certain kinship, since the bombing having lived with the privations of a monk in a small
cell. Whenever he had an audience, Thad would extol
comparisons between a convicted person and a man of the
cloth. A penitentiary was a place of penance. Monks did
penance and so did he. In history, convicts even became
saints.

"Look at Paul of Tarsus," Thad told the Court of

Last Appeal. "He was a sinner, a man who saw the error of his ways, and reformed himself, just like me. He was sentenced by a law that today would seem unjust. The law you are using to decide my fate may one day be unjust. I beseech you to consider this as you look down at the reha-bilitated person before you."

The Justices glanced at one another, then immedi-ately sentenced him to death, "with extreme prejudice." One majority opinion in the law review summarized his crime as "senselessly heinous to the point of disbelief." Another defined Thad's character as "incorrigible, unre-deemable," and his chances of contributing one positive thing to society "nil to impossible."

"No man is completely worthless," wrote one internet cloud reporter. "He can always be used as a bad example." Then he added, "except in the case of one whose crime is so incomprehensible, mankind would be best served by striking the name of Seston Thad from all records, and never having to mention his deeds again."

Thad savored the last of his breakfast and lit up a smoke. He drew the acrid pollutant deep into his lungs and held it until it burned. He exhaled into the last sip of Benedictine in his paper cup, then sloshed it around in his mouth where it found the broken tooth, a little parting gift from Officer Girard. The sting throbbed into his mandible, then went dull. He crunched up the paper cup and threw it against the steel wall across from the steel cot where he laid back to think.

In six hours he would, hopefully, be dead. If he wasn't dead in seven hours it would be horrible. In eight hours, merciless. In nine hours... he didn't want to think about nine hours. He just hoped the surviving victims, those wounded or crippled from the blast, had voted for hanging or a quick bullet through the temple. Even lethal injection wouldn't be so bad, though it lasted several minutes. The gas chamber would be a fitting punishment, but he heard you squirmed in pain as the cyanide gas torched your lungs and ate up your nervous system. No, the bullet was best. Synchronous with the sound came the puncture, then total darkness. He hoped they had voted for the bullet. But the method was kept secret until the appointed hour, when it was revealed simultaneously to the perpetrator and the world at large.

Seston Thad didn't believe in heaven or hell afterlife scenarios. Hell was life on earth, was other people. People who comprehended his failures and could see him for the worthless loss he had made of his life. Hell was living a lie, living a life where he always felt inadequate, afraid, vulnerable to the point of terror. Every day, minute, second of his life, awake or sleep, life haunted him. He was a tortured victim of bad upbringing and worse choices that doomed him to his sociopathic actions and retributive consequences.

That was what the citizens and the reporters were not getting: he was a victim too! He had suffered enough abuse for a hundred victims. The bomb he designed and installed had only killed fifty-five people. By his tally, he was forty-five bodies in arrears.

But there had been mostly women and children, a happy day at the zoo gone terribly wrong. No way he could protest being a soldier at arms, a patriot set against an oppressive establishment. Had he chosen a military base, he could have been tried in a military tribunal where Retribution Day was not a punishment option. In ten years with good behavior he could get transferred to a minimum security base in sunny Florida, his work assignment mowing grass on the officer's golf course.

Thad felt a presence at the bars and looked over to see Officer Girard grinning at him.

"Today's the day, sweetheart."

"Nothing gets by you does it, suck face."

"I heard they got a real nice surprise planned," Girard said, hoping to see Thad squirm. "No bullet. No freeway to heaven. Just a long bloody road with lots of stops."

Thad flipped his butt into the steel commode and stood up. Girard took two steps back from the bars and withdrew his hardwood night stick, thumped it in his hand.

"Looks like boat drinks for me about noonish," Thad mused.

"Way I heard it, you'll still be on worldwide TV at midnight."

Thad gasped and began to shake uncontrollably.

"What's left of you." Girard smirked and eased away, the sound of his squawking boots swallowed by the slam of a heavy steel door.

*   *   *

Dexter Windslow went through the forty-five minutes of calisthenics that had become his morning religion. If God was out there, Windslow didn't want to know him. No god he could fathom would allow a scum bucket like Seston Thad to snuff out his wife and daughters, rob a good man of reason and purpose. Now Windslow was only good for one thing and his talents would be put to use today.

Public executions had become legal in 2025 as terrorist bombings escalated to new levels. Thousands of brainwashed and deluded miscreants, willing to trade existence for infamy, were mustered into service by radical religious factions, political dissidents, self-styled patriotic groups and a hundred other true believer types seeking change through violence. The World Trade Center, the Murrah Building in Oklahoma, The Superbowl Blast, the Ludwig Electric Cruise ship blown up in the middle of the Atlantic Ocean with no survivors, and countless other sites housing innocent noncombatants killed by the suicide cowards, motivated citizens to convince the leaders drastic measures were necessary.

The Retribution Act Bill of 2025 passed unanimously in both houses of Congress in a single day, and was signed by the President the next. The essence of the bill mandated public execution of the perpetrators and allowed free worldwide broadcasting of the event. Three years from the date of crime, at the precise time of the explosion, those convicted would be put to death at the rebuilt location.

The method of execution was decided by a secret vote of all the surviving victims and deceased victims' families. To build suspense, and give the broadcast the attention it deserved, the exact nature of the punishment was not revealed in advance. Neither the convicted nor the audience knew the details, the duration and manner of death. The exigencies of the event were know only to the Victim's Council and its appointed Administrator. The bomber had taken lives. His life too would be taken – in like measure to the grief and pain he caused his fellow human beings.

Dexter had been chosen as Thad's Administrator. The magnitude of his loss, his physical size, iron will and plan of retribution had won him the unanimous vote of the Council. He had waited three long years, holding in his rage, fighting off his passion for revenge which occupied every waking moment. He had held himself in check and obeyed the law. Today, he would obey the law again.

*   *   *

Seston Thad sat on the crapper and emptied his bowels. Magazines scattered around him bore his twisted face with vilifying headlines on the covers: "The Most Hated Man in America," "The Vote is In – Thad is the Worst of All Time." Other magazines boasted the inevitable result: "Adios, Thad!" "Thad's Last Waltz." "Burn Baby Burn."

"Bastards!" Thad spat, tossing the current issue of TIME. He wiped and left the throne flushing. He paced, asserting his life force in every short step between the bars and the sink. None of those journalists had gotten it right. His motives had nothing to do with paramilitary groups or political dissidents he had been linked to in the media. The target he chose was in no way strategic for retaliation against the powers-that-be for grievances done, real or imagined. He was neither a pawn nor a foot soldier in service to someone else's twisted scheme. He was a free agent, a renegade, a lone wolf. He consulted no one and made his own decisions. He was an unsung hero, a modern-day Lee Harvey Oswald, whose name would be remembered.

That's how it would have been, if Thad had not overlooked one crucial detail. His target was anonymous and non-threatening. He had not chosen the White House, a state house or even a school house. He had carefully researched sites with huge publicity potential he could exploit without taking a single human life. Located midway in the Houston-Dallas megapolis accessible by air, rail and road, the Texas Zoo was about as apolitical a place as could be found, designed simply for edification and enjoyment. It was the perfect place to explode a bomb as evidence of his disdain for the world and everything beautiful. People had made his life miserable and ugly, and he would show them what miserable and ugly was all about.

Seston entered the park an hour before closing time and hid in a shed where dry food was kept for the animals. Secreting himself inside a stack of feed bags, he went undetected by both the scout dogs and security personnel. Centrally located behind the polar bears and Bengal tigers, it was also the ideal place to plant the bomb, designed without metal parts so as to defy the entrance metal detector. Thad had laughed to himself as he set the timer the next morning before exiting the zoo, wondering how far away they would find pieces of Rob Roy, their prized white rhinoceros.

Thad thought he had set the timer for 2:45 a.m., a time when the zoo would be empty of all human occupants, thus avoiding a murder charge if caught. Instead, not noticing the little red light on the digital counter, he set the timer for 2:45 p. m. when six buses full of elementary school children were scampering gleefully among the zoological wonders.

He had been riding his motorcycle on the Pan American highway just north of Queretaro, Mexico, when the news came over his headphones on satellite radio. Twenty-six school children had been killed along with dozens of parents and zoo employees. Hundreds had been wounded. The horrendous nature of the deed transcended politics and unified the world in the manhunt. Thad was already a suspect having quit his job as animal feed delivery driver several months prior. The international dragnet with its sophisticated cameras and computers, isolated his location and held him with an observer drone until the troops swarmed and took him into custody. Seston Thad would not retire and live out his life on the sun-kissed beaches of Puerto Angel. He would be slaughtered on live TV before a public assembly at the Texas Zoo.

The outer steel door opened and the murderer locked eyes with the priest.

"It's time, son," the priest said, flanked by a dozen guards eager for the slightest resistance from the condemned. "Do you have anything you would like to confess?"

"Fuck you," Thad spat.

The guards moved in on him with the immobilizer.

*   *   *

Dexter took one last look around his empty room, picked up his two cases and left the clock on the floor by the bed. It read 10:45 a.m. The cases felt heavy as they always did, but today seemed to have a life of their own. They were not filled with cold steel tools, but rather specialized instruments that knew their purpose and would help guide his actions. The tools were his partners, his allies in the work to be done. They would do this thing together.

The carpet yielded to his steel-toed boots as he made his way to the elevator on the 77th floor. The door opened and Dexter entered, oblivious to the others staring at him, glancing down at his titanium cases.

"You're him, aren't you?" One passenger broke the silence as they descended past the 33rd floor.

"Yes."

The man grasped the hand of the woman next to him and squeezed. Their faces were stern, ashen. They were dressed all in black like the others in the car.

"Make him suffer as we have suffered," another man said as the door opened.

They allowed Dexter to depart before they moved. He said nothing and walked straight ahead to the mono-rail station just as the train was pulling up. He selected a seat at the back next to a window. Others filled the car but left the places around him vacant. Out of fear. Out of respect. Occasionally someone would glance at him over their shoulder and nod in appreciation or camaraderie, but it was never acknowledged or returned. They rode in silence, unified in the presence of impending vengeance only humans understand.

*   *   *

At the Retribution Site, an elevated stage had been erected in the center of an octagonal amphitheater with a predetermined number of seats. The black chairs in the inner rows were for those who had survived the blast or lost family members. A wide section was left open at the front for those maimed in wheelchairs. Behind those most affected, were seats painted grey, now filling with spectators who had won the spots by lottery. Each ticket cost a dollar and, after deducting fees and expenses, had raised over twenty million dollars that was evenly distributed to those in the black seats according to an algorithm designed for optimal fairness.

In the center of the stage was a hollow wooden oval with a diameter a foot taller than Seston Thad – a beautiful piece of laminated bent wood construction. It had taken Dexter three months to perfect his design and build the structure that was crowned by a large eight-sided digital clock indicating the time of day. Dozens of remotely-operated cameras were focused on the stage, positioned up under the eaves in the arena. Dexter's work would be broadcast worldwide in HRD (Holographic Reality Definition). Over a billion people had paid in advance for the privilege, the funds used to pay for the event, rebuild the zoo to a level beyond its former glory, the remainder going into the Retribution Day Victims Fund.

Missing from the event was any kind of liquid or solid refreshment except for water, available free of charge from the numerous kiosks stationed around the arena. Afterwards, members of the crowd were free to do as they wished, but during the execution nothing was provided that might interfere with their biochemical perceptions. This was to be a solemn event, a cathartic cleansing of the mind and spirit. No booze. No drugs. Anyone found in violation was immediately removed from the proceedings.

This was to be an eye-for-an-eye Old Testament justice event.

*   *   *

As Dexter Windslow stepped up onto the platform with his two titanium cases, a roar went up from the crowd. He was their surrogate. Through him their need for vengeance would vicariously be assuaged.

Concurrently, Seston Thad, held naked in the immobilizer, was moved through the underground passageway lined with huge aquariums. The air in the passage was cool and damp and awakened fear in Thad's nostrils. A tiger shark swam overhead, its teeth jagged and flashing.

"Ever see what a shark can do to human flesh, Thad?" Officer Girard taunted.

"He's not getting the shark," added the guard driving the immobilizer.

"Yeah, the shark would be too merciful."

"Shut it, clowns!" Thad said.

The driver pushed a button, freezing Thad's face and preventing another sound.

They exited the tunnel into the open air of the amphitheater. The crowd, senses heightened to super-awareness, fell stone silent. The stark reality of what was about to happen slammed against their preconceptions. After three long years of waiting, their day had come. The scene became surreal, as if a movie leapt from the screen and enveloped their minds.

The immobilizer lifted Thad effortlessly up the stairs to the stage.

"Where do you want him?"

"In there," Dexter said, pointing to the oval.

This was the first time he had seen Thad since the trial. He looked at the naked man who had killed his wife and daughters. He thought it strange that he felt nothing, no anger, no hate, no emotion. He thought it strange vitriol failed to rise. He had a job to do. He was the one responsible. A professional.

The guard sergeant guided the immobilizer into the center of the oval. Dexter raised the bolt cutters and saw cold terror fill the killer's eyes.

"Today, you get yours," Dexter said, lowering the bolt cutters toward Thad's naked groin.

"No!" Came the muffled scream.

Dexter brought his hands together, bisecting the convict's waist chain. A second snip temporarily freed Seston's feet.

"Lift up his arms," he commanded the guards.

Dexter set the cutters down, picked up the nail gun

and shot a sixteen penny ring shank nail through a chain link into the oval at ten o'clock. A second nail pinned Thad's left wrist at two o'clock. Dexter fired twice more, securing his ankles to the wooden oval at 4:30 and 7:30, creating a vengeance version of Leonardo DaVinci's Vitruvian Man.

"Release the immobilizer."

The sergeant pushed a button on his service belt and Seston's frozen form again became flesh, blood and bones.

"That's all."

The guards hesitated, not wanting to leave the close proximity to the event they had been waiting for months to witness.

"It's the law," Dexter continued.

"Let's go boys," Officer Girard said. "We'll be close if you need us."

"I've got it," Dexter said. "Leave the belt."

The immobilizer operator dropped his control belt. Girard and his men left the stage and filled the three empty seats behind the black rows, the only open seats in the amphitheater. Thad pulled against his restraints and growled at his executioner, snapped the cerebral slumber of the attendees.

"You bastard!" Yelled a man in a wheelchair in the front row. A cacophony of admonishments followed, each one more vile than the one before – a primal release of man's ignobility.

The Magistrate appeared on the platform and raised his arms. He waited for complete silence and, with every eye on him, read the proclamation. The clock above the oval read 2:43 p. m.

"Seston Gonan Thad, being lawfully tried by jury, and found guilty of senseless public bombing, you are to be put to death, today, April 5th, year of our Lord 2029, by public mutilation with prejudice. Do you have anything to say?"

All eyes were on him, waiting for his last words. Chained naked within the oval, Thad looked out over the assembled and, for a moment, it seemed he was going to tear up and deliver an apology, a plea for mercy. Then, his face drew in, tight and unrepentant.

"What I did I meant to do. Those who were harmed were simply in the wrong place at the wrong time. They were innocent victims, just as I was an innocent victim. The abuse I suffered was transferred back to the society responsible for harming me. I was nothing more than a messenger, an instrument of cause and effect, an unwitting pawn in the game of life. I fucked up. I killed people. But, I have suffered too, much more than you will know. I cannot escape my fate, just as all of you cannot escape yours. I will see you all again in hell!"

The Magistrate looked at those in the black seats who had the vote. They knew what to do. In unison they picked up their remotes and voted. Above Seston Thad came the instantaneous results: 246 votes for no anesthetic, 2 votes yes.

Those in the black seats looked around. It was easy to spot those who voted yes. They wore red arm bands signifying membership in the GARD – The Group Against Retribution Day. Heads shook side-to-side, but it didn't matter.

"The victims have spoken. There will be no administration of anesthetic at any point during the proceedings. May God have no mercy on your soul."

The clock clicked forward to 2:45. The Magistrate nodded to the executioner.

"You may proceed."

Windslow pulled two pairs of vice grips from his case, adjusted the jaws to close around the width of his little finger.

"This is for my daughters," he said, looking Thad straight in the eye. He clamped the jaws of the first vice-grip around one of Thad's testicles and squeezed until locked. Then he applied the other.

Had the earth's surface not be curved, Seston's screams would have been heard in Dallas, a hundred miles away. Some in the crowd stood, raised their fists and jeered. Other winced and slid down in their seats. Several woman fainted and were comforted by those next to them.

Seston was almost unconscious from the pain. Windslow revived his charge with a whiff of smelling salts under his nose. When Seston's eyes cleared, all he saw was a blow torch being lit in front of him.

"This is for my wife."

Dexter sliced off Thad's penis with a razor knife, then quickly cauterized the wound with the torch.

"Can't have you bleeding to death, now can we."

The pain was unimaginable. Thad began to thrash around inside the oval, making it difficult for the handy-man to continue. Dexter reached for the immobilizer belt and pushed a button, freezing Thad inside the oval. Dexter lifted the half inch hammer drill and slid a six-foot-long auger bit into the tool's maw, tightened it. He went to the outer edge of the oval, set the drill point against the wood and squeezed the trigger, the bit twisted its way through the oval and continued to Thad's body, penetrating at the hip bone, cutting through the lower intestines through to the opposite hip bone, out and into the interior rim of the oval. Thad's body was now secure. Dexter opened the chuck and set the hammer drill down.

"Take it like a man," Dexter said. But few men who ever lived had experienced this level of pain.

He pushed the button on the immobilizer belt and Thad screamed until he could scream no more. When the adrenaline and endorphins flooded from his glands, enabling the pain to reach a stabilizing threshold, Dexter raised the circular saw installed with an 80-tooth blade set to a depth of one-quarter inch. He pulled the trigger and the blade whirled like a siren.

"You bastard!" Thad tried to spit, but it got no further than his chin. Dexter set the spinning blade against his navel and drew a red slash upward past his collarbone.

"Take a look out there," Dexter spoke softly. "Look into the eyes of those in the black seats. I am their messenger. I am their instrument."

Thad became transfixed by the collective enmity of those who glared at him, tears running down their faces, their minds and souls locked in the cathartic cleansing of his retributive sacrifice. Dexter's saw droned on mercilessly and when the blade stopped spinning, Thad's entire torso was lined with fifty-six vertical lacerations roughly one-half inch apart.

According to a pre-arranged hand signal, Dexter cued the view screen operator in the control booth. The eight view screens in the amphitheater, simultaneous with a billion screens in homes and pubs around the world, was filled with live footage of a beautiful little girl playing on the beach.

"Mary Jane Anderson," the Magistrate's voice thundered through the arena.

Dexter clamped the channel-lock pliers to the top edge of one of the vertical strips and tore the skin downward.

Seston Thad wailed, but the fight had gone out of him.

Footage of a man, a good man, a family man, appeared next on the view screens.

"Norman J. Boswell," boomed the name as a second strip of skin was removed in recompense.

On and on the names were read and the skin removed. When Dexter made his last downward stroke with the pliers, Seston Thad was nothing but a head separated from two legs by a huge obscene wound.

The crowd was stunned. What was happening before them exceeded their capacity to emotionally process. Some turned away and could look no more. Some got to leave. Others vomited in bags that had been provided.

Dexter dropped the pliers and pulled a leather drawstring bag from his overalls pocket. He opened the bag and poured a small mound of white crystalline powder into his hand.

"The people you murdered were the salt of the earth," Dexter said, dusting Thad's chest, sides and back until all the salt was gone.

Thad screamed until his voice rasped like a broken reed in the dying wind of his breath.

Dexter pulled out his eighteen ounce framing hammer and motioned to a score of people in wheelchairs positioned in the front of those assembled. Some had lost limbs. Otherwise were paralyzed, never to walk again.

"This is for those you crippled."

The hammer was raised and brought down with the force of Thor, pulverizing the murderer's kneecaps.

"Merthy," Thad pleaded beneath the clock that read 5:35 p. m.

"Here's some mercy," Dexter said, using his sabre saw to trim away Seston's hair, the oscillating blade shaving his scalp down to the skull.

"If yooth tuth me agin, I'll kill yooth," Thad lisped through ragged stumps of teeth Dexter had also diminished with the 18-ounce hammer.

"That reminds me," Dexter said, reaching into his titanium case for the bolt cutters. One by one, he separated Thad's fingers from his hands, his toes from his feet.

"Finith me," Thad wheezed. "I beg yooth. Pleeath!"

Dexter sighed and looked deeply into the eyes he purposefully had not damaged. He wanted every possible sensation to be witnessed and transmitted to the brain. To blind him would be too compassionate. His job was not to forgive, but to serve out the mandates of vengeance, the only practice that had proved successful in deterring criminals from committing murder. No more lethal injection, firing squad, gas chamber, or electric chair. Since Retribution Day had been established, homicides were down 78% and senseless bombing a fading nightmare.

"Finith me," came the plea again, as thunder barked overhead. The sky, now dark and sullen, got split by a fusillade of lighting, followed by waves of pelting rain. The audience stood and let the water wash over them, mingling with their tears of ablution, flowing down to the drains around the oval along with the blood of Seston Thad. Screams and wails blended with the cacophony in the sky above them, unifying phenomena and noumena in a crescendo of horrific holiness.

Dexter stood on the stage before the magnificent

oval, strung with his hideous defamation; surrounded by tools he had used to create so many works of beauty. An epiphany of baptism flooded his soul. He felt the anger, the hate, the sorrow lift from him and rise away. He saw himself in a green meadow by a cool spring, playing with his wife and daughters. The sun was warm and bright and lifted his heart. There was a blanket spread out on the soft green grass and she set out plates and napkins with little blue and white squares.

"Almost, my love," she said, smiling the way she did when first they met, when he fell in love with her and wanted her to bear his children.

Dexter looked at what was left of the man in front of him, a wretched soul not unlike himself. He reached into his case one more time, found his pneumatic nail gun and screwed on the compressed air cartridge.

"Forgive me," he said, placing the muzzle against Thad's ragged bony temple. He pulled the trigger twice. Thad's head slumped down, his eyes vacant, no longer mirrors of society's scorn.

Dexter then placed the instrument against his own forehead, looked skyward and rode a sixteen-penny nail to a place, away from this place. A place where his duties of retribution would never again be required.

THE HUNT

"He who laughs last, laughs best."
—Anon

T hrough the molded latex mask, Professor Varner studied the Halloween throng parting around him. Orange and black, fake blood and reptile skin, Nixons, Obamas and O. J.s, maidens and vamps, pirates and poltergeists – every God-awful aberration of the human experience was loose in the open-air zoo of Austin's Sixth Street. The physical compression of the crowd magnified the claustrophobia imposed by Varner's costume – tight black nylon around his legs, hideous bat's feet, webbed wings ribbed with steel spikes sharpened to needle fineness. It had taken Varner a year to design and build the metal frame now strapped around his shoulders and concealed within stretched black fabric. A frame that could be brought together with enough force to crush a small dog... when Varner found the right pair of eyes.

Impossibly blue eyes whose reputation for piracy was superseded only by their effect upon other men's wives. Eyes that had seen Varner's plans for a revolutionary microchip design and his lovely wife Lydia. Eyes that had stolen both and left him a wifeless tenured sot while Dick Sullivan rose to the stratospheric position of a high-tech mogul in a high-tech mogul town.

"Sullivan, my friend!" Varner greeted a satyr. The microchip pirate was attired with pointed horns, cloven hooves, with fake hair glued to his chest and crafted goat loins.

Sullivan recognized the voice and peered into the face of the giant flying mammal that confronted him.

"Varner?"

The bat raised his wings and a dozen apparitions jumped back from around them.

"Yes, Sullivan. It is I, Maxwell Varner, come to take you home."

For years, cramped in his tiny office at the university, Varner had planned his revenge. His trip to Guyana had not been to study the brightly colored folk art of the Ndbele Tribe, but to obtain a small quantity of deadly curare -- a single drop potent enough to stop the heart of a rhinoceros.

"It's been years, Varner. How have you been?"

"Never better, my old fiend. How is Lydia?"

"Gorgeous as ever," Sullivan mocked. "Having a bunch of fun not chained to your boring life."

The giant bat stepped in and wrapped its enormous wings around Sullivan.

"Hey, what's with the wings?"

Sullivan expanded himself against the resistance of the metal skeleton which encompassed him, facilitating the penetration of the sharpened needles into his fleshy loins and haunches.

"This isn't funny, Varner."

"He who laughs last..." Varner flapped his wings once more, feeling the points violate the costume, the epidermis... blood! Then the wings opened and Sullivan stumbled down the block, his impossible eyes glassy with fear, his breath frozen in lungs that wreathed a quivering heart.

The giant bat blended into the crowd and was swept along past the Driskill Hotel.

One block later Varner turned south, aware of a strange attraction that pulled him towards the Congress Avenue bridge where a million kindred souls were returning from their nightly hunt.

Doppelgängera

On a stormy night
    you invade my space dancing
        wind blown slashing rain
           crashing open.

Lightning's lithe fingers
    lick alive my roadmap retinas
        seeping deeply darkly
           my curling essence.

Eyelash curtains thrash
    swirling succubus sense
        mounting my pride
           ride it dry.

Love puddles linger
    passion's spent fragrance
        lipstick ignited gunpowder
        a phantom,
    hungry for mortal man.

CYBERDOC SQUABBLE

"Physician, heal thyself."
–Luke 4:23

Prime time late night in the AOL chat room for "doctors," known as Physicians Online, a couple "professionals" are trying to make an accurate prognosis of one another's credentials...

PathoDoc: Mine was typo and yours was not. You are not a doctor.
MindDoc: Why don't you take your anal retentive personality somewhere else, maybe the spelling room or the vocabulary den?
PathoDoc: Wow, a diagnosis from cyberspace. Amazing. How do you do it? Are you also a psychic?
MindDoc: You don't want to know the rest.

PathoDoc: I was just commenting that you make yourself look like an asshole when you, the MindDoc, don't know how to spell the names of commonly available drugs. It looks ridiculous. You, sir, are a phony.

MindDoc: Typos clown... It's late, and the fingers are thick. No one cares but you.

PathoDoc: Typos my ass.

MindDoc: Why don't you go sit on a rake, fool!

PathoDoc: You can't admit the truth. Misspell those names on the board exam and you don't get licensed.

MindDoc: Mispelled what?

PathoDoc: Amphets and the word that starts with Barb, spell them for me now.

MindDoc: Amphetimines and barbituates, asshole.

PathoDoc: Haha. Amphetamines and barbiturates, jackass. I think I will just print this one up for posterity.

MindDoc: You're too long in path lab. You need some pussy, son.

PathDoc: This is a classical AOL exchange, you even degenerateinto the famous *ad hominem* argument. Can you face up to the misspelling or not?

MindDoc: Why don't you go kick a dog or something.

PathoDoc: What about the misspelling? You still cannot admit it can you. Are you an MD?

MindDoc: I get it. You are one of those doctor wannabes, poor guy who could not make it.

PathoDoc: Meaning what? Are you an MD?

MindDoc: Barbiturates.... No druggist can read the handwriting anyway. Horton cares a who.

PathoDoc: Are you an MD?

MindDoc: I hear the CIA is looking for some pencil push-ers. Some real good spellers. You should apply.

PathoDoc: Simple question. Are you an MD? I guess I know the answer by now.

MindDoc: What I am is of no concern to you. Simply address me as your superior.

PathoDoc: That is what I thought. You are NOT an MD.

MindDoc: There you go thinking again. It's dangerous for one in your condition.

PathoDoc: But, you carry yourself in the room as if you were. It is not really important to me. There are a lot of phony doctors in here. Just wanted to know.

MindDoc: Are you a REAL doctor, that is the question?

PathoDoc: I think you are NOT a doctor, but others in here seem to think you are. If you say you are I am pre-pared to believe it.

MindDoc: More likely you got your little ego bruised in here tonight and you wanted to take it out on a shrink. That's okay. It happens to me every day. We shrinks are the whipping boys of the medical profession. We suffer the arrows and peccadillos in service to humanity.

PathoDoc: Whatever else is going on in here, I speak the truth.

MindDoc: You may speak what you consider to be the truth, but is your truth the real truth?

PathoDoc: I simply asked you if you were a legitimate

MD.

MindDoc: How can I be certain I am receiving the truth from one who is hell bent on attacking me? Physician, heal thyself.

PathoDoc: Okay. I'll stop.

MindDoc: Typos clown... It's late, and the fingers are thick. No one cares but you.

PathoDoc: Mine was typo and yours was not. You are not a doctor.

MindDoc: Would it make any difference to you if I said I was not an MD, that I was a phony?

PathoDoc: No, it really doesn't make any difference to me. I don't give a shit if people in here are MDs or not. In fact, I am growing rather weary of MDs.

MindDoc: That's what I thought. Why don't you tell me what is really bothering you. I am happy to help.

PathoDoc: Most of them are tiresome folks. And I say that from the standpoint of being one. I just became enthralled with your intellectual defensiveness.

MindDoc: Ah hah! A brother of the cloth ranting against his own.

PathoDoc: For some reason you could not admit a simple mistake.

MindDoc: I do now admit it. I persisted only due to your adamance.

PathoDoc: That's what provoked my interest.

MindDoc: I know this. I can read you like a book,

PathoDoc: I made what was perhaps a too-barbed observation.

MindDoc: Have a bad day, doctor?

PathoDoc: But you attempted to "stone wall" ME – a legitimate licensed medical practitioner.

MindDoc: No, I simply made a spelling error.

PathoDoc: Oh, now it doesn't take any advanced degree to know bullshit when you hear it. Here we go again.

MindDoc: It makes no difference what others think of me. I know who I am.

PathoDoc: I will ask you one more time, are you telling me honestly that you did in fact know how to spell barbiturate and that it was all an artifice?

MindDoc: You talk like a baby right out of med school. Yes.

PathoDoc: Then I now sincerely believe you are beyond intellectual redemption and I will desist. Goodnight, sir.

MindDoc: Oh brother, you really are trapped in your own mind. You don't have the mental stones to hang with me, son.

PathoDoc: Could you explain your use of the word "son"? Does that indicate your belief that you are older than I? We will leave intellectual admonishment part for later.

MindDoc: No doubt, by the way you use words.

PathoDoc: Meaning what?

MindDoc: Meaning mentally I am your grandfather.

PathoDoc: Oh, the old "argument from special qualification." Have you been into the old "logical fallacy" section of the philosophy book perhaps? You are hitting them all tonight.

MindDoc: You sound fresh from Philosophy 101. You sure you're not some nerdish college kid, maybe a law school student, playing doctor in the chat room to try and get chicks?

PathoDoc: Please enlighten me as to the reason for the "intentional"misspellings the second time around with barbiturate. I don't think I caught that.

MindDoc: You are like a broken violin – stuck on one note. Perhaps your predilection for barbiturates belies a hidden addiction problem. Been into the medicine chest yourself, Herr Doktor?

PathoDoc: Now you are sounding foolish. I resent that.

MindDoc: You do not understand the ultimate aim of intellect.

PathoDoc: And you do, oh divine one?

MindDoc: Your attempt to mock me falls on barren soil. It will not provoke nor take root.

PathoDoc: How did I know you were going to say something like that?

MindDoc: Because you are 38 years old.

PathoDoc: I must say I am surprised you actually went out on an intellectual limb by saying that. But let me ask sir... Is that just a ploy so when I say how old I am you will say it was just a "mirror" or some such pseudo intellectual garbage?

MindDoc: You say you are honest. Tell me your age.

PathoDoc: I will. But first, venture a little further out on that limb and tell me the meaning if: 1) I am in fact younger; 2) I am in fact older. Sort of the "Greek elder" paradox.

MindDoc: I bet you got an "A" in your logics course.

PathoDoc: Humor me with an answer. Please.

MindDoc: I don't think like you do. It means nothing.

PathoDoc: Clearly, but what if I am older, or what if I am younger than you have stated?

MindDoc: Then your chronological age is askew from your mental.

PathoDoc: What if I told you I was 60?

MindDoc: Then I would say your problem is more advanced than I initially thought.

PathoDoc: Oh god, I love it!!!!!

MindDoc: I'm sure you are a good doctor, cutting up specimens and such. I guess they didn't want to trust you dealing with real live patients, hence the pathology specialization, yes?

PathoDoc: Your patients must LOVE you. You are NEVER wrong. A god among men. Among women too I will wager.

MindDoc: Yes, chicks dig me. But, I do not see appearances in time and space as being "right" or "wrong" per se. To me everything is relative. Women do love me. I am not afraid to look them in the eye

PathoDoc: You cannot answer a simple question, can you?

MindDoc: The spelling bee again? You probably are 60. You manifest classical hang-up profiles for that age. How's the libido?

PathoDoc: But are you an MD? A licensed psychiatrist? You talked about wannabes. Maybe you're the wannbe.

MindDoc: Magna cum lauda, Mod school, 1974.

PathoDoc: Mod school? Another typo I bet.

MindDoc: You're hell with your proofreading, Doc. You missed your calling. Scribners is looking.

PathoDoc: What medical school did you attend?

MindDoc: You seem a little tightly wound to me. I don't need to have you snap and go shoot up a Starbucks somewhere and then blame it on our conversation.

PathoDoc: Damn, you are clever. People must tell you that all the time. Do you always attack people instead of their ideas?

MindDoc: I am not attacking you or your ideas. You have none. I am simply trying to shine a light into that dim cranium of yours, hoping to mop up a damp corner with a thought.

PathoDoc: "Mop up a damp corner with a thought." What the hell does that mean?

MindDoc: It's like a projection test, a Rorschach blot. What does it mean to you is the question?

PathoDoc: Here we go again. I should print this up for the local college logics class and let them analyze it. What a great idea!

MindDoc: The class in which you are currently enrolled,

no doubt.

PathoDoc: Cute. Another blow. I will be back in this room sometime soon and let you know how it turned out.

MindDoc: Ever read The Tao?

PathoDoc: Would you be willing to submit this to a test? Seriously.

MindDoc: Until it becomes boring.

PathoDoc: Would you mind if I submit this in transcript form to some college classes and have analysis done of our verbal exchanges?

MindDoc: One man's ceiling is another man's floor.

PathoDoc: You agree, then, I may use the transcript?

MindDoc: Sure, use it. Whatever blows your skirt up.

PathoDoc: This is truly fascinating to me. Far from boring.

MindDoc: Of course it is fascinating to you. Not often are you handled like a spring pup.

PathoDoc: A "spring pup"? I am not familiar with those rural similes. What does it mean?

MindDoc: You have heard of the season called "spring"?

PathoDoc: Yes, of course.

MindDoc: And you know, being a doctor, a "pup" is a baby dog?

PathoDoc: Yes, of course.

MindDoc: Try to make the leap and string these two concepts together so they form a meaningful phrase in your mind.

PathoDoc: Now you are attempting to mock me.

MindDoc: Not "attempting" doctor, doing it.

PathoDoc: This is another one of your intellectual peregrinations, isn't it?

MindDoc: "Peregrinations." A good word. I bet you have been burning the midnight oil reading the dictionary again. I bet you are revered as a genius in some of the chat rooms.

PathoDoc: Never mind the word. I saw from the beginning, no matter which way I went you had that base covered.

MindDoc: Oneupsmanship bores me. A silly game for little minds.

PathoDoc: Is this another ploy?

MindDoc: Lurking the shadows, hey? Paranoia may be your strong suit.

PathoDoc: So that means I am not an MD? That is really abstruse.

MindDoc: You use "abstruse" incorrectly, doctor. Abstruse means hard to understand. I would have used "inane."

PathoDoc: No, I didn't say "inane." That, sir, would be exactly the wrong word.

MindDoc: Language can be difficult for some.

PathoDoc: Abstruse means only that I cannot understand it.

MindDoc: Now you are using it correctly if it applies to you.

PathoDoc: Which is EXACTLY how I meant it. I will

match vocabulary with anyone.

MindDoc: It is not difficult to understand. Only that you have difficulty in understanding it. Defines "sinecures."

PathoDoc: Conspicuously easy positions that confer advantage without much effort.

MindDoc: Have a lexicographer at the ready down there, do you?

PathoDoc: You've got it all covered, don't you. How about "rodomontade"?

MindDoc: A vulgar word. try "temerity."

PathoDoc: Lack of fear.

MindDoc: Verisimalitude?

PathoDoc: As in the sense of rash truth. But you have to spell it correctly: v-e-r-i-s-i-m-i-l-i-t-u-d-e.

MindDoc: Back to the spelling again. How about "noumena"?

PathoDoc: Any name or naming.

MindDoc: Nope.

PathoDoc: Or phenomenon as in phenomenology. That asshole Kant talked about those.

MindDoc: Way off. No Cohiba.

PathoDoc: Sure it is.

MindDoc: Sorry, but I have a patient on the line and must go. Look up the word "noumena" and study the meaning. I sense this exercise will liberate you from your mental constipation.

PathoDoc: What about your misspelling? You still cannot admit that, can you?

MindDoc: So I misspell sometimes. Good night.

PathoDoc: Thank you. Thank you. Are you really an MD? What med school?

MindDoc: I am not interested in someone of your ilk knowing my true identity.

PathoDoc: I always won spelling bees in school. I believe that good spelling is a sign of high intelligence.

MindDoc: Lots of brilliant dyslexics out there, doc, who cannot put letters in the right order but can run huge corporations. Richard Branson, to name one.

PathoDoc: If you had just said, "I am not a good speller," I would have apologized for my admonitions and begged your pardon. The most intelligent MD I know, a lovely OB-GYN lady I was in love with for a time, was also the shittiest speller I ever knew. I never figured that out. It changed my views on spelling.

MindDoc: In love for a time... bet you drove her nuts correciting her spelling in the bedroom.

PathoDoc: That's not fair.

MindDoc: Yet you have chosen to lambast me for these many minutes about a typo? Called my academic and professional credentials into question?

PathoDoc: Yes, you are right. I apologize.

MindDoc: Apology accepted.

PathoDoc: I usually don't rag on people in these chat rooms. But somehow you provoked me to respond the way I did.

MindDoc: I do use antagonism in my practice to help

reveal a person's inner composure. It helps break down facades. We aim to comfort the afflicted and afflict the comfortable. You seemed too comfortable, stuck in ossified thoughts. You needed a kick in the pants.

PathoDoc: You must be very successful in your practice.

MindDoc: So they tell me.

PathoDoc: It must be fascinating to rummage around all day in the deepest recesses of our little psyches and fantasies. Stripping us metaphorically naked. Worse than felonious mopery with intent to gawk.

MindDoc: See. You can be a funny guy.

PathoDoc: You know, this started out infelicitously, but I really liked it. That's my basic nature, I love the play of the mind and words and ideas and humor found in the most unlikely places.

MindDoc: I commiserate. Must get boring and lonely cutting up specimens all day. Still, you do not have enough originality in your thoughts. Your intellectual programming via the demanding educational system has incumbered you from being the person you secretly wish you could be.

PathoDoc: I have been through lots of therapy and do have a lot more confidence now than I used to have.

MindDoc: You don't seem like an MD. More an artist, a painter perhaps.

PathoDoc: Now you are impressing me. Yes, I am, in fact, a pretty largely frustrated artist. That is my principle love. Damn, "principal."

MindDoc: You are more like 50, not 60, though encumbered with OCD as evidenced by this compulsive spelling disorder of yours.

PathoDoc: Yes, even physically no one ever guesses more than 45 or 46. Wonderful for the Ego. Especially the Id.

MindDoc: What do you paint? Abstracts? Illustrations?

PathoDoc: I do representational art. I'm bringing out a line of hand-painted ties.

MindDoc: Jerry Garcia lives!

PathoDoc: Jerry is dead and I am grateful. Mine have everything from Gene Autry to Special Forces, something to offend everyone.

MindDoc: You say that to defray the possibility of rejection, though you secretly hope and try to make everyone like your ties, and thus you as a person.

PathoDoc: Damn you are insightful!

MindDoc: Good luck with it.

PathoDoc: I'm afraid if people start liking them too much, I would want to dedicate myself to it full time. Then I would discover to my horror I do not have the talent I think I have.

MindDoc: Forget all that nonsense. Just do your best. That's all you can do.

PathoDoc: Thanks. This has been really great. I was going to go to bed early tonight, but your acumen is captivating. Where are you located?

MindDoc: New York City.

PathoDoc: Damn! I'm in the Bay area on the other coast.

I was ready to make an appointment.

MindDoc: Believe in yourself, brother. You are a delightful guy. Keep your acerbic wit holstered in the rooms or you will crush others less wary than I.

PathoDoc: You are wary and very bright.

MindDoc: But am I a real doctor?

PathoDoc: I didn't think so at first, now I'm not sure.

MindDoc: I'll put your mind at ease, my friend. I am NOT. At least not in the traditional sense,

PathoDoc: Oh brother. Good night!

MindDoc: Where can I buy one of your ties?

Night Sounds

dark alone rigid
in fear comes marching
    trampo tramp tramp
scuffed black leather slaps
nameless faceless men
    stampo stamp stamp
imprinting anonimity
disecting individuality
    stampo stampo stamp
bodies wear uncaring
minds wear unknowing
    trampo stampo stamp
coming always coming
nightsticks knock knocking
waiting trembling wondering
    trampo knock knocking
sanity torn asunder
soul rendered souless
    trampo stamp stamp
fading sounds waning
waning sounds wanting
wanting sounds stopping
'til next hour's counting
    tamping tramping tramp.

DEATH OF A DUKE

*"The degree of civilization in a society can be judged
by entering its prisons."*
– Fyodor Dostoevsky

The face was strange, the voice vaguely familiar.
"Hey Fox. Ol' Foxy, come here."

I was heading into the gym to work off a little
tension when I was distracted by a thin black dude in the
lock-up section. The concrete slab serving as the gym's
floor was split in two equal plots by a walkway lined with
heavy gauge chain-link fence. One side teemed with convicts busy at basketball, handball and lifting iron weights.
The other side was vacant except for the gaunt stranger
and another black, locked behind the double mesh. I started to pass.

"Fox. It's me, man!"

I felt it wise to check out the voice so insistent to attract my attention, and walked over. Two liquid brown eyes swam above baggy lower lids dressing an angular face. Sweat streamed from his steel wool hair and ran down to collect in a pair of kerchiefs tied loosely about his throat. A red and a blue. This was significant because you couldn't buy them at the commissary and they were contraband on the unit. They would get you a case if the boss was feeling bitchy.

"It's Earl, man," he said. "From the Dexter Unit."

"Earl?" I still wasn't believing him. The Earl I remembered from Dexter was bigger, lots of flesh and fat and a jolly face.

"I knew an Earl Peterson. 'Earl the Pearl' we called him. But we changed it to—"

"Duke of Earl," he cut me off. "After the song 'cause I was such a bad muthafucka. I lived in H-2, twenty-one cell, bottom bunk. You were next door in twenty-two on top. Your cellie was Ebbie something. Big blond guy who worked in the laundry."

It was Earl all right. I began to piece it together – the voice, the face, the mannerisms – but the changes were numerous.

"You look different," I said. "Thinner, lean even. You've got some muscle tone, a raw edge to you. Before you were flabby. Used to walk with a cane.

"Yeah, well I been workin' out. See."

He flexed his muscles and made a face like a movie
actor. I had to admit he had improved himself consider-
ably. His biceps knotted up into high mounds and lines of
separation outlined his individual muscles in fine definition. I also noticed stretch marks left from the weight he
had dropped.

"You lost some weight, Earl."

"Seventy pounds."

"That's pretty radical. But it's been a year."

"Yeah. Lots of changes, m'man."

It was a cold crawling kind of smirk he flashed me
then, right at home on a face with hate-filled eyes. Something had changed deep inside him. He had been a jiver
and a player, but he used to be able to enjoy himself too.
All that was gone now, replaced by a dark violence I could
feel through the air.

"What are you doing over here in lock-up, Duke?"

"Had some trouble on the chain. Got into with a
dude goin' to the hospital."

I remembered Earl liked to ride the hospital bus. He
was a master hypochondriac and an expert at manipulating
the doctor. Earl had managed to convince him through the
years to get checked out by every specialist the state had
in its prison healthcare stable.

"So, what's the deal?" I asked again, wanting an
update on the mental condition of a fellow convict some
regarded as unpredictable at best.

Earl the Pearl displayed the basis for his early nickname as his facial muscles pulled his cheeks tight over the bones to reveal huge teeth like a cartoon walrus. He was smiling, but his eyes were cold and mirthless.

"The other dude stayed at the hospital. Doctor's orders. Something about broken bones. I think he'll be there a while. Brought me back in shackles and stuck me in lock-up. Took away all my shit. Haven't even got a fan. The run is loaded with crazies who scream all night, throw food and piss, break out the windows and run around like psychos at shower time. Last night they tore up their fuckin' sheets and jammed up the shitters and flooded the place. I wake up and step right into a fucking puddle."

Earl was getting agitated. Foam started to form at the corners of his mouth. His eyes were steady but wild. He stuck his fingers through the woven mess and squeezed his knuckles white.

"You got to take it easy, Earl. Cool down. Already they've got you in lock-up. They can turn the screws to you, Earl."

"Let'em start turnin' then, 'cause I had about all I can take. Time to fight back, I been thinking. The Duke is takin' it no more. From anybody."

Talk like that always unnerves me, because I understand what can happen when a man reaches that point. The point where a man doesn't care any longer to exercise control and restraint over himself. Th point where he feels he is backed into a corner and has nothing to lose. The point where a man starts to become dangerous – unpredictably, savagely dangerous. Earl was near to reaching that point if he hadn't already. I got the feeling an old homeboy like myself would not be immune from his fury should it break loose any time soon. Suddenly I realized the sanity of the chain-link fence.

"I don't see it that way, Earl. This place to me is like quicksand, like one of those Chinese finger stretchers. The more you struggle, the deeper you go or the tighter it gets. But you can be cool and make your way through it and get out of here."

"Yeah, unless you're man enough to bust that finger stretcher right off. Tear it up. Rip it right off your fingers and your hands will be free."

"Only it's not straw in here, Earl. The chains in here are tempered steel. You're not Superman."

"Yeah? Who the fuck says I ain't?"

Earl had an answer for everything. I was beginning to see that my words were having no effect. His hatred was too deeply rooted and was growing like a cancer inside him.

As if to bleed off some of the tension forming in the air around us, the silent mulatto inside the cage with Earl got up and started to work the heavy bag with his fists. His blows thudded like quick snaps of thunder. Earl looked pleased at the support for his tirade. The one-man rebellion had been increased to two.

*   *   *

A job came open in the Major's office and I sent in the proper form for an interview. Ol' Jonesy had made his parole third time up after doing six flat on twenty. The Major called me down for an interview at six o'clock in the morning. I stood outside in the hallway for half an hour before I heard him boom "Come in" through the closed door.

I entered quickly and stood in a respectful position before his desk. The Major was struggling to assemble some kind of printed report into a colored tag board binder. Lieutenant Green, a younger white field boss, sat off to the side scraping mud from his boot into a trash can.

"What did you have on your mind there, Ol' Fox?" The Major questioned me condescendingly.

"Bookkeeper's job, sir. I'm strong in math, good with ledgers, numbers. Can type sixty words a minute, have a college degree, sir. Used to run a construction company in the world."

The brief summary of what I thought would be pertinent credentials seemed to irritate him. The stack of pages burst from his hands and spread out all over the floor of the room.

"Damn!" The Major glared at me like it was my fault. I sensed my opportunity was at hand.

"Let me help you, sir," I said, bending down to gather the sheets. I worked rapidly and in a moment had the offending pages ordered and bound. I set the completed report before him and employed my best imitation of obsequiousness.

"There you are, sir. No problem."

Lieutenant Green looked up over his buck knife. I noticed his big toe was poking through his sock on the foot where the muddy boot was missing. He articulated his version of a command.

"There's a stack of them books that needs puttin' tagatha."

He nodded to the stack and spit into the trash can, releasing a stream of dark amber from the wad in his cheek that dribbled on his chin.

"Yes, sir. Right away, sir." I sounded like a new recruit eager to please his superiors.

I sat down at a small table against the wall and began to silently organize and collate copies of a report detailing updated sexual harassment complaint procedures. The two prison officers verbally evaluated my person in their own brand of code.

"You know 'im?" The Major inquired of the Lieutenant.

"Naw. Seen 'im around."

Pause... Buck knife scraping mud. Desk chair rocking, squeaking.

"Looks like he's got some snap."

"Yup."

"Be pretty hard to replace Ol' Jonesy."

"Jonesy was a good hand."

Pause... Buck knife folding. Foot squeezing into boot.

"Jonesy minded his own business. Never gave us any guff."

"Jonesy was awright."

"This one looks pretty good too."

"He might be able to cut it, Major."

"Why don't we give him a shot, LT."

"Okay by me."

The flow of words changed direction to include the one being observed during the dialogue.

"Where you workin' now, Ol' Fox?"

"Garment factory, Major," I said.

"What's a convict like you doing sewing overalls?"

"That's where they assigned me, Major."

"Makes a lot of sense, doesn't it Fox?" quizzed the Lieutenant.

I sensed a test of some kind in his question. It seemed designed to measure my true opinion of their system. From my answer they would be able to tell whether or not I would fit in as the new bookkeeper. A sincere, comprehensively evasive answer wrapped in respect was my ticket out of the garment factory.

"Well, sir, they process a thousand or so men through Diagnostics every two weeks. They have to analyze a lot of data and make the best decisions they can. I'm sure it's hard to find the perfect slot for everybody. I think what they do is just try to get close and once you get to your unit you're supposed to use a little initiative and find the right spot for yourself. That's why I'm here this morning, Major. I'd like to work in a capacity that utilizes some of my skills, where I'd be of maximum service to the institution. That way we both benefit."

When I turned around and set the completed stack of bound reports on his desk, the Major's eyes were wide and his expression blank, as if he was attempting to fathom some great mystery.

"There you are, sir," I said calmly, eagerly. "What's next?"

The Major glanced at the reports that had baffled him, then up at me. He seemed to be perceiving me from a renewed perspective.

"Get down to the laundry, Fox," he ordered. "Get yourself some pressed clothes. If you're going to work in this office you can't look like you just fell off the turnip truck. What's your number?"

"H-17-223-83."

The Major made a move for the phone.

"Take off, Fox. Get the clothes and come right back. Ol' Jonesy left things a mess and you seem like the one to get them straight. I'm callin' Garment right now and having you transferred."

"Yes, sir. Thank you, sir." A closing expression of anticipated gratitude. I skipped out through the heavy plate door and headed for the laundry. This was going to be easier than I had thought. The Major needed me.

*   *   *

Weeks rolled by and I adjusted to a somewhat
civilized setting. The main difference was being out of
earshot from the hatcheting machines and lint dust that,
in two minutes, would settle a quarter-inch thick on a cup
of coffee. The Major was right about things being a mess.
Whether it had been Jonesy or someone else, it was hard
to tell. But Jonesy took the blame. It's always that way
when a guy goes home. He was the dumbest clown to
have hit the unit that decade.

It took a while to gain the Major's trust, and that
was, at best, dependent upon his coarse vicissitudes of
mood. But soon I was able to help effect certain changes.
Little things, like moving one-legged men off top bunks,
weren't too difficult to convince the Major about. Getting
a guy with reoccurring hepatitis out of the food-prepara-
tion area was a little harder. But with back-up from medical records, and case law indicating how the unit could get
in trouble with the Federal examiners, the Major begrudg-
ingly saw his way clear to make the change.

In prison, the status quo is the rule. No procedures
ever change except under duress. Only emergencies receive extra attention and in them lies the only hope of
modifying procedure for the good. To see the Major was
hard, at best inconvenient. It was purposefully made that
way. If you were hurting bad enough, you would stand

on the wall for hours waiting, or come back four and five times to see him. Twelve years in the prison business had given the Major a keen acumen to bust about any act or facade. Working as his bookkeeper, I was party to many of his interviews and over time developed a special respect for his perceptiveness. But once in a while a convict was able to get over on him. The Duke of Earl was just such a convict.

I had not seen Earl since that day in the gym, but had been able to track him though the move slips that crossed my desk. About three weeks after I took over Jonesy's job, Earl was moved from lock-up over to D-Building, the skid row block, home of the most violent and incorrigible prisoners. Our unit was classified as medium-minimum security and Earl would have been on a maximum unit like Dexter but for his medical problems. This was the infirmary unit and when inmates like Earl had to be here they were sequestered in D-Building.

The problem was Johnny Boy. The pretty mulatto had been moved from lock-up to A-Building and this interrupted what I found out was a heavy sexual thing he had with Earl.

Earl had held out for the first three or four years thinking his appeal would come through, but when it got denied. leading to the futile anxieties of climbing the judicial ladder to the Supreme Court, Earl needed sexual release. A need that grew stronger day by day in reverse ratio to his desire to wait for a woman. With a 75-year sentence, Earl would have to do at least twelve flat to come up for parole, but with his lengthy record of prior offenses, he could bet on several set-offs. That was fifteen years without sex, and Earl soon became convinced that a pretty young boy was a hell of a lot better than his fading memories.

Johnny Boy had not been the first, but was the current favorite of the Duke. Earl was actually in love with Johnny and was insanely jealous and possessive. I was getting out soon and could wait for a woman's touch, but I guess I could understand Earl's fascination. Slim but taut, cafe au lait coloring, dazzling green eyes and ripe full lips that frequently parted into a smile that must have said "I dare you" to Earl when they first met. Johnny loved Earl too, in his own kind of way, and was down with twenty for killing a pimp. They needed each other. They were good together. I saw that the first day in the gym. So Earl came to see the Major about a move.

"What is it Peterson?"

"I want to integrate, Major," Earl said after waiting two hours on the wall. "Need your permission for the move."

Getting moved in with a friend was next to impossible or the Major would have daily lines waiting a hundred deep. Integration was another story. It looked good when the races were mixing voluntarily. The Federal monitors ate it up. It made the prison's socialization process appear to be working.

I looked up from my computer when I heard Earl come on with his approach. It was a brilliant tactic.

"Who's the other inmate, Peterson?"

"John Randall, sir. Lives in A4-21."

"Randall... Randall. Doesn't ring a bell. Pull his tag, Fox."

I went over to the master board that filled an entire wall. Every bunk in the entire unit was located in complex diagram. I pulled the tag under bunk A4-21 and brought it over to the Major.

"Randall, John," the Major read. "Caucasian. Stewart's Dept. Where's Randall now, Peterson? Why isn't he here with you?"

"Sick call. He's having medical problems. That's why I want him with me. He needs someone to look after him. He gets these fainting spells, Major. Has to take special medicine."

The Major scrutinized the Duke. Something was amiss, but he couldn't put his finger on it.

"Who is your cellie now, Peterson?"

"Don't have one, sir. He went home yesterday."

Earl had all his ducks in a row. He made things attractive to the institution, and thus the Major. No third party to move, an integration. How Earl had gotten Johnny's race designated as "Caucasian" was another indication of his skill as a politician. Earl had passed the night bookkeeper a taste of some chronic weed he bribed a guard to smuggle in.

"Make out a move slip, Fox," the Major decided.

I rolled it through the typewriter, imprinted both names, numbers and cell locations. The Major took it, checked it and slid it across his desk.

"Okay, sign it."

Earl Peterson made his obligatory mark.

"Have Randall come by and sign it and I'll authorize the move."

"But, Major," Earl said. "You're going on vacation tomorrow. If you would, sir, could you sign it while I'm here and I'll have John come in later? Lieutenant Green will be here."

The master stroke. The Major would never lay eyes on mulatto Johnny. He grabbed the paper and scrawled his signature.

"Okay. Dismissed, Peterson. I got better things to do than spend another minute with your goat-smellin' ass."

"Thank you, Major," Earl fawned.

Only I saw his sly smirk as he slid through the door. The Duke of Earl.

Johnny went in the next day as planned and signed the move slip before Lieutenant Green, consenting to the integration. Green was stumbling around, power-tripping and trying to fill the Major's shoes. The Major's signature on the slip was all he needed to pass it right through. I made up some new bed tags, slid them in the proper slots on the big board, and went about my business.

An hour later Earl and his mulatto were hot after it behind a bedsheet hung up over the bars. This was the beginning of the end for both of them, but you never would have known it then. They were just another happy couple.

*   *   *

Earl had been having his toenails cut out one at a time at a month's lay-in from work apiece. Johnny Boy kept them supplied with goods from the Steward's Department they traded on the block. Earl gambled at dominoes in the day room while Johnny cooked for the guards. In the afternoons they'd go to the gym, pump iron for a couple hours, then shower and be back on the run for the evening's business. D1-25 was on ground level at the very end of the run, the perfect location as headquarters for all kinds of illicit activities.

The Duke ruled fairly over his minions and enterprises, but came down iron-handed on those who broke their word or crossed him in any way. Maintaining control was a matter of image and the Duke was frighteningly adept at inducing loyalty and respect in those with whom he had dealings. He had given up on his appeal and had steeled himself to do the long run. If he had to do fifteen or twenty years flat, he'd do it on his own terms.

He felt he really had nothing to lose. Earl was discreet in his dealings and the bosses left him alone. He was new on this unit and hadn't caused any trouble since the hospital chain. Little things like that are quickly forgotten. D-Block was rough anyway and the guards didn't like to come too far inside without official business. And then they never came alone.

Earl was a natural leader and organizer. He had boundless energy and an unlimited capacity for managing his ventures designed to beat the Man at his own game. Once he got going, Duke's reputation spread quickly.

Before long he had established working relationships with everybody who was anybody. He didn't deal with short timers or fools, but every solid dude knew the Duke and treated him with respect. There weren't many inside who would back up their play with their life, but the Duke of Earl was concrete. Minor players hung around him like flies. He got big, real big, too fast. And that was the problem.

Competition. Things had been operating fine long before Earl arrived on the unit and the old power structure didn't like the rapid rise of the new kid on the block. Steaks had always been available on D-Block for three decks of real world cigarettes, but Earl provided them hot and seasoned. Marijuana joints were four decks, but the Duke's stash would stone three or four guys instead of one. Duke had prettier punks, many he had turned out himself. During football season, parlays paid five-to-one with the Duke, while Bumblebee still paid four-to-one.

Bumblebee. Six-foot-four, two-forty, could bench press 460 pounds and wore size thirteen triple-E brogans. Bumblebee had inherited D-Block from Wolfman four years back when Wolf finally discharged an 80-year sentence after serving twenty-five flat. So called because of his dark saucer-sized sunglasses and teeth of pollen gold, the Bee lived at the roof of the world in D5-25, right above Earl, five open tiers upward. He felt the drain caused by Duke's action from day one but, to save face, blew it off in front of his runners and supplicants. But inside, the lava was beginning to flow.

It wasn't until Magpie, Bumblebee's cellie and educated book man, did some figuring and found that business was the lowest ever. Bumblebee dispatched Highside, his A-number-one handyman and all-around snoop. A few days later Highside had uncovered an exploitable crack in the Duke's organization that bubbled with the emotional intensity necessary to get the Duke to blow his cool.

Earl was at the hospital getting his sixth toenail removed when Highside slid up next to Johnny Boy as he was coming back from the kitchen.

"Johnny Boy. Where's the Duke?"

"Hospital. What's up?"

"Something special jus come in. Gotta find Duke or he's goin' miss it."

"He won't be back 'til afta chow."

"That's too bad, 'cause it's real pretty. Too bad you can't handle it."

That was the barb that finally got to Johnny Boy. He was tired of people thinking he was just the Duke's "gal" and nothing more.

"Sure. I can handle it. What's the deal?"

"Sinsemilla. Fresh and strong. Two ounces."

"You know the Duke always likes to test it first himself."

"Thought you said you could handle it."

"Who's the man?"

"Bumblebee. But, Streaker from C-Block is on his way over to take a look."

Johnny Boy drew himself up to a new height.

"All right. Let's go."

I know this dialogue is accurate. A little bird told me. An old convict we call Fossil who sweeps the runs and has powers of hearing equal to a sophisticated eaves-dropping device the police might use. Fossil is half snitch, half self-appointed peacemaker. He's been know to give up a minor asshole to the Man so bigger fish can swim and feed in the deep. He's been around since before half the guys in here were born and is considered almost a tradi-tion, an exhibit like in a museum.

According to Fossil, Johnny Boy followed Highside up to D5-25 to see Bumblebee and test the weed. Bumblebee came on real cordial, had a fat one already rolled and told Johnny Boy, if he liked it, he could make the deal in Duke's place. Said he'd been watching, and thought Johnny's talents were going unappreciated, that he had more potential than was being utilized.

Johnny Boy enjoyed this banter, and as he smoked

the reefer, his feelings of self-importance soared. Johnny Boy played the big shot, smoked the joint deep and fast, said he could handle it no matter how strong it was. What he didn't realize was that Bumblebee had laced the joint with a heavy hit of hog tranquilizer, angel dust, a hit that would have knocked a donkey's dick in the dirt. A few minutes later the pretty mulatto slid down glassy-eyed in Bumblebee's bunk, like his body was suddenly robbed of all its bones.

Bumblebee brutalized the poor boy that afternoon, asserting his territorial rights again and again for over two hours. Later, the autopsy report would show his internal organs had been ruptured. That was before Bumblebee stood outside his cell with Johnny Boy held high over his head and rattled the barred windows with his blood-curdling yell. The echoes continued after the body had fallen five stories and landed in front of cell D1-25, just as Earl was entering the run. He threw his cane aside and started running toward the blur of tan flesh. When he reached the body, the shrieking started and didn't stop until the Duke was dead.

A call came into the Major's office from the building sergeant about then and I watched Lieutenant Green's face go white with fear.

"Seal off the block!" he barked into the phone. "I'm calling SORT." Special Operations Retention and Tactics.

The Lieutenant began dialing furiously, bracing himself with thoughts of what the Major would do. I slipped out the door and eased my way down to D-Block. The crash gates were locked tight when I got there and I joined the crush of inmates looking up through the bars at the open stairway. I heard a noise, but couldn't place it. Then Earl ran by and I saw that he was screaming. It was an inhuman sound, one a hyena might make after tearing off its leg in the jaws of a steel trap. The riot squad ran up and stopped. Not one of them wanted to go inside D-block.

"Let'em cool off a little," said a helmeted corpsman as he slapped a stout oak club into his other palm.

The Duke took the stairs three at a time, with one foot swathed in bandages. He carried a length of hollow pipe, flattened and sharpened like a spear. In his other hand was a shorter shiv with a double-sided blade ground shiny at the edges. The Duke didn't see me. He didn't see anything but the broken body of Johnny Boy magnified by his rage.

Duke met Bumblebee halfway down 5 run and drove the spear through his mouth and out the back of his head. Bumblebee was weakened by his sex and other exertions, but still managed to drive a shank under Earl's rib cage before the Duke toppled him over the railing. He landed about twenty feet from us inside the bars with a thud I could feel through my shoes.

A moment later Duke stumbled down the stairs, eyes wide and spitting up blood. He wore Bumblebee's shank rooted in a wet stain on his left side. Red gauze bandages trailed from his foot like an obscene tail. He reached the body, stunning everyone to silence as he went to work with the short knife. Metal scraped concrete. The Duke stood up, limped toward where we stood watching, convicts and the cops. He dragged his left foot and held up Bumblebee's head by the black knotty hair. He approached the bars and pointed at the head with his bloody shiv.

"This guy has been fucking with me," the Duke said.

Then he fell against the bars and slid to the floor.

To A Pulp

After 22 years on Prolixin
Clifton begs through the bars
a light for his state issued twist.

He was a fine son once, a worker
who could go all day. Loved his
mother, father, brother, sister...
But he heard strange noises
a buzzing along the hairline
told him to look inside his
grandfather's head.

The answer was to give him LIFE
without parole; LIFE with a chance
and saving himself; LIFE for a life.

No good for work any more, he paces
back and forth, up and down,
all day and sleepless night
hoping someone will offer a
shot of coffee a smoke a chocolate.

"Maybe I get some mail today or a
money slip." He wrote his sister
seven years ago for $10. "Maybe I'll
        write back and ask for five."

His head is like his grandfather's
        now... beat to a pulp.

ME AND BOB

"I am convinced that basically dogs think humans are nuts."
–John Steinbeck

I was relaxing on top of the comfy sofa watching snow drift down outside the front window when Bob pulled up the driveway in his shiny black SUV. My ears perked up as he got out and opened the hatch, disappeared for a moment, then marched toward the front door. Little plastic bags stuffed with groceries hung from his arms like sausages. I could tell there was some meat and a box of those ginger biscuits Mary brought Bob with his tea. If I was nearby, I could usually cajole Bob out of a biscuit or two, depending upon how many Mary brought and how

fat he thought he was. Bob was always worrying about his
waistline. More often than not, a cookie or a piece of meat
was dropped on the floor in front of me due to his dietary
guilt.

"Damn!" Bob said.

I heard his key turn in the lock just before a bag
dropped on the foyer tile, putting an end to his fancy mustard. I knew it was fancy mustard, not the cheap yellow
kind, from the sound of the crash, the odor of mustard,
and from the way Bob articulated "Damn." If it were the
cheap yellow kind, he wouldn't have cared so much. Plus
it came in plastic tubs and would have bounced. I know
a bounce from a crash, just like I know the scratch of a
raccoon against the trash can or a mouse scampering from
the dining room to the little crack in the kitchen baseboard
he squeezes through when the cat is after him.

I watched Bob struggle with the bags as he kicked
the front door open with his foot. What a clown! He
always tries to carry the maximum amount to save trips,
then ends up crashing the mustard, or the apple juice like
he did last week. One time he had a birthday cake for little
Alice balanced on top of a case of beer and it slid off. Bob
tried to catch it with his foot, but the toe of his wing tip
caught in his pant cuff, and he ended up kicking the cake
up in the air. He sure looked funny when the cake came
down on his head with a crown of blue and white icing.
Some more profane cursing that day for sure, but I helped
him clean up, licking that sweet icing off the tile until it

was gone. Mary threw me out of the bed that night I was farting so much.

Bob set his load in the kitchen and went outside for the rest, when Mary came down the stairs.

"Oh. Bob. Not the mustard. Glass and everything. I told you to get the squeeze bottle."

"It tastes better in the glass," Bob said, sidestepping her, his arms heavy with the bags. "No worries. There's some Gulden's in the fridge."

Mary looked down at the mess, her hands on her hips, then she looked up at me.

"What are you looking at? Big help you are."

I wasn't going to help. I never did and it wasn't expected of me. If I started helping out and doing things, God knows where it would all end. They would have kept me busy from morning to night. No, best just to play dumb and let them handle it. It was fun watching them manage their lives and yell at each other. Sometimes after a terrible row they would go up to the bedroom and lock the door. I'd listen outside and hear noises that didn't make sense.

It seemed like Bob was hurting her, but after they came out Mary always seemed happy and dreamy, like the way she looked when she came back from her tennis lesson.

Bob got a mop and broom and cleaned up his mess as Mary prepared dinner in the kitchen. I was curious about the menu and strolled in through the dining room, my alleged purpose to get a drink of water. I heard the soft rub of fur just in time to alter my course as Opie lashed out with a paw where he was hiding in a velvet chair. It was a game we played. I controlled the floor and he controlled the space above.

When he did manage to give me a scratch on the ear or snout, I would remember it the next time Bob and Mary went out. Then he had better stay high or get a nip. One time I chased him through the closet and got a coat hanger stuck in my collar. Bob and Mary got a laugh out of that when they got home and talked about it for weeks. How it got in my collar they never could figure out.

I scratched at the door and Mary let me out on the deck. The wood was cold under my paws, but I had to piss. The ground was visible under the bare magnolia tree. I picked my way over, stomping through the snow that came up to my chest. I watched the flakes flutter down as I stood there, all peaceful and white. No odor in snowflakes.

Bob caught my eye as I approached the kitchen door and let me in.

"Get in here, girl. What are you doing out there?"

"She's relieving herself, what do you think?" Mary added. "You don't want her to go in the house do you?"

To me, that was a dumb question. But that was just Mary's way of riding Bob and keeping him under control. Dogs and cats do it too. All species do. It's how nature has things designed to maintain balance and order.

I could smell the meatloaf cooking and started to

salivate.

"Think I'll watch the game," Bob said, looking toward the fridge. At this point he had to make a decision: beer and chips or tea and cookies. I moved in and blocked the fridge, wagging my tail and looking at Bob all droopy-eyed. Bob tried to get in the fridge but I stood my ground. He soon gave up, my presence tipping the scales.

"Some tea when you get a chance," Bob said.

"Yes, dear."

"And a few of those ginger snaps."

"Sure."

I like Mary okay, she's a good wife to Bob and always cleans my bowls before she sets my food out at night. But me and Bob are pals.

I followed Bob into the living room and we assumed our usual positions on the sofa. He grabbed the remote and found the game. I don't personally get anything out of watching a football game, or watching anything on television for that matter. How humans can sit for hours and look at a flat screen with images jumping around accompanied by irritating sounds, is beyond me. I'd rather Bob watch the game than play the game like they do next door, bouncing a ball and throwing it up into what looks like a thick spider's web. You never know where that ball will come down and it's best to stay way out of the way or you're in for a tumultuous round of cursing, maybe even a kick or two. Besides, I know Mary will eventually bring tea and cookies, and Bob will share what he has with me.

We watched the game awhile, or Bob watched it and I watched for Mary with the refreshments. Finally they came. Mary always wanted attention from Bob when she brought him something, and this time it came in what must have been a real important part of the game. Bob tried to get her to be quiet for a minute, but Mary doesn't like it when she has to play second fiddle to a stupid ball game on TV. She carried on and on, making a big deal out of what could have been avoided by a polite sentence or two and totally ruined the rest of the game.

Bob got up in a huff, went out to the garage and starting tinkering with some of his gadgets. Mary went up to her room.

That left me with the plate of ginger snaps.

Who's running the show here? Tell me. I'd really like to know. When's that meat loaf going to be ready?

BAGGAGE

"Courage is not the absence of fear, but rather the assessment that something else is more important than fear."
–Franklin D. Roosevelt

"Carry the bag or we'll kill you."

My hands and feet were tied, a dirty kerchief stuffed in my mouth. Grey duct tape smothered my face like an oppressive hand. The guy with the gun ripped the tape away. Then the blindfold.

"What'll it be?"

My mouth was dry as a nest of powder. I spit out the kerchief. I tried to speak, but the words stuck in my throat. I swallowed hard and blinked, trying to get my eyes to focus.

"I… ah."

The small man became impatient, turned and tore away the impediments from Jose's eyes and mouth.

"What about you? Will you carry the bags?"

"What's in them?" Jose's voice cracked.

"It doesn't matter what's in the bags." The man hit him with the pistol, cocked it and jabbed the barrel into Jose's mouth.

"I'll take them," I croaked, hoping to lessen the violence.

The man glared at me, assessing my sincerity. He pointed the pistol at the rusted tin ceiling and let the hammer slowly drop to safe. Jose gasped and started muttering to himself.

We had been in the hovel for three days waiting for the coyote before realizing we were given bad directions, or misunderstood them, and chose the wrong house. The drug smuggler's house. They snuck in when we were sleeping, threw blankets over us and beat us with bats. Then tied us up.

Every once in a while they would grab one of us to drag outside. There would be loud words and screams. Sometimes gunshots. Looking around I counted three of us. Me, Jose and one other bound and gagged on the dirt floor against the wall. We once had been twelve.

"Get up," the man said, hauling the rope that secured my hands behind my back. His strength was surprising and his breath foul. His eyes were brown, like smooth stones you'd find in a stream.

He shoved me into the wall, held my face against the plaster while he untied the knots. The plaster was rough and hurt my face. My arms were cramped and stiff and I moved them slowly, loosening the joints, working life back into the muscles.

"Pick it up." The man nodded to a case on the dirt floor. It was dark grey Samsonite with key locks.

"He's too weak," said the other man, a tall thin gringo with blond hair. A blue steel machine gun with a banana clip was slung across his chest.

"He can do it," the first man said. "You can do it, right boy?"

"Yes. I can do it."

"Pick up the bag and follow me," the second man said.

My legs were weak from all the sitting. My right calf cramped and I bent to massage it. He snap-kicked his boot into my ribs and sent me sprawling.

"Leave the kid alone, Zack," the first man said.

"Shut up, Lou. I want to see if he can really carry the bag. He has to carry it a long way."

"I can carry it," I said.

"Saying is one thing. Doing is another."

I got up, gripped the plastic handle and lifted the bag off the ground. It was heavy, like it was filled with dirt. It must have weighed 20 kilos. I walked it around the room, switching hands to show my capability.

"How about the other one?" Zack said, wiping sweat from his pale blue eyes above a thick sandy mustache. The late afternoon heat made the shack seems like a chimera.

"Jose can do it too," I said. "He can carry the bag." They looked at me, then at Jose.

"Can you do it?" the first man said, glaring at Jose, his patience wearing thin.

Jose looked up at them. He was afraid. He was small and thin without much muscle.

"A pussy," Zack said. "We should shoot him and bury him with the others."

"Get up, Jose," I said. "Get up and show them you can carry the bag."

Jose struggled to his feet and held his hands out so the man could cut the rope. He flexed his hands, grabbed the handle and lifted the bag off the ground. He walked in a tight circle in demonstration.

"See, he can do it," Lou said.

"He can in here," said Zack. "But can he carry it all the way to the river? Cross the river and tote it another mile to the meeting place?"

"I can do it," Jose said, realizing it was do or die.

"If you wimp out you will get a bullet right here."

Zack touched the middle of his forehead with the tip of his middle finger. Jose shivered and lifted the bag higher as he circled.

Lou went to the edge of the room, reached down

and dragged the girl out by her long hair.

"What about this one?" Lou asked.

Zack glared at Jose. "Do you know this girl?"

"Yes," Jose spoke slowly. "She is my cousin, Yolanda."

"Your cousin! Yolanda! Such a pretty thing, hey Zack." Lou pulled her hair back, then kissed her hard on the mouth.

Yolanda bit his lip, turned away and spit. Lou slapped her down in the dirt. Then reached down and tore away her dress, exposing her breasts.

"Please, señor," Jose said. "Let her go and I will do whatever you say."

"See how easy it is, Anglo?" Lou grinned at Zack. "Push the right buttons they become donkeys."

"We need donkeys to carry the bags." Zack gave Lou a stern look.

Lou stared down at Yolanda, whimpering and trying to cover herself. "What do we do with her? We can't let her live, she has seen our faces."

Zack cocked his weapon and pointed it at her chest.

"Wait," I said. "I know Yolanda. She is the strongest girl in Topolobampo. She was the captain of her soccer team. She can carry a bag. You would get three bags to the meeting place instead of two."

I could see the wheels turning behind their eyes, greed overpowered their love of brutality and extortion.

"Getting sixty kilos of product across the border

would be a better choice, señor."

Lou looked at me. "What is your name?"

"Martinez," I lied in my best Spanish accent. "Pedro Martinez."

"You want to be a vato, Pedro?"

"I want to live, señor."

"Smart boy."

Lou picked up a blanket, folded it in half and cut a slice in the middle with a sheaf knife. He opened the cut and slipped the blanket over Yolanda's head like a serape to cover her nakedness. Then he cut away the ropes from her hands, grabbed her wrist and pulled her to her feet.

"Pick up the bag."

Yolanda gripped the handle and pulled up. Strain flooded her face, but she stood erect and walked the bag around the room.

"No es nada," she said.

The banditos exchanged a shrug.

"We will make it, señor," Jose said, asserting himself. "It would be good if we could have some food. To build strength to carry the bags."

Lou slid his pistol into his waistband, took two steps to the door and yelled outside.

"Carmela! Frijoles!"

"Agua, señor," I added. We had gone without water for a day.

"Mas agua!"

Lou turned back at us and smiled. "You will get

some food, some water. We treat you right and you treat us right. A good arrangement, yes?"

He looked straight at me. I saw a glimmer of fake kindness within the hardness. There were many tales of banditos chopping off heads. I had to keep them interested in our value to them.

Carmela brought food and water and we consumed it ravenously. She was older and wore compassion in her face. She lingered to make sure we were cared for then left.

"When we carry the bags to the meeting place," I asked, "what then?"

"Then… you are free to go," Lou said.

"Yes, but we will have nothing," Jose added. "You took our money and our papers. We will be stuck in the desert with no place to go and no way to get there."

Zack laughed. "If you have no place to go, what does it matter how you get there?"

Jose sighed and put on his best hangdog look.

"You are right, Jose," Lou said. "We are not monsters. We are businessmen. You do us a service and should be paid. Maybe you will do us a service again."

"That would be very agreeable, señor," Jose spoke up.

"When you bring the product to the meeting place, I will pay you five hundred American dollars for each bag." He tried hard to reflect the authenticity of his promise on his face.

"You are very generous, señor," I said, realizing no matter how well we performed he was going to kill us after the delivery.

*   *   *

The three of us rode in the back of an open truck with the suitcases, Lou and Zack in the cab. They had us handcuffed to metal rings in the bed to prevent escape.

The moon was full in the clear October sky, illuminating the river ahead like a long silver serpent. A stench rose from the Rio Grande, a mix of fertilizer and rotting garbage caused by the flotsam collecting on the river bank.

After many minutes of bouncing on a dirt road we came to a spot of concealment behind a stand of scrub cedar. Lou slammed the truck into park and opened the rusty door. A cool breeze swept in from the west and carried the dust away.

Zack got out and turned on an orange light he had strapped around his head. Lou unlocked our cuffs. He motioned with the machine gun. "Get out and grab the bags."

I hopped over the side and Jose passed me the three suitcases. I then helped Yolanda down. We exchanged a look that told me she was ready for what we must do.

"These too," Lou ordered. He opened the rear cab door. I walked over and peered inside. There were three more suitcases.

"That makes six bags, not three," I said.

"Smart little monkey," Lou responded. "Two each."

"How can we carry two bags?" Jose stammered.

"You will find the strength, or..." Zack set his hand on Yolanda's shoulder.

"If we carry two bags, we should be paid for two bags," I said.

"Did you hear that, Lou?" Zack scoffed at my boldness. "He wants to be paid for two bags."

"He is lucky we are letting him carry one bag," Lou said.

"We should kill them like the others," Zack threatened, panning us with the machine gun.

"Wait a second," I said, climbing back in the truck bed to fish out a length of hemp rope. "We can do it."

I hopped down and scrambled under the base of a cedar tree looking for a stout branch. I found one and tried to break it, but it held firm.

A machete appeared bathed in an orange light. I stepped back. Zack severed the branch with several expert chops, then looked at me and smiled.

"Two more," I said. "To carry the bags."

Zack went to work on the tree and in a moment I had three perfect wooden poles. I measured the rope, held it out and Zack severed it into three pieces. I quickly tied the rope across the poles, knotted it at each end so a length hung down.

"Come here, Jose."

I slid the pole across his shoulders and tied the bags

so they would swing off the ground. The weight was supported by his back muscles and he could steady the ropes with his hands.

"Clever, boy," Lou said, as I fashioned a similar support for Yolanda, then myself.

Zack nodded and slid his machete in a leather sheath strapped to his pant leg. "Vamanos!"

"Wait," Jose said. Everyone looked at him. "We should be paid one thousand dollars. I want to hear you say it."

Blood rose in Zack's face, but Lou put a hand on his arm. "He's right, Zack. Two bags, twice the wages."

"It doesn't matter anyway," Zack spat. "Let's get on with it."

Lou led the way down the dirt path toward the river, Zack close at our backs. Lou carried a yellow cube of rubber I assumed was an inflatable raft.

"You have done this before, Lou?" I asked him.

"Many times."

"What about the patrols?"

"They are no problem."

"How do you do it?"

"We have our ways."

I sensed resistance to the question and changed tact.

"I don't mind this work," I said. "It is exciting and pays well."

Lou glanced at me again, like I was missing something.

"Yes. The pay is good," he said, hiding a smirk.

We broke through the last stand of brush and cactus and down below was the once mighty Rio Grande. The summer had been dry and land owners upstream diverted water to feed their crops and herds. The sharp cliffs carved in the bank spoke of the river's former prominence, reduced to a rivulet with a deep portion in the middle no wider than a highway.

"Wait," Lou said, turning. "Take a rest." He motioned with his hand and we set the bags down.

Lou scanned the riverbank with binoculars. Zack took a canteen from his belt, took a deep drink then handed it to Jose. Jose handed it to Yolanda. She took it and drank her fill and handed it back. Jose handed it to me.

"You first."

"No you." We shared a look that told me he and Yolanda understood and that we were together in whatever we had to do. I drank and Jose finished it.

"This next part is tricky," Zack said as a flashlight blinked twice from the other side of the river. "Let's go."

We hefted our yokes and the bags swung just off the ground. They were heavy but we got used to them. We had to. The dirt was dry leading to the narrow stream and crumbled as we descended from the rise. Zack went on ahead and inflated the raft at the water's edge.

"Put the bags in the raft."

I put mine in then helped Jose and we both helped

Yolanda. She started to get in the raft.

"No," Lou commanded. "The raft is for the bags."

He swiveled his head and the orange light painted a stripe across the river.

"Let's carry the yokes," I said. "We can help each other."

I went first and stepped into the gently flowing water. It was chilly and not too deep. I waded out to my chest.

Yolanda followed holding the end of my yoke in one hand, her yoke in the other. Jose grabbed her yoke and extended his for Lou. He grabbed it and we formed a line.

Zack pushed the raft ahead and the current played with it.

I stepped ahead and my feet no longer touched the river bottom. "It's deep," I said. "Can you swim?"

"Yes," Yolanda nodded and started to kick the water.

"Hold on to the raft," Zack said.

The raft came toward us and bumped off Yolanda. She grabbed the side and pulled Jose up to it with the yoke.

"You said it was shallow," Lou yelled at Zack. "I can't swim!" He let go of the yoke and was thrashing about on the surface.

That was the opportunity we had been waiting for. Yolanda jabbed the end of her yoke hard into Lou's face as Jose swarmed over him in the dark, holding him under.

"Lou?" Zack shouted as I hit him with my yoke in the back of the head. Zack went under water for a second then came up with the machete. He swung it and I moved in time so it glanced off my shoulder. I managed to grab him around the neck with my left forearm and battered him mercilessly with my right fist until he went limp. I pushed him under until his lungs filled with water then let the current take him away.

By then we were several hundred yards downstream from where we saw the flashlight. Yolanda and Jose were clinging to the raft. I joined them.

"Good work," I said. I saw exhilaration in their faces, their white teeth shining in the moonlight.

"What do we do now?" Jose asked.

"We complete the transaction," I said.

"You sure?" Yolanda added. "We could let the raft go, swim back to our side and take the truck home."

We considered the options there in the moonlight, clinging to the raft with sixty kilos of product.

"I wish we had a gun," Jose said.

I raised the Mac-10 I had wrestled away from Zack. "We made it this far. Why not?"

Yolanda sighed. "I always wanted to go to America."

Jose grinned. "But we have no papers."

"Cash makes no enemies, amigos," I said, patting the bags.

We frog-kicked the raft across what was left of the

Rio Grande to the American shore and lugged the bags
back upstream to where the contacts were waiting.

"What happened?"scrutinized the dark Hispanic
with the beard. "Thought we lost you."

"Just had to get rid of some baggage," I answered.

There were three of them and they took the six bags
up to a black Suburban concealed back in the brush. Inside
under the dome light they snapped the latches. The bags
were stuffed with one-kilo bundles of heroin.

"Nice job, Agent Green," the muscular one with the
blond crew cut said to me. Under the light Jose and Yolanda could see the military fatigues, vests and badges. They
looked at me like I had betrayed them.

"Jose and Yolanda were essential to the operation,"
I said. "They saved my life, lieutenant. They need sanctu-
ary."

"Not a problem," he said, turning to my companions. "Welcome to the United States."

BABY SHOES NEVER WORN

"People rarely bring flowers to a suicide."
–Jennifer Niven

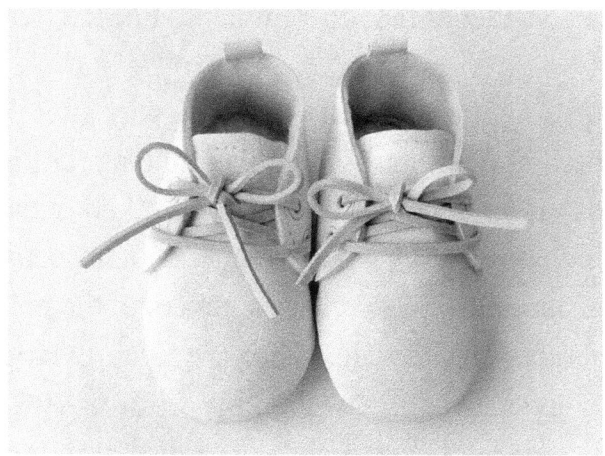

Hemingway liked to tease new writers he en-countered, usually at a bar, that he could write a complete short story in ten words or less.

"Pick a number between one and ten."

"Six," said the writer from *The Miami Herald,* sit-ting next to the aging bearded Nobel Laureate on his fifth rum-infused Papa Doble, still celebrating accolades from *The Old Man and the Sea.*

"Baby shoes for sale, never worn," Hemingway

grinned, his sun-baked face wrinkled around eyes floating above his fish-belly-white beard. "Tragedy foretold in six words."

Hemingway's love for brevity came from his early work as an overseas war correspondent. Sending words by telegraph was expensive, so he relied on nouns and verbs. Then, when adjectives were inserted, they were "like a blow under the heart." Often imitated, Hemingway's prose style was considered the most influential of the twentieth century.

Birdsong had read all of Hemingway after college and credited him with providing the impetus for his modest success as a man of letters, having hacked out a living writing copy for TV ads, brochures, menus and table tents at restaurants, press releases, letters to the editor, the occasional freelance article, and more recently blog and website copy.

His one published novel was a dismal failure, skewered by one reviewer: "Birdsong has about as much business being a writer as the moon has thinking it's the sun."

Drink-fueled outbursts separated him from his only promising relationship with a New York agent. And like Hemingway, as life went on, Birdsong sank deeper and deeper into depression thinking about his hero.

Hemingway was a horrendous drunk, though he would stop around ten p.m. to allow his mind to sober up enough to attack the page at the crack of dawn. Just as he eschewed cigars as they dulled his sense of smell, he never drank when crafting phrases. He could always tell where in a paragraph F. Scott broke discipline as the tension slid into indulgent lassitude.

But these great writers drank for different reasons than he did. They drank to celebrate their success, to maintain image, to accentuate bravado. Birdsong drank to assuage the guilt and pain of failure. They had great sweeping lives which spanned the globe in high circles of art and society. Birdsong had a little apartment in a big city and was virtually unknown. They had people clamoring to know them, to gain their favor or throw cash at them for their next project. Birdsong had to scrap out every assignment he ever got. People dodged him when he tried to collect.

His mind decimated by decades of abuse, Ernest attempted to alleviate his depression through the insanity of shock treatments at the Mayo Clinic. Two days later he returned to his home in Ketchum and tripped both triggers of his double-barreled pigeon gun in the foyer.

Hemingway's weapon was later destroyed, the remnants buried in a field where Birdsong now stood with a gun of his own.

To a Lady I Once Knew

Upon the winds of fate I wandered, one;
  No harbor called me home, a fearful dread
My constant friend; an emptiness, dark sun;
  I thought I'd be better off quite dead.

And then, from out of gloom, you did appear,
  My heart was borne away upon a wing,
I trembled, could not breathe with you so near
  I'd found my queen with you I could be king!

Together we rode high on top a wave,
  But at the crest your ornament shown through,
A mighty castle crashed as if a knave,
  Had tried to show the world just what was true.

And now at sea again, bereft and tossed,
My soul laced not with gold, but yet embossed.

THE THREE GRACES

"The beauty one can find in art is one of the pitifully few real and lasting products of human endeavor."
–J. Paul Getty

Wiggins crouched among the rocks, slippery with the rising surf, gazing up at the balcony jutting from the mansion over the ocean. Security cameras covered the inland drive, so the dangerous shore break was his only point of access. He ducked down as the rotating beacon from the lighthouse swept over him, his dark camouflage facilitating concealment.

The former Mrs. Wiggins thought she saw something move among the rocks below. She wore nothing under the silk negligee and the cool ocean breeze felt good.

"Come back to bed," a raspy voice called.

"In a minute." She had lied about the abuse and convinced the jury with fake photographs that Wiggins was a brutal bastard. She had taken everything from him and moved to the island with her lover, whose villa overlooked the sea.

A wave rose up and crashed down, sucking Wiggins toward the dark cold waters of the north Atlantic. His hands fought for purchase. A rough line went around his neck. He grabbed it and hauled himself back on shore. A lobster trap. The lighthouse on the reef illuminated the coastline once again, along with the beautiful ass of his beloved as she disappeared through the double glass doors.

Belinda allowed Roger to service her again.

"You're the best," she lied.

Belinda was sick of men. Roger's villa provided plush refuge. When the time came she would move on, with the Canova sculpture, beaming elegance from the marble Doric column next to the bed where she moaned like a skilled thespian.

Wiggins didn't care about the house he lost or the money her greedy lawyers managed to usurp. He knew how to create wealth using other people's assets. But the one thing he could not abide was Belinda's theft of *The Three Graces.*

In 1814, the 6th Duke of Bedford traveled to the art studio Antonio Canova in Rome and was blown away by a neoclassical sculpture done for Napoleon's Josephine. It depicted the mythological daughters of Zeus in white Carrara marble. The three nude figures represented Thalia (youth and beauty), Aglaia (elegance) and Euphrosyne (mirth), iconic images of art and literature. The Duke commissioned a second sculpture for Scotland, the original sold to the Russians for permanent display at The Hermitage in St. Petersburg.

Canova also produced a third version, hidden from history for over 150 years. It appeared on the black market and was offered to Wiggins for $5 million. A quick authentication of provenance, money wired to a Swiss account and the treasure was his. The Graces was the most valuable thing he ever possessed. It moved him in a way nothing human had ever done. Until he met Belinda.

On their first date, she had stripped naked and posed next to the sculpture, mimicking each of the three graces. Wiggins was mesmerized. She was the woman of his dreams. He proposed and she strung him along until he dropped the idea of a pre-nup. While he worked his ass off, she spent money, ran around and extorted him for sex. She called him an ape and made him shave his back. His ideal woman transmogrified into a seductress of Satan.

Belinda lit a cigarette on the balcony and watched the cone of light slide toward her. The ocean breeze was welcome relief from the insatiable workout between her thighs. She knew that last session would appease Roger for the night, as revolting as these sessions had become. Her money was gone and she had to sell the Canova to get away. Maybe Italy this time, or a Russian mobster with a mansion on the Black Sea. She liked dark men from the dark side. They asked no questions her body couldn't answer. A buyer for the Graces had been after her since the divorce. She would call him in the morning.

Wiggins clung to the rocky wall, staring up at the naked succubus. The eighty-foot climb was treacherous, but he had trained for months and bought the best equipment. Slowly, maintaining three-point contact with the rocks, he inched up the jagged limestone face. He could smell her as the breeze shifted, and almost lost his footing. But his loathing steadied him and he climbed on, eager to empty the syringe of succinylcholine into the neck that once had mesmerized him so. The neck that led to her mouth of deception.

Belinda felt a chill and looked down. Something seemed different in the configuration of the cliff beneath her. Visions of Wiggins flashed through her mind: the first time she allowed him to kiss her, then take her, and the many other times as revulsion gained mass in her psyche. She was glad she took the bastard for all he had. She earned every cent as she had with every man before him. She learned that sex trumped love every time.

She flicked her cigarette butt, watched as the oxygen rich air made it a glow bug, then went back inside and closed the door.

Wiggins got a hand on the edge of the balcony, then two hands, and silently pulled himself up and over the iron railing. His heavy breathing was undetectable inside the sound of waves crashing below. He calmed himself, listening for any movement inside the bedroom, concealed from the sweeping spotlight behind a potted evergreen tree.

Just then the glass door slid open. Roger strode out, butt naked, and began to relieve himself over the railing. He belched loudly and the whiff of prime rib and bourbon drifted into Wiggins' nostrils. Roger leaned forward against the railing, and raised his arms into a full stretch, shaking his long hair as if to untangle the mental lassitude from too much sex.

Wiggins rushed in, grabbed Roger's ankles and flipped him over the rail. The Lothario twisted in the air, eyes wide and arms flailing, his anguished cry silenced as he hit the rocks below.

Exhilarated, Wiggins charged into the bedroom, withdrawing the syringe from a special pocket in his vest. A spotlight in the ceiling illuminated *The Three Graces* in regal splendor, causing Wiggins to pause in awe.

"Looking for me?" Belinda said, walking naked from the bathroom.

Wiggins froze and started to tremble, her hold over him still potent and powerful.

"Thanks," she said, coming up to him, her perfect breasts equal to Canova's vision. "Roger was a bore, just like you, baby." She threw her arms around his neck and pulled him close, too self-absorbed to notice as Wiggins inserted the needle.

The paralysis began immediately. She slid to the floor, her eyes frozen in disbelief as Wiggins went to the column and hefted *The Three Graces* over his shoulder.

"Bye love," he smiled down at her. "I'll be taking the Ferrari."

Wiggins hooked the keys off the dresser and moved for the door.

WIZNET

*"People see what they want to see and what people want
to see never has anything to do with the truth."*
–Roberto Bolaño

Wiznet was a dancer. When she met people,
conversation would always come around to what they did
for a living and Wiznet would announce her profession
proudly. Once, at a fancy affair where the men looked like
penguins and the ladies tried to outdo one another with
jewelry and satin gowns, four high society gals cornered
her by the bandstand during a break.

"Oh, a dancer! That must be exciting!" effused a
lady with hair so silver it could be melted into metal bars.

"What kind of dancer?"

"Most any kind," Wiznet replied, a whimsical twinkle in her eyes.

They peered at her, wanting more information. A lady with a diamond the size of Dallas made a lilting wave, bouncing a rainbow of colors off the tops of her shiny breasts.

"Ballet?" she innuendoed. "I saw Giselle at the Met. All those dancers in white… magnificent!"

"Not an easy performance," Wiznet said smiling, sipping her champagne.

The tony gals looked at one another, unable to ascertain the status of the gorgeous creature in front of them. Poured into a red dress which left little to the imagination, Wiznet snagged a fresh glass of champagne from a passing tray and downed half of it.

"I just love the tango, especially the Argentinian," ventured a tall lady with alabaster skin in a black gown, eyes blue as a robin's egg. "Robert Duval is quite a tango dancer.'"

"Did you see that scene in 'Scent of a Woman'?" the third lady effused. "Al Pacino was blind and guided that young lady across the parquet floor without missing a step."

"But he wasn't really blind," said the silver lady.

"Of course not! It was a movie," corrected Diamond Lil as she was known around town. Her husband had a west Texas ranch, fifty miles by fifty miles, covered with oil wells.

"The thing about the tango is," Wiznet interjected, "'if you make a mistake you just tango on'."

"Right! That's the one." The third gal with the make-up problem said. Wiznet couldn't figure out whether her thin eyebrows were overplucked or tattooed.

"Where have you performed?" The first lady was becoming impatient, her right hand in a death grip around a whiskey sour.

"My last performance was in here, in Washington," Wiznet insisted.

"Fabulous!"

"At the Warner?"

"No."

"The Parilla?"

"Not this time."

"You were in *Sleeping Beauty* then?" guessed the comely middle-aged wife of a Capitol Hill lawyer, his obnoxious fees dazzling around her neck and wrists.

"Sleeping beauty. Yes, I've played that role," Wiznet answered, trading her empty glass for a full one as the passing waiter caught her eye.

The ladies stared at her with scrunched up faces – the words coming from the mouth of this stranger were incongruous with what their intuition told them about her.

"It must be exciting, a life on the stage, traveling around, meeting new people," said Diamond Lil, open to what might follow.

"Yes, it's quite exciting," Wiznet explained. "You never really know what's going to happen next."

"I considered a career in the theater when I attended Yale," said the alabaster statue. "Then the agency called and I was off to New York working the runway. You ever work a runway, Miss...?"

"Wiznet," she said. "I have done some runway, but was probably not in your league."

"Dancing always eluded me. It was hard to find men tall enough." She adjusted the shoulder strap on her black gown which fell like a shroud around her.

"Excuse me, ladies." Wiznet left the bon tons to their gossip and cut her away across the dance floor to the bar, turning every head in her wake.

"Bye now!" they called after, mystified.

Her attraction was universal. She felt the eyes of the barmen and the barristers, the magnates and malefactors, the congressmen and the lobbyists, their wives or companions – all comb her body with equal scrutiny or desire. She seemed at once accessible, yet an enigma.

"Vodka martini," she winked at the barman, trading her sparkling wine for something more substantial.

"Right up!"

Wiznet opened her bag and checked her lipstick in the compact mirror, angling it to watch a tall heavy-set man straighten his bow tie and move in her direction.

"Thank you," she said as the barman held out the funnel glass filled with clear cold liquid. She dropped a fiver in the champagne bucket serving as a tip jar and took a hearty sip.

"Hello there, li'l darlin'," ventured a deep voice with a country twang.

Wiznet turned and looked up into the weathered face she recognized from TV.

"Thurston Sanders, from Tennessee," he offered his hand.

She gave him more of a grip than he anticipated.

"Why, you've got one helluva grip there, little lady."

"Congressman?" she asked rhetorically, knowing exactly who he was.

"I've represented the fine folks in the 4th Congressional district for over 20 years," he said.

"That's Nashville, right?" Wiznet purposefully erred to make him feel comfortable. Men loved to correct and loved to talk about themselves.

"Jasper, darlin', Chattanooga area," he took pleasure in correcting her. "Named after William Jasper, Revolutionary War hero. Town was ak'quired with a one dollar lease from Cherokee Indian legend Elizabeth aka 'Betsy' Pack, daughter of Chief John Lowery and the beloved Cherokee woman Nannie Watts."

"That's fascinating," Wiznet drew him out. "Your area certainly has come a long way from way back then."

Sanders chuckled. "We certainly have, yes indeedy." He took a long pull on his bourbon and water, thick eyebrows rising and falling as he panned up and down her supple form. "So, young lady, what line of work are you in?

"I'm a dancer," she said coyly, with a hint of mischief in her eyes.

"Dancer! Well doggone." He paused briefly. "That explains your fine physique."

"It's quite demanding, all the stretching and jumping. Makes me really strong in through here," she illustrated by drawing her red tipped fingers slowly across her lower abdomen.

He replied quickly: "The little lady likes the ballet and drags me there at least once a season." He laid all his cards on the table – open to discreet liaison should she wish to explore it. She didn't, but saw an immediate use for the old bugger.

"It's really something to see," Wiznet said. "How long have you been married?" Wiznet stifled a yawn, enduring the big buffoon who kept the wolves away while she scouted the scene.

Representative Sanders held up his hand to show his band of gold. "Forty-seven years. Two of the best years of my life." An involuntary chuckle was followed immediately by another involuntary sound below his belt.

"Ex-cuse me," he blushed. "Musta been the crab cakes."

"Must have." Wiznet raised her arm high, looked past the congressman's shoulder and waved to an imaginary someone across the room. "If you'll pardon me, I think I see my director."

"Your director?" He looked around, expecting to see someone important and artistic when his wife appeared.

"Who was that, dear?" asked Susan Sanders, thin as a willow wisp in a blue brocade jacket.

"A dancer! She's in the ballet."

"The ballet!" The dignified lady exclaimed, watching the red dress cross the room and thread her way through a stand of black suits like a fox disappearing in a forest. "I heard they might be here. I'm just dying to meet them."

A congressman from Maryland, a lobbyist for a big food conglomerate, and their wives joined Rep. and Mrs. Sanders, enjoying the sight of Wiznet walking away.

"Who is she, Susan?" asked the wife of the lobbyist, adjusting her Dior gown to plump up her cleavage.

"She's the lead in the ballet at the Kennedy Center," Susan offered.

"Must be *Swan Lake*!" interjected Bill Minton's wife, Kelly, who worked as a Constitutional lawyer on K Street. "We saw that last week, remember, Bill?"

"Why yes, yes I do," Minton mustered fake enthusiasm, but his mind was on the night he spent with a luscious mulatto during the recent corporate junket to the Bahamas – all free of charge.

"She certainly is something," Susan added. "Good

with conversation too, wasn't she Thurston?"

"Quite knowledgeable about many things," the representative played the game, easing away to the bar with his empty glass.

"Dancers aren't stupid," Susan added.

"Look at Ginger Rogers," Milly, the Maryland Senator's wife, offered in example.

"Isadora Duncan."

"Absolutely!"

"Sally Rand."

Polite laughter.

"We don't have to mention her now, do we ladies?" Susan smiled.

All of a sudden, the haunting beat of 'Buscándote' erupted from the bandstand. Everyone stopped and stared at the far end of the dance floor where Wiznet was moving in time with the music. The slim tall junior congressman from Colorado was next to her, his guiding hand at the small of her back.

As the music rose and fell, the dancers illustrated the perfect tango. The whirling red dress, her breasts pushed tight against his satin tuxedo… they dipped and twirled, mesmerizing the crowd with unreal fluidity.

When 'Buscándote' ended, even the band stood up to applaud.

"Bravo!" cried the conductor, his nods causing others to increase the volume and tempo of their clapping.

"What a classy young lady!" proclaimed Susan

Sanders.

"And such a dancer!"

"Quite a catch, I would say," added Milly.

Wiznet hurried through the admiring crowd, towing the young senator by the hand toward the back door.

"Where are you going?" he asked.

"I have an engagement," she replied, stopping to kiss him on the cheek.

"I want to see you again," he pleaded. "Take my card."

Wiznet glanced down, seemingly unimpressed by the address on Capitol Hill. "I'll call you." She started to leave.

"Wait!" he said, pulling the card from her nimble fingers and scrawling on the back. "My private number," he whispered.

She saw the desire and longing in his eyes and knew she would call, but not for a week or so to make him want her more. Then she would have her way with him, like she had with so many others along the tour. She kissed him again, this time full on the mouth. His arms went around her and pulled her crushingly close. She could feel the thumping of his heart, the trembling in his loins. Then she pushed him away.

"Gotta go, sweetie."

"I don't know your name," he gasped, catching his breath.

He was tall, dark and gorgeous, the perfect playmate, she thought.

"Wiznet."

"Wiznet?" He pondered. "You're a whiz at the internet?"

"Something like that," she smiled, licking her smudged lipstick in remembrance of his special moment.

"Call me!" he said.

"You bet." She winked and flowed past the big man with the wire running from his ear down his shirt collar who held the door open for her.

She glanced back; the look she expected was on the young senator's face. She laughed quietly to herself and stepped outside.

It was a cool spring evening and a slight breeze carried the scent of cherry blossoms from the Potomac through the city. She loved Washington, the power and the energy which emanated from the streets and buildings. This was headquarters, where the fate of the country was decided. She would do well here, she thought to herself as she covered the three blocks to her venue. Her high heels made sharp crisp sounds on the sidewalk, followed by a comfortable echo like someone was watching over her, protecting her. She reached the stage door, knocked three times and it was pushed open.

"Hi Wiznet," said the guard in the black leather coat. He wore a full beard and smelled of expensive cologne.

"Hi, Bruce," she said. "Good crowd?"

"Nothing but the finest."

She climbed the steps and made her way to the dressing room she shared with several others. The backstage was tumultuous as always, dancers stretching and cajoling, attendants fetching, admirers held at bay by the burly guards on the periphery.

Wiznet removed her red dress, slid it on a hanger, and placed it on a rack with the others. She chatted with her fellow dancers as she prepared her make-up, staring into a mirror with light bulbs set around the frame. Satisfied, she stepped into her costume and walked to her spot behind the curtain, listening for the music to wind down.

"And now, ladies and gentlemen, put your hands together and give a big round of applause for Wiznet!" came the booming voice of the announcer.

The audience reaction was loud and enthusiastic.

She whipped the curtain behind her and strode boldly onto the stage.

The men in the front rose to their feet and clapped wildly.

Wiznet took three smooth strides, leapt into the air, and grabbed the brass pole with her thighs.

Repaired

Leaden cotton slumber

dishwasher thoughts

   high-centered

   doldrummed

sails hang in sad cheeks

   cargo soul rotting.

Personality Electra

   supercharged winds

   sails tauten

   enabled by chaos

   we leave the reef

      screaming.

THE WALK

"Travel is fatal to prejudice, bigotry, and narrow-mindedness."
–Mark Twain

It rained all morning and I had to delay my walk until midafternoon. By then the dark clouds had broken into little gray clumps that hung in the air like dots from a painter's brush. I opened the door and the thick wet air hit me like a damp cloth. The storm invigorated the fecund smell of rotting leaves and fresh grass which rose to greet me when I stepped down from the porch onto the sidewalk. The concrete was slick and shiny and was glad I wore the high shoes with rubber soles.

The tug on the leash pulled me as Gekko sprang forward, eager to leave the stuffy confines of our house and push his nose into places only he could perceive. The heavy rain had reorganized the fallen leaves into drifts against the curb, some gold or bronze and wet like lacquer. I allowed Gekko to set the pace and pulled him in only to avoid traffic. At eleven years his ears no longer caught sounds, but his eyes were sharp and his smelling acute.

A squirrel was rolling two nuts toward a hollow tree, then froze as Gekko came round and pointed. It would be sport to release him from the leash, but it would be trouble getting him back and I was not up for a quick dash that might disrupt the good work the doctor had done on my leg.

The break was severe, the bone cracked straight through by a black guy who clipped me during a volley-ball game. I had been serving and chiding the other team and when we switched sides between games he fell, feigning an accident, and took out my fibula. The prison doctor said the new way was not to set the bone but rather let it heal where it came together inside the cast. I explained that would make my right leg shorter than the left. Then he went on about budgets and lack of personnel and that I was lucky to get any treatment at all for an injury that was undoubtedly my fault.

"It will keep you out of the fields," he said, as not slaving away chopping roots that didn't need chopping and breaking hard ground was a blessing. "Don't look a gift horse in the mouth."

Not every doctor was top of his class and those gathered near the bottom found employment in prisons and welfare centers where the clients' complaints were easily buried. It made no difference to him that, should I ever be shackled and blindfolded and set out in the middle of a desert, I would not walk straight ahead as my short leg would cause me to move in a wide circle.

But that was way back in my past and, while I had reformed myself in many ways, old memories still lingered and colored my view of the world.

The rain made the break ache and it took a while to get the muscles loose. I lived at the edge of downtown where the nice big houses quickly degenerated into smaller not so nice houses, then slums and leftover FEMA trailers for section eighters. I liked to walk away from the nice neighborhood into the tenderloin with Gekko. He was a pit bull with the sweetest disposition you'd ever see, but loyal and protective.

I ambled through the trailers and could see people inside peer out, checking to see if I was the law. Hookers lived in the trailers and dealers and fugitives who skipped parole. They didn't bother me. I had been inside and realized they were just poor slobs who had made a lot of bad choices they rationalized as bad luck.

"Luck is when preparation meets opportunity," I had told one of them once standing in the chow line in a red brick building surrounded by forty-foot walls. The line moved slowly and it was better to lead a conversation than allow dead air to breed the notion I was weak and a potential victim. Bullies were like that. They sense rabbit in you, they push until they find a way in. Then you're inconvenienced and have to prove yourself. Stand up to them from the start and they move on to someone else.

"If it wernt fer bad luck I wouldn't have any luck at all," he said back. This guy wore his trousers so low his genitals were ready to burst over the top of his belt. He chewed on a tooth brush like it was a stick of candy and had a thick black comb stuck sideways in his nappy hair. Prisoner's rights groups had got the heavy combs allowed for cultural reasons, but they also made horrific shanks that would evade metal detectors.

"You make your own luck, amigo," I replied. This guy was not my friend, nor would he ever be, but he didn't know that and squinted at me like I had useful knowledge he had overlooked in the third grade.

"How's dat?" His polished incisors chomped on the brush – another shank in disguise.

"Think about it," I said, in the spirit of service to my fellow man. "You get what you deserve in life. Penalties or rewards come from the behavior you choose."

"For you, maybe," he scowled. "I grows up in da prajeks. Daddy was a junkie. Mama turn twenty dolla tricks."

"So sad. You can let that drag you down. Or you can pull up your shorts and do something different. Obey the laws and earn an honest living."

He stopped chewing, cocked his head at a slant and removed the toothbrush. "You dat smart white boy."

"Yep. You dat dumb nigger. Let's move it." I turned and made my way past a row of steaming square pots filled with different colored substances inmates with ladles plopped into cavities in my stainless steel tray. The guy chomped on his toothbrush and followed, not knowing whether to assault me or shit himself.

An old rusty truck with a bad muffler filled with used appliances roared by and I had to jerk the leash to keep Gekko from getting his head torn off. He led me along a cracked sidewalk past a row of clapboard houses built in the '50s. One had a faded black POW flag furled down from front pole stuck slanted in porch support. The next house had a child's bicycle with two flat tires on its side in the mud. High weeds obfuscated the next shelter where plywood was nailed over window frames. The destitute, the disenfranchised, runaways and habitual users inhaled the white snake behind the plywood on rotten mattresses where rough sex was exchanged for an hour of opiate bliss. I passed, shouldering a horrible truth I could do nothing about.

Three men stood on the next block talking about a football game, drinking beer out of a cooler set in a shiny new pick-up. We nodded, knowing our worlds were different, a glance of respect all that was needed to avoid confrontation. Gekko and I walked past the triangle corner

where the ironworker's shop had been for fifty years, torn down to make way for a new freeway exchange; bulldozers chugged dirt three stories high into a pile that would become an overpass. Gekko sniffed a black cat and tried to pull me toward the first trailer, but I held him back.
He sniffed wildly, the cornucopia of odors a stimulating treat. I let him wander into the edge of the woods and he spooked a groundhog. It loped away like a big brown caterpillar and disappeared inside a thicket.

My presence was noticed at the next FEMA trailer and I saw the curtain push aside, then close. A screen door opened and a thin aging black hooker came out, her belt undone, her flimsy shirt but a nuisance.

"Whatcha doin' heer, boy?"

"What's it look like."

She flopped down the wooden steps and stood at the end of her walk. Her pupils were big as her irises, jet black like her straight oily hair. She eyed me and lit up a cigarette, drawing the smoke in deeply through a rack of missing teeth.

"You gotta a fiver?"

"Nope sorry," I said, as Gekko stopped and started to empty his bowels on her lawn.

"Whadtha fuck!"

"It's your lucky day," I said.

"Youa crazy, nigga," she said, her face scrunched up, eying me as if to take a psychic reading.

"No, really," I said. "Gekko is blessing your

house."

"Bulllllsheeet! He's takin' a sheet en my yard."

"It's the oldest of tributes," I said smiling, my into-
nation similar to the guy from Publisher's Clearing House
who shows up unannounced and gives you a big check.
"He could have chosen another spot, but he chose *your*
yard."

She stared at me, her cracked lips rolling the cigarette around until the filter was coated in red lipstick.

"Gekko? Wha kinds dawg is dat?"

"AmStaff."

"Bullshit, dats a pit."

"American Staffordshire Terrier is the breed name,"
I spoke in proper English by way of distancing myself
from her. "He's pure bred. Papers."

"Youz in da hood now, nigga." She got real sweet,
her mouth extended, her glazed eyes dreamy as a pot of
black tar. "Weze homies. Come in a minit."

She made a motion with her hand, indicating a skill
for which she usually extracted a fee in advance.

"Thanks, another time maybe."

About then a big black man appeared at her door.
His shirt was off and he was building a shed over his tools.
"Comes back in, Pauline," he said, his eyes trying to bore
a hole through my shades.

Gekko tensed, alerted by the man's energy. He finished his business and scratched his paws back against the
grass.

"Hey!" The man said, coming toward us. "What you mean lettin' dat dog take a shit!"

"It's the oldest of tributes," I said, hoping for a reaction.

The man rushed up and stood over me. He was a head taller, unshaven, his breath fouled with God knows what.

"Why you be comin' down here, boy?"

"Talkin' to your lady friend. She invited me inside."

He looked at her. "You crazy, bitch! He Five-0."

I forgot I had worn a gag DEA hat I had gotten on Venice Beach. I looked at her. "Sure. I'll have that beer now."

I started past them, drawing in the leash to keep Gekko close. He growled and eyed the big guy, followed me up the wooden steps into the trailer.

The inside was trashed as you might imagine, but I ignored it, went to the fridge and found a cold PBR in a can. I washed it in the sink to be sure, popped it and sat on the couch at the end where I had full view of everything. Gekko climbed up and sat next to me. Through the window I could see them arguing, then he hushed her and they came in together.

She licked her lips and became an actress. Through the years she had developed a certain way of moving her body and facial expressions, her tools to draw men in. I pretended to go for it and sat calmly drinking my beer.

The big guy loomed over her shoulder and glared at me, his game upset by my lack of fear and willingness to play their game.

"Nice place you got here," I said. "Bit of a mess, but you must be busy. Hustling and shooting drugs and probably dealing. Not much time to tidy up for guests."

The hooker was impervious to my comments. She only heard the tone in my voice and it was anything but threatening. She slid over and sat next to Gekko on the couch and started to scratch his ears.

"Pretty baby."

The big guy was at a loss for words and disappeared into the far end of the trailer, separated by the front with a hanging bedsheet. I suddenly had the thought I might have made a huge mistake. He could have gone for a shotgun and that would be it. He would probably hit me first, then pump and take out Gekko. Gun blasts came from this part of town all the time. I could hear them from my third story skylights late night after the bars closed. Sometimes the sirens came right away. Sometimes they didn't come at all and you didn't know about the bodies until the early morning news.

My senses became acute. My eyes darted around the tiny trailer, taking in every crack in the ceiling, every candy wrapper on the rug. I breathed deep, trying to detect the odor of marijuana or crack or chemicals dealers used to make speed. My ears picked up the sound of Gekko breathing and the gal next to me murmuring something quietly. I could hear the big guy in the back rummaging around, maybe opening a case and pulling out a shotgun. Then I heard his footsteps on the carpet as he came closer.

With a flourish, the bedsheet was brushed aside and man appeared, carrying something metal and shiny in his right hand. I felt my life race before me in my mind's eye, and said a silent prayer. One last attempt at mercy or salvation.

The muscles in the man's face twitched as he brought the metal object up to take aim. I shut my eyes not wanting to see the blast and pulled Gekko close.

"I love you, Gek," I said as I heard the blast.

But it wasn't the blast from a shotgun that jolted my senses. Rather, it was the sweet sound made by a brass trumpet in the hands of someone who knew how to use it.

I sat back and was entertained for more than an hour as this incredible musician played everything from Dixieland jazz to Herb Alpert to Miles Davis. I felt like a bigoted fool sitting there in the company of a talent who could have played the Iridium Club in New York. And blown them away.

There was a knock at the door, followed by the entrance of beautifully groomed young woman carrying a tin foil wrapped tray.

"Hi mama," she said to the lady sitting next to Gekko. She looked at the young woman like she didn't recognize her.

"Forgive Lydia's appearance, sir," the young woman said to me. "She's got Alzheimer's."

A little girl came in and climbed up in her grand-mother's lap. The elder lady's face lit up when she saw her and gave her a big hug.

"My chacha," she said.

"Would you care for some lasagna?" Michelle asked.

"I would indeed," I said. "Let me help you."

We spent a pleasant evening talking about all sorts of interesting things. The little girl and Gekko ran around the trailer and set everyone laughing when they got tangled up in some Christmas decorations that remained up year round because Lydia liked them.

After dinner she got tired and the trumpet player said it was time to put grandma down. I helped them clean up and told them if there was anything I could ever do to let me know, and gave them my phone number.

When Gekko and I wandered back to our nice house on our nice wide street, I was humbled by the humanity I had encountered and what I had learned in such a short period of time. Initial perceptions can be misleading and previous experiences can miscolor your judgement about people you meet. It's best to keep your mind open, your mouth shut and your palette clean.

Moby Dick

Rather wait

    than rush unprepared

Rather thought dumb

    than speak too soon

Rather do nothing

    than ruin what's made.

I am wandering

    listening

    gathering

    waiting

    to throw the harpoon.

PERIPETEIA

"The love of money is the root of all evil."
–Timothy 6:10

"Where's grandma?" Sophie asked, sluffing off her heavy coat still powdered with snow.

"In her bedroom. Where do you think." Belinda barked from the sofa in the enormous play room, stuffing another chocolate cupcake in a yap that had processed way too many cupcakes, Ho-Hos, Twinkies, pieces of pie, eclairs for way too many years.

"Thanks, blimp." Sophie flung her coat over the Lazyboy and made for the loo, followed by the sound of a heavy stream splashing into the bowl.

"Shut the fucking door!" Belinda raised the TV's volume with the remote to drown out the flush, water splashing in the sink. Jerry Springer was on the flat screen. Two women in ridiculously short skirts were trying to tear out each other's hair as the bouncers hung back.

Sophie plopped down next to her sister. "Do we have to watch that crap?" She grabbed the remote and changed it to a closed-circuit feed at the other end of the mansion. The sisters watched for a moment in silence. An old lady was asleep in a gigantic bed.

"Why doesn't she die, already?" Belinda said, un-screwing the top to a diet soda.

"How cruel!" Sophie answered. "You'd have nothing without her."

"Yeah? And you're a big success. Forty-five and an assistant professor at a junior college."

"At least I don't sit around all day stuffing my face."

"How rude!"

*   *   *

Ellen Margaret Brown, heir to the Brown Candy fortune, sensed something moving around the bed where she dozed and raised a lid. It was a familiar shadow which became clearer as she blinked.

"Sophie?"

"Yes, grandma. I'm here."

"Sit by me, child."

She saw Sophie sit, but felt no weight on the bed.

"Where's your mother?" Ellen reached for where her hand should be, but grasped only air.

"Mom will be along," Sophie said.

Up at the top of the wall mounted over the antique armoire, Ellen noticed a little red light below a glassy black circle on a tan box. She pointed a boney finger, blue veins visible through translucent skin.

"They're watching me."

"They love you, grandma. They want to make sure you are all right."

"They want to see when I'm dead," she spat. "So they can get my money."

*   *   *

Lawyer James Makepeace arrived with Crystal. They were laughing and went straight to the bar. Crystal filled two tumblers with bourbon.

"What's so funny, mother?" Sophie asked.

"Ellen's delusions are become stronger, more frequent," the lawyer stated.

"Won't be long now." Crystal poured three fingers. "Jimmy will have her declared incompetent and..."

"You bitch!" Sophie fumed. "You would do that to your own mother?"

"Grow up, dear. She's been in bed for nine months. She's not about to give birth!"

"I'm telling the doctor."

Crystal and Jimmy shared an amused smile.

*   *   *

Dr. Brian Shields, noted neurologist and highly paid expert court witness, remotely adjusted the strength of the implant frequency in Ellen Brown's brain. He had inserted the device 90 days previous through a small tube into Brodmann area 17 on the medial side of the occipital lobe within the calcarine sulcus. Crystal held her mother's hand, limp from the anesthesia.

"It will stimulate images, people, whatever we place in front of the camera," he confided.

"We record her. Show it to the judge," Jimmy Makepeace added, enjoying how smoothly the plan was coming together.

"It will look like she is talking to ghosts," Crystal conjectured.

"Bat shit crazy," said Makepeace.

"Dementia," Dr. Shields nodded.

"Can't have an insane woman in charge of the family fortune, can we," Crystal smiled.

"No, Ms. Brown," the counselor deadpanned. "It would not be in the best interest of the children."

*   *   *

She was riding her favorite horse, White Star, a
long-legged Arabian her father had purchased for her in
Kentucky.

"Come on, baby," she whispered in his ear, her
hands entwined in his mane as he galloped through the
snow. Her thighs gripped tight around his bare back. The
cold wind made her eyes water, but her chest was warm
under the thick coat her mother had saved for. She was a
girl from modest means, but her parents wanted her life to
be a pleasant dream filled with good things and fun times.

"Go White Star. You can do it!"

The snow was deep, up to his knees, his breath
came in heavy gasps. She could feel the strength of his
heartbeat through her loins. On they rode over the lush
fields, dormant now under a thick blanket of snow. Little
Ellen knew the fields well and guided White Star along
the fence line between the stands of poplar and the frozen
stream. It was an exhilarating ride and she pushed her
steed on.

"Faster, boy! Come on Star!"

Leaves slid across her helmet as the passage nar-
rowed. She reached out and grazed the fence with the
tips of her fingers. Pounding hooves were muffled by the
deep powder, the only sound hot breath shooting from the
horse's nostrils.

Suddenly, a startled buck rose up, struggled to

evade, but was tangled in the underbrush, sharp points of its rack piercing White Star's chest. Ellen was thrown tumbling over the melee, into a drift of snow. She struggled up, looking back in horror at the fountain of blood pumping red from White Star's heart.

"Noooo…..!"

* * *

The video was being shown in the judge's chambers. Centenarian Ellen Brown seemed delusional, re-enacting an episode from her childhood. She waved her arms over the bed where she was confined as if to ward off evil spirits.

"White Star! My baby!" A torrent of tears rained down her weathered old cheeks, her mouth twisted in anguish.

"Fractured memory recall, confusion with place and time, are symptoms typically associated with degenerative Alzheimer's disease," Dr. Shields explained. "Changes in mood and personality, along with increasingly poor judgement, are also manifest in this patient."

Judge Waters stared into the monitor, his face pursed in concern. "I've known Ellen for forty years. It hurts me to see her in this condition."

Crystal Brown gave her attorney a nod.

"It's time the legal system stepped in to protect the interests of the family, judge," Makepeace urged.

Judge Waters switched off the video, leaned back in his padded leather desk chair. "Rendering a person incompetent is a delicate matter, Mr. Makepeace. It's a decision encumbered with responsibility. How current is her will?"

"Five years, Judge."

"And the beneficiaries are…?"

Makepeace withdrew a document from his briefcase, passed it over. The judge flipped through it quickly.

"That's a lot of money for such a simple will." Then he stopped and sat upright. "I cannot rule on this today. It will require a hearing."

*   *   *

Young Ellen was getting dressed for the high school spring dance, gazing at herself in the full length mirror. Her mother, Margaret, watched proudly over her shoulder.

"You look like a dream, my darling!"

"I hope Steve likes it," Ellen said bashfully.

The doorbell rang. They went to the window and looked down. A handsome well-dressed young man stood at the front door holding an orchid corsage.

*   *   *

Crystal and Belinda huddled around a TV inside a locked bedroom, one of sixteen spread out among the three floors of the mansion. A mounted camera pointed down at an illuminated photograph of young Ellen Brown in a peach satin dress as her date pinned on a corsage. A cable ran from the camera into a metal box fronted with knobs and gauges. Crystal pushed the rocker switch and the camera zoomed into for a tighter shot of the orchid.

"The camera encodes the image into the converter which sends a wireless signal to the implant in her brain," Crystal explained to her favorite daughter.

"She thinks she is sixteen again," Belinda smiled.

"Yep. It causes her mind to locate the memory and bring it into present time as a simulation."

"Pretty clever."

They watched intently as the family matriarch, propped sitting up in the grand bed, raised her elbow as if to offer it to a prince taking her to an inauguration ball.

"Sophie know about this?"

"No! And don't tell her," Crystal advised. "You're the only one I can trust."

*   *   *

For the past forty years, since the death of her husband, Beacon "Bob" Brown, founder of Brown Candy Corporation, Ellen Brown served as the company's President, CEO and Chairman of the Board. Under her guidance, a small mom and pop candy store with a great product grew into a multinational powerhouse with distribution centers across American and over 3,000 workers on the payroll. When she retired at 92, the company went public, Ellen cashed out and became almost instantly one of the richest women in the country.

But life has a strange way of compensation. Three of Bob and Ellen's children passed before their time – drug overdose, car crash and hunting accident – leaving only Crystal, the youngest, to carry on the family genes. But after a series of failed marriages, rehabs, extravagant spendthrift compulsions and inveterate alcoholism, Ellen accepted her failure as a parent, and except for a monthly stipend to remove worry, cut Crystal out of the will. The majority of her eight figure estate was going to charity, except for modest sums to keep her two granddaughters safe and sound.

"Can you believe this bullshit!" Crystal cried to her lawyer when he first showed her the revised will.

Makepeace leaned back in his chair, measured his words carefully. "How far are you willing to go to make things right?"

"All the way," Crystal replied without hesitation.

Makepeace picked up the phone and dialed a private number. "Shields," the lawyer said into his landline. "It's on."

Crystal paid no attention to the details Makepeace and his doctor friend were discussing. She was engrossed in photos on the Yacht Trader website showing amenities of the Princess, a 155-foot yacht for sale, once owned by the Sheikh of Dubai. Sixty was supposed to be the new forty, and at 61 she needed to live out her fantasies while she could still get around. But she needed the long green. The measly hundred grand a year barely kept her old Jaguar running and her liquor cabinet full of Pappy Van Winkle.

*   *   *

Crystal lit a cigarette in her big bed on the third floor next to the video room, and pushed Jimmy Makepeace off her naked body.

"What is it?" Her lawyer said, half-drunk from the booze and the sex.

"I'm sick of waiting!" She could barely conceal her boredom, but had to keep things going until she became executor of her mother's estate.

"The hearing is Tuesday, Crystal. You'll get everything you want."

"You better hope so," she said, flipping back the sheet and climbing down. "Or I'm getting another lawyer!"

Jimmy watched her pad across the thick carpet to the shower, hoping this was the last time he had to service the old broad to keep himself in the game.

*   *   *

"Would you like some tea, Grandma?"

Sophie was at the door with a silver service, china cups and a little plate of butter cookies.

"Why yes, dear. Come in."

Sophie set the tray down, helped Ellen sit up and poured her a cup. Ellen grabbed her arm and felt her hand close around the warm flesh.

"It's really you, child," she smiled warmly.

"It's me, Grandma."

"Tell me about yourself. What have you been doing?" She sipped her tea and bit into a cookie, slowly chewing and savoring the taste.

Sophie pulled the old velvet arm chair close. "I teach anthropology at the college. It's a rewarding job. I learn more from my students than they learn from me sometimes. I get to travel some, do research. I really like research."

"That's wonderful, dear," Ellen's eyes brightened into deep green pools of wisdom and experience. "When Bob and I were starting out, we drove around America to see what people thought about our candy. We found that different regions liked their own type of product, so we produced what they wanted and became frighteningly successful."

"I know," Sophie said. "Brown Confectionaries are everywhere."

"It has made me a very rich old woman and I am about to die."

Sophie's eyes welled up. "Don't say that Grandma."

Ellen took her hand. "Nothing to be sad about, dear. I've had a great life. Time catches us all."

They sipped and talked for almost an hour until the tea was gone and Ellen passed out from the exertion. Sophie cleaned up, kissed her grandmother on the forehead, and quietly shut the door.

*   *   *

"That little snake!" Crystal fumed, having watched the little scenario play out on the video.

"No worries, babe," Makepeace said. "Court tomorrow. In a month we'll be on that yacht cruising the Greek Isles with all the little playmates we want."

"I can't wait," Crystal said, thinking as soon as the papers were signed she would never have to see Jimmy Makepeace again.

*   *   *

The courtroom was packed with Brown employees, TV news people, bloggers, distant relatives and friends, all wanting to see what would legally become of the vast fortune. Crystal, Belinda, Makepeace and Dr. Shields sat at counsel's table as Judge Waters began his final proclamation.

"I have seen the videos admitted into evidence which depict Mrs. Ellen Brown experiencing the delusions described in the neurologist's report, and it seems reasonable to conclude that Mrs. Brown has become mentally incompetent and can no longer legally manage her financial affairs, as stated in 18 U. S. Code 4241(a). But where is Mrs. Brown now?"

Makepeace stood to address the bench. "Bedridden, your honor. She is unable to be moved without danger to her health."

"Is that also your assessment, Dr. Shields?"

He stood. "Yes, it is, Judge."

"Very well then, this court orders that…" his words were halted by a commotion at the back of the courtroom.

All heads turned as Sophie pushed her grandmother in a wheelchair down the center aisle.

"Excuse us, Judge Waters," called a tall man in a dark suit followed by a cadre of other lawyers on his.

"Mr. Greathouse!" Judge Waters brightened. "And Mrs. Brown. How are you, Ellen?"

"Never better, Judge. Good to be here."

The group took up residence at the opposing counsel table as Crystal glared.

"My client is here to refute the evidence presented by these miscreants and declare it to be a fraud," said Greathouse.

"Objection!" Makepeace shouted.

"Sit down and shut up!" the judge ordered. "Go

ahead, sir."

Greathouse then presented his evidence – surveillance video taken from an old system Ellen had installed fifteen years before, designed to record what happened in every room of the mansion.

THE NEIGHBOR

"Going home must be like going to render an account."
–Joseph Conrad

Walter Wilkins was watering hydrangeas when his new neighbor backed his moving vehicle into his driveway. No bright yellow truck or shiny steel POD for this guy, rather a large wooden box strapped to a flatbed trailer towed behind a black 1950s Cadillac hearse.

"Howdy, neighbor," Wilkins waved.

The tall gaunt man touched the brim of his ballcap as he got out and unhooked the trailer, engine running.

Wilkins twisted off the water and stepped to the property line ready to shake hands.

"Welcome to Quail Hollow."

"Later," the tall man said. He slid back behind the wheel, goosed it, and the old hearse disappeared in a cloud of black smoke.

"He's an odd sort," Wanda Wilkins said, joining her husband. "Wonder what's inside the box."

"Don't know," Wilkins said. "But I think I just saw it move."

Later that night a strange noise brought Wilkins to his upstairs bedroom window. He watched as his new neighbor pushed the box off the flatbed onto a dolly and rolled it into the garage.

*   *   *

Morning coffee in the breakfast room. The hearse was parked in the driveway beyond the French doors. No trailer.

"Maybe I'll bake some cookies."

"Good idea," Wilkins said as the doorbell rang.

The FedEx man was climbing back into his truck as Wilkins opened the door. He picked up the heavy package from the porch and carried it inside.

"Our neighbor is Reginald Blackstone," Wilkins read the label as Wanda flipped eggs in the pan. "Telemetric Instruments, Corp."

"No need for cookies then," she said.

"Right."

Quail Hollow was an older upper middle-class neighborhood with large brick homes artfully arranged on well-landscaped curvy streets, where children played after school and American flags were stuck next to mailboxes every 4th of July. Residents took pride in mowing and painting, and when 604 Shadow Wood became vacant, everyone was anxious for occupancy.

Surprisingly, it sold in one day.

Ding dong. Walter pressed the bell again. Noise inside, door swung open.

Thin and striking, barefoot in a black robe, Reginald peered at the little man, his head stooped below the door jamb.

"Special delivery!" Walter said with the tone of a good neighbor.

Dark eyes scanned the label, boney fingers removed the heavy package from Walter's hands.

"Thank you." And, with a flourish, Blackstone withdrew, like a moray eel dragging a crab into a hole, and closed the door.

*   *   *

Wanda was the neighborhood gossip and soon everyone was on guard about the new resident. Cars would cruise slowly round the cul-de-sac hoping for a glimpse of the mysterious stranger. His outside lights remained on until the wee hours and loud noises punctuated the silence.

Rumors grew about the large wooden box, and one night when the hearse was gone from the driveway, two teenagers crept up to the garage window and peered inside. A moment later they ran screaming away when the stranger's face appeared. And so the legend grew...
Blackstone was:

"A hitman for the CIA."

"An ex-convict planning revenge."

"With the Russian mafia."

"An alien in human form."

"An Islamic terrorist."

"Not his real name."

A police detective was appraised of the situation, ran "Reginald Blackstone" through the database and came up cold. The matter was referred to the FBI. Still nothing.

The old black hearse would disappear for days at a time, then remain in the driveway for weeks. Other than the weekly lawn service and sporadic package deliveries, there was no movement.

Except in the garage.

Day and night rumblings, poundings and scrapings. At times the tremors were so great Wanda would wake Walter up in the bed.

"What is he doing over there?"

"I don't know, dear."

"Well, go find out!"

So Walter got up, changed into warm clothes, grabbed a flashlight and went outside.

It was a windy night with a bright gibbous moon. A thick wall of bamboo outside a high wood fence bracketed the back of Blackstone's house from the garage to the far side, assuring complete privacy.

But Watkins had lived next door all his life and knew a secret way in. He peaked through a hole in the fence, eased through his garden gate, crept round to the corner, slid through a split in the bamboo and pushed the hinged panel he and Bobby Greenwood had installed before his mother went missing and he was shipped off to military school forty years ago.

Splintered boards from the wooden box were stacked outside. Emanating light was cut by cross-hatching on the window in the back garage door. The rumbling noise drew Watkins closer and he peered inside.

Blackstone was stripped to the waist, operating a machine that brought up dirt through a big hole in the concrete floor. A conveyer deposited dirt in a series of screens. Samples were sucked through a pneumatic tube into a box where meters indicated the results of quick analysis. Tested dirt was sent back into the hole or piled around the inside walls of the garage.

Just then the digger hit a solid patch and stuck. The machine trembled violently as Blackstone worked the levers to get it free. He backed the conveyer, swung its carriage, and lowered it churning into softer ground.

Wilkins gazed intently through the window. Sweat dripped from his neighbor's beard and mixed with the dirt to form a gray paste that covered his torso like cracked plaster. There was something familiar about that man, but Wilkins could not make the connection.

Then a dirt sample brought a high-pitched squeal like a dog whistle from the analyzer and Blackstone hopped off to look, disappearing from view.

The garage door was yanked open. Wilkins fell forward toward the crevice, but Blackstone grabbed his collar, and hauled him up.

"Hello, Walter."

Then it hit him. "Bobby? Bobby Greenwood?"

"Been a long time," Blackstone smiled.

Wilkins was relieved. "We were what – seven?"

"You were. I was ten."

"What the hell are you doing, Bobby?"

"Come look." He stuck a long muscled arm into the hole and brought up a large bone. A human femur.

"Dad killed mom then killed himself," he said somberly. "I've come to find her and take her home."

BLEDSOE

"Peace is the product of justice and love."
– Oscar Romero

Bledsoe was frum Hangtown. Got its name frum all da hangin's happen'd dare. Lots of 'em. Eighteen one year. Rustlers, rapists, robbers, murdrers, a sodomites, one goat fuckin'. Bad year fer most places, but en Hangtown et brought biz. Money frum all da backwoods scrapin', sheep raisin', cow herd wranglin', dirt farmin' peeps come ta see'em swing.

Sherriff Dooger charge uffitall. Mean sumbitch, meaner dan a tree-legged coyot, tough like armadilla hide. First report he'd ride out en lassoo dem bastards en brings'em in, hogtied en wide-eyed. Even Big Bill Drake fell ta Dooger's lash, a fifteen-footer worn smooth frum redneck circlin'. Got Bill rushin' troo da pines, hidin' back enda bush. Den da black leather tongue lick out en neck pull em right offa steed. Crack a rib frum da fall, den two moor draggin' o'er da brush back inta town.

Gallows Pete kept'em purty. Fresh cedar provided fra-grance. I like ta stan close. Et was bess right up next ta da edge'da platform. You could hear da metal latch pullin' back, releasin' dat wood trap, da whoosh en da fall, da signal crack wen da rope pull taut. Ev'ry neck had a leettle diff'rnt twang. Sum louder, sum sof'n'sweet like spankin' a baby's bottom.

Den da twitchin'. Dat was da bess part.

Ol'Mike Foster hezes fiddle ready en wood match da jumpin' legs widda a tune. Drake's dance was da leese disappoinin'. He was so beeg his girth stuck in da square hole en his fall was interrupted, so dere was no crissp snap. A simpfunny of gyratin' as he choked enda noose.

Mike got troo his whole repertoire and starts back again 'fore Big Bill finally quit dancin' da two-step stuck in dat hole. Just a silent swingin' and da hemp rope creakin. Et wass majakel!

Mary make a livin' sellin' pies. Her oven roar'd two day befo, her winda sill so crowded crows wood bop in and steal a peck. Boysenberry, blueberry, blackberry – berry pies sold well at a hangin'. For sum reason custard pies weren't all the rage, though Darkie Sam Greer would be first in line if Mary offer'd peach.

Mary's kids picked da berries frum bushes 'long Miller Lane where dey grew tangl'd en da split rail fences ran east side Fancy Dweller's place.

Fancy es the rich guy. He wass born into it, name his daddy give'em, like his daddy called him Duke. Duke Dweller, son of King Dweller. Folks been here longest say da King made it first in dry goods, then Duke xpanded da family fortune troo land grabbin' en claim jumpin'. Had a stable of grimy boys who ran folks off en da night after sellin' out. Mighty shitty bizness datg Dwella clan.

But dis was Hangtown en people cum frum all over ta free der souls and seek ablution frum dare evil deeds. Dey return'd home cleanse' 'til da next time when they reupped, da evil too much ta bear. Hangtown provided a unique service ta mankind. A little taste a hell turned folks back ta der heavenly ways.

Preacher was always dere. He'd climb da wooden steps en deliver a final admonishment frum da good book. Den he'd ask fur repentance, a last chance at redemption, 'for da lever pulled en da condemned man dropped ten feet closer to his final restin' place. Dat devil smiled up at Hangtown. We were his favorite supplier of lost souls.

But poor Bledsoe getting' hung for somethin' he didn't do. Not dat it mattered much to da neighbors, 'specially da muthers whose daughters Bled had comman-deered via his charmin' ways and prodigious gift. Once dey got sight of it, they had to try it, and dat was usually da end of dare wholesome en descen' ways.

All da hangin's meant da mens was in short supply, da odds growing more favorable each passin' year
fer Hangtown's Cassanova, its Jack-the-lad, as a passin'
Englishman once conveyed.

Muthers in need with husbands hung alzo came callin' on the sly.

Bledsoe evaded da noose while runnin' da hen
house 'til his twenty-fifth birthday. Valentine's Day, ta be
ironic. God doth hava sensa humor.

The audience swooned as Bledsoe took da stage.
His tight black leather pants replaced by a burlap sack, out
of kindness for da women folk whose dauhers weep en
called out his name… "Bleddddds ooooo."

Yep, it was kewhite asight. A sunny day early
turned cloudy then misty as Preacher began his tepid ora-
tion.

"Putta sock in et," Bledsoe cursed.

Preacher glance' over, but continued with a hack-
eyed phrase frum Revolashun, da noose hangin' like a
halo. Bledsoe hopped up, grabbed da wood beam, den
trew his chained ankles 'round dat Preacher's neck. Pure
sinew en grit, Bledsoe twisted violently, snappin' dat
frock'd man's head pedestal, den released him down da
chute. His puffy corpse thudded en da dirt like a wet cot-
tun sack.

Da audience was stunned. Bledsoe stood defiant,
eyes half-lidded, his smile wide en devious. If they was

goin' hang'em, might as well be fer sumpem' he *did* do.

"String 'em up," cried Sullivan da undertaker, salivating at da tought of a double pay day.

Sherriff Dooger looked at Fancy who gave an urgent nod. Dooger stepp' in, deliver'd a roundhouse ta Bledsoe's gut dat doubled him over, his last meal becoming a baptizen cascade ta doze in da fron' row.

Dooger slipped da noose 'round Bledsoe's neck as da hangman held his arms, and pulled it chokin' tight. Bledsoe knew what was comin' en lifted his legs up to his chess jus as da Hangman pull'd da lever.

Bledsoe's cuffed hands sped 'round his feet, shot up en grabbed da rope juss as da slack ended, stoppin' dat snappin' fall. He pull'd himself up, like en eel wedgin' itself off a spear, open'd da noose with one hand en slid out.

Dat crowd was in an uproar. Young girls screamed. Dare mothers screamed louder. Horses rear'd en bucked. Sherriff Dooger looked down da hole so far he fell in, breaking his fadass backside.

"Get'em!" Sullivan yelled. But no one was brave enough ta move.

Bledsoe hopp'd on da waitin' buckboard, knocked da undertaker off his seat, grabb'd and snapp'd da reins. Da four-horse rig leapt forward, speedin' Bledsoe 'way as bullets whizzed by.

Fancy's pistol empty, he nodded ta his grimy boys. Dey mounted up en clomp'd after da 'scapin' Lothario, never to be seen or heard frum again.

Dat was da lass hangin' in Hangtown. People had nuff ada violance. Bledsoe's deparshure heralded a wave of kindness en beneficence which emanated out en sanctified da county.

Da gallows was torn down, da wood converted into park benches where lovers could sit after a stroll 'round a garden park, created where da hangman us'd ta 'ply his trade.

Stroll en'eat pie.

Mary's enterprisin' sons perceiv'd an opportunity, a void created by Bledsoe's departure. No need ta curtail da flow of traffic. Bess to utilize dat profitable publicity.

Da image of Hangtown faded amid a renaysince af pastry. People came frum far en wide to enjoy storees mellowed with age, much like outlaw tales a Jesse James en Billy da Kid, back-shooters histry toins inta folk hee-rows.

Turism encrees, Mary's Pies grew inta an industry, employin' half da town. Mary invents tales 'bout how 'er pies was enspir'd by er secrt lover. Dose'ho etter pies 'came imbued widda resurgence of desire.

Awhole gen'ration a peece'en beautiful childrens 'merged frum many unmarr'd ladies, who remain'd troo to da man who rebirth da town, dat renam'd itself en his 'onor.

Bledsoe.

MARIPOSA

"When the going gets weird, the weird turn pro."
– Hunter Thompson

Mariposa found dandelions amusing. She thought dragonflies should have houses. Licorice was too strange for her. It was often said coffee was the color of her skin.

Her ice blue eyes were startling when the sun caught them laughing. She liked leopards, and had one once. It ate a crocodile and she had the dressmaker at the corner make her a crocodile tunic she wore with polished red boots and a broad silver belt.

She was an eye-turner, a striking long-legged beauty with two hearts. Her mother had taken Thalidomide for anxiety when pregnant, thus affecting the strange anomaly. She had been studied by scientists and doctors and given money to live, providing they could periodically check her physical well-being once a year. She agreed, took the annual stipend, and never had to get a real job.

Mariposa played the game of amazement, was sought after for media interviews and by other freaks of nature with whom she felt a special bond.

There was Charlie with a third eye that smiled in his forehead, and stumpy Pete who transported himself on a rolling board by slapping the floor with gloved hands. Brenda had extended scapulae which resembled wings and had special dresses made with clip-on extensions made of Styrofoam and feathers. And Hopscotch whose joints could dislocate, allowing him to curl up in a ball and roll down a hill.

Halloween was their favorite holiday.

The group got together Wednesdays at Buster's Bake and Shake down on Euclid, two blocks off Main. It was a lively place with quick waitresses, yellow leather booths and lots of windows. The clientele was eclectic and the food was good. Buster's started serving drinks at noon and by four the bar was packed, standing three deep.

Dr. Feverdish came after surgery still in scrubs with a stethoscope draped round his neck so people could hear Mariposa's two hearts. It cost a round of drinks and the disbelievers were happy to pay.

When things juiced up, Pete would roll over to the juke, ply it with quarters and punch up hits like Journey's "Who's Crying Now," and everyone would sing when the line came round to "two hearts born to run, who will be the lonely one."

Once a trucker took Mariposa for a ride down to Allendale and back in his 18-wheeler, and nicknamed her "Big Two-Hearted River" in honor of his favorite writer Ernest Hemingway.

Men never stayed with her for long, and when they broke up, Mariposa was said to have suffered twice the pain.

Jokes did not affect her, nor did the incessant curiosity of news people who maintained a vigil at the periphery in case she would falter. Her condition doomed her to a short life and the subsequent autopsy would make the medical textbooks.

Mariposa felt differently. She felt two hearts gave her twice the strength and stamina, thus twice the longevity.

Bookmakers in Vegas ran a special sheet on her with odds increasing each succeeding year.

Mariposa was determined to live an ordinary life filled with ordinary things ordinary people did every day. She had a small apartment with a great view of the park and would drink coffee on the balcony, macramé and watch people move about down below.

Early mornings dark-suited men carrying briefcases would cross the paved diagonal, the sound of their slapping leather soles in Doppler delay with their moving legs.

Midmorning mothers would emerge in loose-fitting dresses pushing strollers with new babies.

The tennis courts would fill on a pretty day and skateboarders worked the cement course of bumps and curves after school.

There were derelicts too, and users who would crowd in the hedges and come out woozy. And at night the lovers would stroll and find places to explore intimacy, caring less and less about someone observing as they lost themselves in blinding passion.

From the balcony Mariposa selected in advance those she wished to know. She studied their routines and chose the right time to enter their lives. She decided she wanted to know a young mother who pushed a special stroller so her triplets could ride abreast. She lived in one of the big old Victorian houses lining the opposite side of the park and rolled in religiously around ten when her housekeeper arrived. She wore running shoes and a track suit and jogged behind the carriage, making five laps around the baseball field, then resting by the water fountain next to the gazebo.

"Hi," Mariposa said as the young mother sat on the bench where Mariposa had been waiting.

"Oh, hello." Her faced was flushed from exertion and her eyes were bright. She began rocking the stroller with her foot.

Mariposa gazed into the stroller. "Three girls?"

"Two girls and a boy."

"Ah, just right!"

"Oh?"

Mariposa pulled three knitted wraps from her bag, two with designs in pink and one in blue.

"For me?" She accepted the wraps graciously. "Why thank you. How did you know?"

"Lucky guess." Mariposa did not tell her she had three of each color just in case.

"Such fine work," the lady said as she examined the stitches. "Here, let me give you something." She reached into her purse and found a bill.

"No money," Mariposa said. "Something personal. But only if you wish. I expected nothing in return."

The woman eyed her curiously, trying to decide if the stranger was for real. "I'm Belinda," she offered her hand.

"Mariposa."

"What a lovely name. May I offer you tea?"

Tea was what Mariposa had hoped for, a glimpse inside her fine old house. They walked together pushing the babies ahead of them across the park and up the ramp of new concrete.

"My husband had it built."

"A thoughtful man, your husband."

"Do you live around here?"

"Just there," Mariposa pointed to her apartment, barely visible through the tree tops. The modern flat roof of her building and simple lines stood in sharp contrast to the wonderful ornate woodwork of the old houses.

"I've often wondered about those," Belinda said. "I remember when they put them up about seven years ago. We all had a fit, but the builder had permits and paid the right people. Now we're all used to them."

"The trees help too."

"Yes they do."

"Except in the winter, of course."

They shared a polite laugh as they entered the drawing room from the foyer. Mariposa stared at a full-length portrait of a young girl in a white summer dress standing in a rose garden.

"It's me. Daddy had it done when I was eight. Out back."

"Beautiful."

"Look around all you like. I'm going to put the babies down and wash up a bit."

The housekeeper appeared and helped Belinda remove the newborns from the stroller.

"Be right back."

They left Mariposa alone and she walked to the window. The view of the park was less distorted by distance and she saw flaws not obvious from her balcony on the eighth floor. Breaks in the hedges and paper litter and broken swings in the playscape. An old man she watched go for coffee every morning now had a limp. The park attendant overlooked refuse he had appeared to conscientiously remove.

The clatter of cups and saucers drew Mariposa away from the window across the parlor into the spacious kitchen filled with bright light from the wall of south windows. Belinda draped strings from half a dozen teabags over the edge of a silver pot and twisted the knob of the gas stove. A flame rose and flattened out against the bottom of the copper kettle heavy with water.

"My husband is an architect," Belinda said, her face fresh. "He specializes in restoring old houses."

"He did a great job on this kitchen." Mariposa admired the bright tile and new cabinets rubbed with white paint to look like driftwood. She moved to the windows. "Is that where –"

"Yes. My father established the rose garden when he and mother had the house. My brother and sister also had their portraits painted there."

The kettle whistled and Belinda set it on a silver tray between cups on saucers and a basket of biscuits. "Let's sit in the garden."

Mariposa found the door and held it open. In a moment they were sitting at a wrought iron table within a horseshoe hedge of large blooming roses.

"So, how about you?" Belinda said after the first sip. "What's your story?"

"I was born in the back of a Greyhound bus."

Belinda started to laugh, then bit her lip.

"I know. Sounds like an Allman Brothers song. But it's true. Dad was a rambling man and mom was, well… let's just say she didn't come from a house like this one."

"I'm sorry."

"Don't be. I'm not asking for pity. I came to grips with it long ago. I've had an interesting life."

"Do tell." Belinda was becoming fascinated with her new acquaintance, someone out of the ordinary.

"I have two hearts."

Belinda's eyebrows shot up. "Two hearts?"

"I'm not joking. One here and one here." Mariposa touched both sides of her chest above her breasts.

"How does that feel?"

"They don't beat in unison. It's like this." She tapped a rhythm on the table that resembled the clack-clack of an elevated train.

"That's amazing. Are you in –"

"Danger from dying?"

"Yes."

"No more than you are. We all die. My doctors are ambivalent. Some say I won't make it through the year. Others say I'll live to be a hundred. I figure in case something happens to one of my hearts, I've got a spare."

"A girl I went to college with had three kidneys. I guess it's happening more and more. All the chemicals in the food and water."

They had a laugh and settled into a free-flowing

conversation without pretense. Mariposa liked her new friend and felt she had finally found someone she could be completely honest with. Someone who wanted nothing from her but her company.

Someone she could be herself with who didn't think she was a freak.

Winter Virus

Microbes like Lilliputians
    ensnare this Gulliver
        within forty hours
            thrashing sleep;
weak,
    aching from a
    three story
    window fall
dead,
    a sack of stones
    immobile
    incommunicable.

Dreams... disjointed, horrid;
    sour thoughts
    anisette visions
    ugly phrases,
        fever roasts joints
        stiffens memories;

Air... still as tundra frost biting
    burning breath,
        beaten
            careless.
Hope lies in springtime,
    love simmers for summer;

Icicles lurk
    a symbolic reminder;
        best to shuffle in silence,
            hide the inner gleam.

THE PLAN

"The best laid plans of mice and men oft' go awry."
– Robert Burns

On Monday morning Rex Rider decided he would kill the alligator. The stench coming from Jenkin's place next door was unbearable. The damn thing groaned all weekend like a dinosaur stuck in a tar pit. The splashing and flopping around caused Sparkie to bark like the mailman stole his Alpo. It was only a matter of time before the gator would break through the thin cedar fence and eat them both.

Rex wondered what Jenkins was up to when he started hauling in rock and planting palm trees. He thought maybe the guy had gone nostalgic and missed his old home in Florida. Or maybe his floozy was pressuring him to fix up the back yard. The bitch screamed at the poor bastard half the time and told him what a loser he was, before he told her to go perform an impossible unnatural act to a rolling donut. Then doors would slam, the TV would blast, and Jenkins would screech out in his beautiful red Corvette. She'd wade into the booze, call her sister and run the poor boy down. Good thing they didn't have any kids to grow up and find out what a joke their father was.

Jenkins shouldn't have an alligator. It was against the code. Whenever someone painted their house with an obnoxious color, added a carport or planted the wrong kind of tree, the neighbors always said "that's against the code." As far as Rex knew no one ever bothered to look up the code and see what it said. Where the hell would you look up a code anyway? Wherever and whatever the code was, the alligator was definitely against it. It was just common sense. A quality evidently in short supply next door in the Jenkins family.

Screw the code. The alligator needed taking out. But Rex didn't want to get caught. It might be a criminal offense with jail time attached, and he couldn't afford to lose his government job. Alligators didn't come cheap and he didn't want be on the hook for some long green when the reptile rolled belly up.

He had to make a plan.

Rider took Mondays off from his job at the post office as he preferred the Saturday route. The mail was lighter and so was the traffic, and he could get around in four hours. If magazines or catalogues came in, he could pass them along to the Monday carrier, as the brick and mortar site was closed on Saturdays due to the cutback and the supervisor was off. Plus, he had put in eighteen years and was the senior man. So, while young Fitzgerald lugged the heavy Monday sack, Rider sat in his cool home office researching on the computer.

First thing he had to find out was how alligators died naturally in the wild. This might offer a clue to a method that would survive the most subtle detection by the authorities. He typed in a Google search: "alligators + death." That turned out to be a bad choice as the 643,000 results returned in .55 seconds were all about people who were killed by alligators, not the other way around. He simplified his thinking and typed "alligator," figuring he'd start at the bottom and get to know a little something about his nemesis.

However, as Rider read on, a healthy respect began form in his mind about the nature of a creature whose ancestry reached back 37 million years to the Oligocene epoch, earlier variations having outlived the dinosaurs. The word "alligator" was derived from el lagarto, "the lizard," coined by Spanish explorers who encountered the beasts in Florida in the 16th century, when Ponce de Leon was seeking the fabled fountain of youth. In the wilds, alligators were atop the food chain and had no natural predators. Only man was capable of inventing devices and methods to take out this master of survival. This was not going to be an easy kill. Maybe he should take out Jenkins instead?

Rider read on, looking for a weakness, a point of entry into the physicality of the resilient reptile. The average weight of a male alligator was 490 pounds with a length of 13 feet. Jenkins' pet was only about eight feet which meant the damn thing had a lot of growing to do. Soon it would gnaw through the fence and come after Sparkie, his ten-year-old beagle, who would disappear whole inside the monster's yap. He had to save Sparkie and possibly himself, as after it tasted mammal, the gator would surely rearrange its menu and have a predilection for warm living flesh.

The off-duty postman logged off the internet and went to the closet where he kept his 12-gauge pump-action Mossburg shotgun as Sparkie watched him curiously. He laid the leather case on the bed and unzipped it, releasing the sweet odor of gun oil. Rider racked the slide and found the breach empty as he remembered. He pulled out his nightstand drawer, found a box of double-ought shells and stubbed six, one at a time, into the magazine until it was full.

He slid open the glass door of his bedroom, tucked the butt of the stock into his shoulder and panned the backyard along the fence line. If the gator came for him he could probably get off three or four shots before its mangled hide would lose its value to the luggage-briefcase-handbag-and-belt man. He would be free of the curse which vexed him more every day and ate away his sanity like salty sea water splashing against a steel rampart. Satisfied his protection was ready, he set the shotgun in the corner, closed and locked the door.

Rider wondered what Jenkins fed his gator. That might be the answer. Surely there was some kind of poison that would promote death – even to a creature sturdy as a prehistoric reptile. He decided to listen carefully to the goings on next door and take a good peck when it was feeding time.

That night, at dusk, when purple clouds swelled with rain and lightning made a laser show on the horizon, Rider heard Jenkins calling to his beast.

"Come here, baby. Over here, sweetheart."

Fucking idiot. Rider slipped out the glass door and eased over to the fence. He pressed his face up against the cedar board where his right eye could peer through a knothole.

Chickens! Standing high up on his deck, Jenkins pulled a limp feathered hen from a cardboard box and held it out like a steak bone to a dog. The alligator knew the drill and hurried over, its thick tail wagging in unison with the pad of its stubby feet. When it got to the edge of the deck it opened its yap and Jenkins dropped the dead bird from his perch behind the railing. Two chomps and the chicken was gone. Then its jaws spread wide for another. And another.

The box empty, the gator scurried a one-eighty and

slithered back into the muddy waterhole where it took a deep drink.

Rex smiled as he crept away from the fence. Now all he had to do was get a bucket of chicken from the Colonel, season it with the right poison, flip the tasty wings, thighs and breasts over the fence and the gator would eat the evidence. Who is going to autopsy an alligator anyway? As far as Rider knew CSI didn't do gator calls. And should the poison drive the gator crazy and he started thrashing through his fence in the throes of death, he had his 12-gauge Mossberg to seal the deal.

Rex went back inside to search the internet for the exact poison required to do the job and the location of its distributor. He was a postman and could easy have a package sent to a fictitious address and claim it before anyone was the wiser.

After a few minutes on the internet, Rider became despondent. He had located a promising website: "How to Kill Alligators with Poison, Gun or Knife." But as he read on, several things which hadn't occurred to him caused him to rethink his plan.

First, he had to be a really good shot to hit a moving alligator who was scampering quick and low. He had the 12-guage loaded with buck shot, but what if it was night and the light was dim? He hadn't fired that gun for ten years. The damn gator could be on top of him with its jaws clamped around his leg before he could sight it in.

Poison was no sure fire way either the website

warned, as "There have been many situations in which domestic pets or other animals have been accidentally killed by people trying to place poison."

And killing it with a knife was a solution too ridiculous to consider, unless your name was Oceola and you grew up in the Everglades.

No, he couldn't kill the gator. He was not capable of executing such an enterprise and remaining calm in the aftermath. The investigators would know he did by the look in the alligator's eye. He was an honest man and would easily crack under interrogation. He had to find someone else to accomplish the deed. A professional.

Maybe the guy who provided the advice in the web article he was reading?

Rex read on, becoming convinced this guy knew what he was talking about, especially when he read the one sure fire recommendation: "hire an expert." Yes, there were people trained in catching and disposing of these perilous reptiles, people who made a living at it and were still in possession of all their limbs.

Professionals.

The website was owned by just such a man, Trapper Dan. He certainly looked the part dressed in camouflage Army Ranger gear, his combat boot resting on the elongated head of the dead 12-footer, rifle butt on his thigh with the deadly muzzle pointed skyward.

Rider sent Dan an email and waited for a reply. It came within an hour and included a phone number.

"Trapper Dan," said the gruff voice at the other of the line.

"Hi, Dan, Rex Rider here. I've got a little problem."

"Ain't no problems, Rex. Only solutions."

"My neighbor's alligator is chewing through my fence."

"That's an odd one," Dan paused. "You live in town?"

"I do."

"It's illegal to have a gator within a residential area. Why not call the cops and let them handle it?"

"I hadn't thought of that," Rider confessed.

"Guess I talked myself out of a job," Dan chuckled.

"Maybe not. What if I wanted to handle this another way? I don't particularly like dealing with the cops."

"Been in trouble, hey? Got a rap sheet? Rider... I get it. Been there meself."

"No no. My sheet is clean. I just don't want any trouble."

"I see. I'm a do-it-yourselfer myself."

"If I snitch out Jenkins, he's liable to retaliate. He's nuts and his wife is worse."

"I'm beginning to get the picture."

"So, what would you charge and how would you do it?"

"Snatch and grab might be best."

"I like the sound of that."

"I need to bring my partner."

"How much?"

"Five bills should cover it."

"Deal."

"Up front," Dan suggested.

"Two up front. Balance when you have the fucking thing loaded and are backing out of my driveway."

"That'll work."

"When do you want to do it?"

"I need to scout the location. How about tomorrow noon?"

"Six o'clock is better."

"Let me check my calendar."

Dan, the alligator wrangler, was gone a minute to, by the sound of it, walk to the fridge and get a beer.

"Okay, you're in luck. Six sharp tomorrow. Have the cash ready."

"No worries." Rex then gave Dan his address and driving instructions.

*   *   *

After 6:30 the next day, an old mud splattered pickup with door panels filled with body putty pulled up in Rider's driveway. Rex peered out his front window, standing a yard back in the shadow, and observed two men on the other side of the cracked windshield chug the last of their beers before exiting the cab.

The driver, he assumed to be Dan, was a barrel-chested bearded fellow in faded blue denims and jungle mesh boots. His sidekick was small, wiry and clean-shaven and had the look of a ferret. He sniffed the air and pointed in the direction of Jenkin's house as if to confirm they had come to the source of their payday.

Rider met them at the door, glanced down at his watch.

"Yeah, sorry. Had an emergency this morning," Dan's face held the lie well. "Gator on a golf course."

"Yeah, the eighth hole," the short guy added. "A par five."

"I see," Rex said, thinking maybe punctuality and integrity were not qualities requisite to professional alligator wranglers.

"I'm Dan, this here's my partner, Leroy."

They shook hands, an unpleasant experience for Rider who shuddered to imagine where those hands had been.

"Wipe your feet and come on in."

The gator men scrubbed their soles on the mat and followed Rider through the house. Rex stopped at the sink to squirt hand sanitizer and pointed to the glass doors leading to the back yard.

"That the fence?" Dan said rhetorically.

"There's a knothole. You can get a look."

"Stinks out here," Leroy noticed.

"Yep. Gator stink," Dan concluded.

The men shuffled over and Dan pressed his eye to the hole. He backed away and gave a Leroy a chance.

"You got a gator problem, all right," Dan said, walking back.

"He's a big one," Leroy added. "Mean too."

"So, what's the plan?"

Rider didn't like these men and wanted to get the business over with. He could tell they sensed his aversion and would try to extort him with their presence unless he diffused it. "You guys want a beer?"

"Sure," the gator guys said in unison, their crusty demeanor assuaged by the thought of the cool beverage.

Rider retrieved the beers from the kitchen and brought them to the round table on the patio with the umbrella. The men sat down.

"Thanks," Dan said, popping the top and swallowing half of it in a gulp. "We could sneak in and grab thegator, or poison him, but your neighbor..."

"Jenkins."

"Yes, Jenkins, would suspect you first. If he's big sumbitch as you say, he'll rag you 'til you give it up."

"I'll be the first one he'll question."

"Or the cops," Leroy added, Dan having briefed him about Rex's concerns.

"Made cracks about the gator, have ya?" Dan said, finishing his beer and squashing the can like it was a big metal bug.

"Jenkins knows I don't like it. But he doesn't give a

shit."

"Guy's an asshole," Leroy offered.

"Yep. Chrome plated," Dan added. "Got another beer?"

"Sure. Help yourself."

Dan got up, lumbered inside and brought the rest of the six-pack back to the table. Rex surmised the planning session would last the duration of the beers and was glad he hadn't bought more. Dan popped a couple and handed one to his pal, who was also empty.

"So," Rex continued. "You can't poison the gator and you don't want to hook and grab him. What's next?"

"It's kinda unique situation," Dan said, the golden liquid boosting his mental clarity.

"Yeah," Leroy confirmed.

"Most time we catch gators where they shouldn't be– golf courses, boat docks, swimmin' pools, you know."

"Big ones in swimmin' pools," Leroy nodded.

"But here, you gotta gator a man has as a pet," Dan continued. "He wants gator to stay where it's at."

"It's his gator," Leroy shrugged.

"That's the whole point of you guys coming out here," Rex said, getting a bit weary. These guys were taking up space and not paying any rent.

"You got a gator owner here, Rex. It's not a nuisance case."

"Not a nuisance case," Leroy confirmed.

"The fucking thing is dangerous. To me and to

Sparkie."

Hearing its name the dog trotted over and got up on his hind legs.

"His dog," Dan summarized.

"Couple bites at best," Leroy noted like a battle-field surgeon who had lost too many wounded soldiers.

"Hey!" Rex took Sparkie in his lap and scratched behind his ear as if to assuage the mention of such a thing.

"Sorry, man."

"Just kiddin'"

"It's against the law," Rex said, starting to get per-turbed.

Dan and Leroy shared a glance. "No cops you said."

"No cops," added Leroy.

"Look, you guys are the experts. Handle it."

He pulled two hundred dollar bills from his pocket and flopped them on the table.

Dan drained another can, squashed it and set it next to the others. It was beginning to look like a junk yard of miniature cars. He eyed the money, but Rex could sense he was trying not to seem too anxious about picking it up. Dan popped another beer.

"What if gator ate through your fence and escaped into the street?" Dan mused.

"Go on," Rex prodded.

"You look out the window and call it in."

"Right. Then the gator trespassed on your property," Dan smiled.

"Then I'm still the snitch. I don't want Jenkins on my ass. It's gotta be a clean deal."

Dan tipped the beer up and poured it down his throat.

"What if you don't call it in?"

"Yeah," Leroy picked it up. "Gator's got to go somewhere, right? Neighbor sees it, makes the call. Then he's the snitch."

"The neighbor's the snitch, not you," Dan nodded.

Rex grabbed the last beer for himself. "Not bad." The pull he took on the can was appreciated by his new associates. "I leave the side gate open. The gator breaks through the wood fence and paws its way out into the road."

"You got it," Dan smiled. "It's genius."

"Genius!" Leroy effused.

Rex was thinking… "So, how do we time it? How do we know when he's going to break through fence so I can leave the gate open? We gotta do it when Jenkins isn't here or he'll corral the gator and bring it back."

The gator wranglers scrunched their faces and looked at each other for a long minute. Then Dan snapped his fingers.

"Jenkins is an asshole right? He gets into it with his old lady."

"Right," Rex confirmed.

"Then Jenkins leaves in his Corvette?"

"Most of the time."

"Probably has sum cooze 'cross town," Leroy interjected.

"Jenkins leaves, we dangle a chicken over the fence, then pull it back. Damn gator will tear dat fence down to get it! But, we have it tied to a fishing line…"

"I'm likin' this, Dan," Leroy sat up.

Dan continued… "I'm in the bushes outside your gate with rod and reel, a good one, like one you catch marlin. Gator busts through, I reel in the chicken, gator follows… No, wait. Leroy, you got da rod, I'm in the truck drivin'. You hop in back and we lead that damn gator down the street away from Mr. Rex here. Neighbor sees 'em, calls it in."

They sat back and looked at Rex, their heads bobbing up and down to sell the workability of their plan.

Rex sighed. These clowns were all he had to work with.

"What the hell," Rex said, swigging the brew and twisting the empty into the grave yard. "I'm in."

Dan slapped the table and picked up the two hundred dollars. "Okay, this is what you need to do…"

*   *   *

Dan thought it was a good idea to get the gator accustomed to the luring bait, so Rex picked up a bucket of chicken from the Colonel and waited until midnight to test its efficacy on the gator. With his eye pressed into the hole it the fence he lobbed an original recipe thigh over toward the mud hole but it was snared by a leafy tree limb. He felt around in the paper bucket for a breast and gave it the same motion, like LeBron would hook one outside the three-point line. It landed in front of the sleeping gator on the mud bank. The gator didn't move.

Rex rapidly emptied the bucket in a series of arcs, the chicken pieces landing around and on the gator, but the gator didn't twitch an eye.

"Dammit!" Rex muttered to himself, concerned about the $14.95 he laid out for the family bucket in tandem with the potential discovery by Jenkins of the professionally prepared poultry. If the gator didn't eat the chicken he would have to get it back or Jenkins would think he was up to something.

Then a lucky thing happened. The thigh Rex tossed in the tree came lose and landed directly on the gator's snout. Gators can take a lot of abuse, they've survived on earth for millions of years, often finding food in murky waters by their smell. Evidently the Colonel's original recipe communicated with the gator's DNA as the tasty thigh disappeared in its yap in a blink of an eye.

Rex thought he saw the gator twitch its ancient nostrils as it began to slowly move around its domain and, one by one, seek out and disappear the chicken pieces into its gullet.

"It works!" Rex laughed to himself. He would feed

the gator a bucket every day for a week as Dan instructed
and the plan would be ready to progress to the next step.

A week later Rex waited for the event he knew
would come.

"You bastard!" Came the shriek from Jenkins'
house, followed by the sound of plates crashing against
the kitchen tile.

"You're nuts! I'm outta here," came Jenkins reply.

Rex went to the window, saw the garage door open
and the Corvette back out. Jenkins had a smile on his face
and his clothes were fresh as his shave. Rex picked up his
phone and dialed.

"How long is he usually gone?" Dan asked.

"Four hours or so."

"Good. Hang tight. We'll be there in about an
hour."

"Do I need to get more chicken?"

"I thought you knew that."

"Okay, I'll pick up a bucket."

"You got the other three hundred."

"Don't worry about that, just get over here."

"Keep your shorts on, chief." Dan hung up.

Rex got the chicken from the Colonel and kept it
warm in the oven on low.

About an hour later Dan's old truck pulled up
towing a shiny black enclosed trailer. Leroy hopped out,
opened the back of the trailer and pulled out the ramp. Rex
watched from the window then met them at the side gate

in the chain link fence off the garage. The dog barked as they lumbered up.

"Sparkie's on the job," Dan said.

"Glad to see you guys are," Rex said.

"We'll have this wrapped up before your asshole neighbor gets home from the cooze."

"Did you loosen the fence boards?" Leroy asked.

"Thought you guys were going to do that."

Leroy shrugged, ambled back to the truck and grabbed a crow bar out of the back.

"What's with the trailer?" Rex asked as Leroy was prying loose enough boards to accommodate the gator's girth.

"Change of plans," Dan said.

"How do you mean?"

"We are taking it alive."

"Alive? Are you fucking nuts," Rex moaned. "The plan was to lure it out with the chicken, let it run in the street, then kill it."

"Plans change," Dan answered. "And, no, I am not fucking nuts. That's a big alligator with a couple square yards of hide. They want to skin him fresh."

"Who wants to skin him fresh?"

Dan and Leroy looked at one another.

"You want the gator gone, the gator's going to be gone," Dan said. "What we do with it is our business."

Rex eyed them up and down. "You are going to sell the gator."

"That's right," Leroy chimed in.

"How much?"

"Doesn't matter how much."

"So, I am paying you $500 to take the gator away and you are going to sell it for what, another $500?"

"You got a problem with that?"

Rex was flummoxed. "I don't know. I don't know if that's fair."

"You never said nothin' 'bout whats we does with the gator," Leroy added.

The three of them stood there looking at one another, letting the exigencies of the new deal solidify.

"Guess I never thought about it," Rex said finally.

Leroy elbowed Dan in the ribs and smiled. "He never thought about it."

"A deal's a deal," Dan concluded. "Get the chicken."

Rex padded empty-headed into the house and brought the family bucket out to where Leroy had four vertical fence boards hanging loosely by a screw.

"You fed him a bucket every night for a week, right?"

"Right. A bucket a night."

"Okay," Dan said, his eye to the knot hole. "Toss him a piece."

Lex flipped a breast over the fence with practiced skill, landing it right in front of the gator. The gator opened its jaws, turned its head at a workable angle, chomped twice and the chicken was gone.

"Okay, toss another piece about a foot away in line with the fence."

Lex did. The gator moved toward the bait and chomped it down.

"Another one. Halfway to the fence."

Lex lead the gator piece by piece toward the section of fence with the loosened boards until its snout starting testing the sanctity of the wooden boundary.

"How much chicken you got left?" Dan asked.

Rex slid his hand around inside the greasy paper bucket and pulled out an original recipe breast. "Just this."

Dan nodded and Leroy snatched the breast from Rex's hand and threaded a three-pronged fish hook through the tender meat. The hook was attached to a braided wire leader tied to a fishing line a deep sea guy would use to haul in a marlin.

"Okay, better get out of the way," Dan warned. Leroy let the chicken rest on the ground inside the rack of loose boards and backed out through the chain link gate.

Lex grabbed Sparkie and went inside through the glass doors, leaving a crack for the muzzle of the Mossberg. He racked a shell into the breach and stood ranger ready.

Dan went to the side and pivoted a loose board from the top so the gator could see and smell the bait. Its appetite whetted by the rest of the bucket, the gator stuck its head through the boards and opened its jaws, its short stubby feet propelling the beast ahead. Leroy reeled in the line and the gator followed.

Sparkie started barking and jumping up and down against the glass doors as the gator's girth took out the loose boards and entered the yard. Dan remained still at the side, letting the gator pass en route to the Colonel's original recipe breast Leroy dragged toward him with the fishing line.

Then the gator's eye caught sight of Sparkie, swiveled ninety degrees and headed for the glass door.

"Oh shit!" Rex exclaimed. He pointed the shotgun at the gator through the crack in the door frame and fired. The buckshot tore into the ground in front of the gator, sending up a screen of dirt and grass over the reptile's face. The force of the blast knocked Rex back into the kitchen table, the barrel wedging the door halfway open.

Now incensed, the gator picked up speed and forced its way into the kitchen. Sparkie jumped up on the counter as Rex backpeddled through the living room toward the front door.

"Sparkie!" The dog leapt from the counter and the gator followed, its thrashing tail knocking over tables with lamps, anything in its path.

Dan, seeing his pay day turning to disaster, ran around through the chain link gate, grabbed Leroy and met Rex as he was hauling ass out the front door, Sparkie in the lead.

"Take this," Rex tossed Dan the gun and kept running.

Dan caught the weapon, chambered a round and fired, missing the gator and taking out Rex's front window.

The gator went for Dan, who fled toward his parked trailer. Leroy was fighting with the fishing line. The hook had come out of the chicken breast and was caught in the fence.

Just then Jenkins' Corvette came cruising down the street with the radio blaring "Gimme Shelter," Mick Jagger's inimitable pipes adding a fitting undertone to the melee unraveling ahead.

"What the fuck!" Jenkins sat up as he saw his gator chomping after a guy scrambling inside a lawn service truck. A shotgun blast issued forth from inside the trailer, sending Jenkins' left front fiberglass quarter panel and headlight into oblivion.

Jenkins hit the brakes.

Leroy got his hook loose, and cast the chicken, missing the gator and landing inside Jenkins' vest, throwing him off balance.

Trapper Dan fired again, severing the gator's left hind leg amid a divot of macadam.

Rex watched from across the street behind a stone mailbox holding Sparkie.

Two police cars, sirens blasting and lights flashing, converged from both ends of the streets. The officers hopped out, guns drawn.

Houses emptied. Neighbors eased cautiously toward the spectacle.

Without the stabilizing left rear limb, the gator dragged itself around in a sad circle.

Dan emerged from the trailer with a rope. He eased up to the gator, slipped it around its jaws and pulled it close.

The officers holstered their weapons.

"Does someone want to tell me what the hell is going on here?" Asked the officer with rocker stripes on his sleeve.

Jenkins stood quietly by his hissing radiator trying to figure it out for himself.

Sensing his fee and pelt were still retrievable, Dan took the lead. "Gator call, Officer."

The officer noted the writing on the side of his truck: Trapper Dan's Landscaping and Gator Removal Service, and moved around to look inside. Packed against the back wall were mowers, weed eaters, lawn tools, and rope.

"You Trapper Dan?"

"Yes, sir. This here's a mean one. Chased that poor man over there through his house. Almost ate his dog."

Rex waved a hand and stayed put. Better let Dan handle it.

"Get the tape," Dan ordered Leroy as he approached and stowed his rod.

"Where did that alligator come from?" the taller

more inquisitive officer asked, his gaze falling on each of the players in turn.

Jenkins shrugged. "Beats me. But look what that jackass did to my car."

"Bad luck," Dan said. "He drove up as I fired."

The officer glanced back and forth from Dan to the Corvette to the blast hole in the road where the gator's leg lay twitching.

"Not much of a shot, pal."

"You ever try to hit a moving gator hot to take off your leg?" Dan offered as a defense, now straddling the gator and holding his jaws shut as Leroy secured them by rolling the duct tape around. The gator groaned.

"Where did that gator come from, that's what I want to know," the sergeant queried and expanded the scope of his vision to the two closest houses. "What's that over there?"

Jenkins clambered out of the Corvette and stepped between the officer and the secret gator paradise behind his house.

"What I want to know is who is going to pay for my car?" His demonstrations were effective enough to divert the officers' attention to the antifreeze mist rising through cracks in the hood.

"That looks like a civil matter."

"Yep, civil," said the sargeant." He turned his attention to Dan who was busy lashing the gator in the trailer with Leroy.

"You got a license for the shotgun?"

"Not mine," Dan wheezed. "Guy with the dog." He nodded toward the mailbox across the street. Rex noticed their attention and ambled over.

"What's the problem?"

"The shotgun," the officer said. "You got a license?"

"Sure do. In the house. Want me to get it?"

"That would be good."

An urgent message came over the cop's radio: "All units, possible 10-54 at Maple and Red River."

The cops looked at one another. "That's us." They charged for their cruisers.

"Hey, what about the damage to my car?" Jenkins shouted.

"Gotta go. You guys figure it out." Cruiser doors slammed and they burned rubber.

Dan had the gator secure in the trailer and was raising the ramp when he felt a hand on his shoulder.

"My gator," Jenkins said.

Dan let the latch drop. "Sure, buddy. Take the fucking thing."

Jenkins paused, looked at the gator's stump, the trail of blood. "Naw. Keep it. I was sick of that thing anyway." Dan raised the ramp and threw the latch.

Rex came up holding Sparkie. "Your gator tried to eat my dog."

Jenkins scratched Sparkie behind his ears. "Sorry

about that. Sorry about the whole thing really. I got the gator to piss off my wife."

As if she knew what he was thinking, Jenkins' wife screamed at him from their front door. "What the hell did you do now, Malcolm?"

"Malcolm?" Rex smiled.

"Nothing, dear. Go back in the house."

Instead she came running out in a night dress, her hair up in rollers. "Your car. What did you do to your car?"

"I did it, miss," Rex said.

"What?"

"No, I did," Trapper Dan stepped forward. "Gator was about to eat his dog."

"I told you that damn gator was nothing but trouble." She fumed.

"Go back in the house, Glenda. I'll handle this."

"You're all fucking nuts," she said and flopped back toward the gatorless abode.

"Glenda," Rex repeated. "The good witch."

"Your insurance should cover the car," Dan said. "I'll give you a statement."

The three disparate fellows stood there watching Glenda pad back to the house as Leroy lashed the gator to the tie-down bar inside the trailer. Dan bent down, picked up the gator's severed leg and tossed it carelessly towards its owner. It hit Leroy in the neck.

"Hey!" Leroy said. Then he noticed the flying object. "Fuck this."

"Sorry," Dan replied. "Let's pack it up and get going."

Rex slipped Dan an envelope containing the balance of his fee.

"What's that for?" Jenkins said suspiciously.

"Fence repair." Dan pointed to the wood barrier
where the gator had "broken through."

Jenkins squinted at the damage then turned to Rex.
"No, I'll pay for that."

"It's okay," Rex said. "Dan is going to do some
landscaping too." He pointed to the sign painted on the
side of the trailer.

"I insist, man. My gator caused the damage. It's
only right that I cover it."

"If you insist."

Jenkins came over, put his arm around Rex's shoulder, looked into his eyes, and spoke with the utmost sincerity. "I had afterthoughts about putting in the gator pond
and how it might upset you. You have always been a good
neighbor and I'm sorry about the whole thing."

"It's okay."

"No, really. I mean it. I got the gator on a drunk-
en whim to irritate the old lady. Thought maybe it would
cause her to leave me." Jenkins nodded to the house where
Glenda's hind end had disappeared through the closing
door. "As you can see, it didn't work."

"Too bad you can't work things out with her."

"That's not important. Tell you what. I'm going to hire your guys to redo my backyard. Take out the crocodile habitat and put in something else. Maybe a swimming pool."

"Sure," Dan spoke up. "I can help you with that."

Rex had a nervous realization. Jenkins would be paying Dan and Leroy way more than he did to remove the gator. These wranglers were drunks and loose at the mouth. Jenkins was a slick operator who could get people to talk. Eventually Jenkins would learn he hired them to dispatch the gator. Things would get ugly. Next maybe he would get a shark for his pool. Or an anaconda.

"You know, Jenkins," Rex confessed. "I never liked you until now. I appreciate what you said. Now I have to tell you something."

Jenkins grinned. "That you hired Dan to steal my gator?"

"What?" Rex was shocked.

Jenkins removed his arm. He face changed to pure menace. "You think I'm a fool, son? You've been stalkin' my gator for months. I've seen your pitiful attempts at bravado. Heard the deal you made with Dan. I called him up and made another deal."

Jenkins looked at Dan for confirmation.

"Sorry, man." Dan shrugged.

"A confederacy of assholes," Rex replied, the bile rising in his gullet.

The betrayal was overwhelming. Rex grabbed the

machete off Dan's belt, pulled the pins and the trailer ramp
fell. He rushed inside and with a couple swift strokes freed
the three-legged gator. Sensing its destiny as handbags
and briefcases, the gator charged for the opening, ignoring
Rex the liberator. Rex, with the adroitness of a matador,
fell back against the side of the trailer and slashed the duct
tape.

Jaws wide open, the gator charged toward Dan who
stood dumbstruck until the last second then leapt just in
time, hurdling over the incensed beast as it sunk its incisors into Jenkins lower leg.

Jenkins screamed and went down on the macadam,
his hands trying desperately to pry open the puncturing
vise.

"Help me!" Jenkins cried.

Leroy came round the side with the shotgun,
pressed the barrel between the raised beady eyes.

"No," Jenkins screamed. "You'll shoot my leg."

Leroy moved the muzzle away toward the center of
the beast when he was knocked over by its thrashing tail.
He dropped the shotgun and it went off, ripping through
the back of Dan's vest. Dan went down.

Rex moved to the front of the truck, reached in and
took his envelop full of cash.

"Good luck with all that. Come on, Sparkie."

The dog followed Rex into the house. He closed the
door, went to the fridge and opened a beer.

Attitude

Disaster

    special food

        for my character.

Destruction

    a tonic

        for my rebirth.

Success

    warning sign

        against complacency.

Complacency

    waiting room

    of disaster.

THE CHAMPIONSHIP

"Talent wins games; but teamwork and intelligence
wins championships."
– Michael Jordan

The rain fell like lances down on the prison yard, metamorphosing into a rising pool of quicksilver at the bottom of the surly gray sky. The yard was macadam, square and confined within buildings – the prison chapel, the infirmary, the library, and C-block where Shooter peered out through the bars from a third tier window.

"Fuk-ing weather," Shooter said to his bunk mate who lay reading a Jack Reacher novel.

"Be all right, Shooter," Nick said without looking up. "All things pass, even this obnoxious rain."

It had rained for a solid week but was supposed to let up for the weekend. Independence Day. The annual volleyball tournament. Shooter wanted to win.

"Cap'm ain't goin' let us play in the rain." Shooter stared down where a rivulet ran fast around the basketball pole, splitting in two then reforming into a steady stream that fell down a welded drain grate. Clyde Barrow of Bonnie and Clyde fame, was once rumored to have lathered himself with lard, lifted the grate and slithered in, thinking it was a sluice to the outside. Bosses caught him, nearly half drowned a day later, hanging onto a metal rod above the sewer drop. Poor bastard. Later cut off his toes with an ax so he wouldn't have to pull time in the hoe squad. Guy was a coward, nothing glamorous like in the Warren Beatty movie.

"It's six a.m., Shooter. Give it a rest."

The whistle blew atop the garment factory and the cell gates rolled back. Shooter hopped down from his top bunk. "Goin' for chow?"

"I'll pass," Nick said, not wanting to leave his book.

"Fourtha July. Ham and eggs."

Nick bent a page and set his book down. "Forgot about that!"

Four days were special in the life of a Texas convict: Thanksgiving, Christmas, Easter, and the Fourth of July. On those days the dinner food was edible, turkey or steak, but on the Fourth of July there was the added bonus of a good breakfast. It was either a gift of the warden, or his sadistic ploy at further dispiriting those incarcerated under his charge. Independence Day. *Right.*

After breakfast the rain stopped, clouds were whisked away by a stout southern breeze, and by eleven convicts were push brooming the remaining water into flower beds. At twelve sharp Lt. Barker followed Jimmy Legs carrying a ladder to the hoop, fresh nylon net in hand. He climbed up and curled the new loops into the slots under the rim, completing the tradition. Every year the basketball players were treated to a new net on Independence Day – the system's promise its heart was in the right place. *Sure it was.*

Shooter walked through the tunnel, passed the metal detector and stood at the edge of the yard. It was a day off and spirits were high. All the work details were suspended and a long table was set up with watermelon slices, canned soft drinks in ice and snack cakes. On the back wall fronting the infirmary, the flower garden was livid with bright peonies and periwinkles, the pride of Ol'Yeller, an octoroon life-timer who took pride in his spring planting and maintained the beds through the first freeze in the fall.

On the left side by the Chaplin's office bare-chested convicts pumped iron, purple tattoos coming alive under the glistening sweat. Round the corner past the infirmary entrance was a U-shaped area perfect for handball where the Mexicans played a closed game. On the right side under the high wall of C-block, teams of black men in shirts and skins were at it with the round ball, enjoying the swish of the new net. But in the center of the yard was the volleyball court where players for the annual tournament were warming up.

"I'm on your team, Shooter," Mikey said, heading for the weight rack.

"You gotta draw, man. Yunno that." Shooter extended his arms wide and leaned back to look up at the sun, getting a full stretch through his midsection.

Shooter was the best volleyball player on the unit with a fast overhand serve; it skimmed the net then sunk quick like a German submarine. Only way you could stop it was jump when he smacked it and hope you guessed the trajectory just right so it hit your flat palms and shot down like a spike, straight at the feet of your opponent in the front row.

Shooter could also dig and set. An all-around all-star, down for ten years for shooting three guys who tried to break into his car. Had the car been in front of Shooter's house and had he a permit for the handgun, and had one of the thugs not been the cousin of the town constable he might have gotten away with it

The tournament consisted of six-man teams. Everyone who wanted to play wrote their name on a slip of paper and dropped it in a butt can. At 12:30, Lt. Barker counted the number of players, divided by six and drew out the names of the team captains. The captains then drew one-at-a-time in unison, picking the members of their team. This year there were 48 players which meant eight teams. And as luck would have it, the six best players on the unit ended up on one team with Shooter as the captain.

"It ain't fair," was the common reaction.

"How the fuck did that happen?"

"It's a lock."

"Don't worry," Shooter smiled, "it's double 'limination."

"Wazzat mean?"

"You gotta lose two games," Copper Coon said, one of Shooter's elite six, a tall lithe mongrel of a man down for killing his wife, his best friend and his wife's lover, the latter two being the same unlucky dude, whose last memory was the feeling a crowbar made when it caved in the front of his skull.

An all-star cadre of misfits rounded out Shooter's team. Buddy Sims, down for auto theft, his fifth stretch, small and wiry with a nervous tic born from excessive sport with crystal meth; but fast, and would dive into the macadam to retrieve a ball rather than lose a point. Nickie Green once played semi-pro ball in south Texas, had reflexes like a cobra, but was played out of position one night in Eagle Pass, when the big pot distributor from Dallas turned out to be a DEA Special Agent who brought lots of friends with weapons.

Jim-Jam was a spiker, in more ways than one,

which brought him down to petty theft to stay well; but set the ball high anywhere in front of him and the point was automatic. And Speedy Lane was a lanky mouth-breather from Texarkana who could gather in the toughest shot with his storklike arms. He was also infamous for six-fingered discounts from high-end diamond shops when the dark suit covered his tattoos allowing the mistaken image of a banker.

Cellblock bookies had the field even against Shooter's team, meaning you could take Shooter or take all the rest for even odds. It slid 2 to 1 for Shooter's, then 3 to 1. Betting got so lopsided, Bunky had to lay off the action with Drake Fellows on D-Block, a guy you didn't want to get behind to.

Like did Mitzy Prago, a misplaced wop who lost five cartons one weekend betting NFL games. Next day his cell was stripped of everything but the state issued sheets, including a fine radio, a new pair of Adidas, and a half-full commissary sack. Mitzy complained and was found the next day spinning around in a commercial dryer in the laundry, unconscious. He lay in the infirmary two weeks before he could remember his name. But he may have been goldbricking to miss work in the license plate factory.

The games kept a furious pace throughout the afternoon. By five o'clock four teams were out, Team Grasshog and two others had lost one game while Shooter's team remained undefeated. Team Grasshog was a sleeper team made of second tier players. None were too tall, too fast or too anything, just good solid middle level players who worked well together as a unit. Unlike Team Shooter, they had no prima donnas. None of them thought they were the best, so it didn't bother them when they made mistakes. They just kept on playing and encouraging one another.

In the next round Team Shooter and Team Grasshog both won and would face each other in the finals.

"One more and you're toast, Grasshogs," Speedy Lane taunted as balls flew over the net during the warm-up.

"Don't listen to him," advised Charlie Wade, Team Grasshog captain. Charlie was serving a five-year sentence for running an illegal high-stakes Texas Hold-em game that was fine as long as the county comissioner with a gambling habit was winning. When real players caused him to lose his car and almost his house, the game was rousted and the cash disappeared along with the commissioner's financial troubles.

"We don't have a chance," offered Cappy Saunders, a former captain of a Gulf shrimp trawler who was busted with a hold full of square grouper. The marijuana weighed almost a ton and Cappy was sentenced to a day a pound.

"There's always a chance," Lane Boggs said, a stocky ex-boxer who took the fall for his boss on a larceny beef and was due for release next month.

"Never say die," said Denny Martin, a repeat drunk

driver down for a nickel who served time overseas as a Marine.

Lt. Barker blew his whistle and the extra balls were slapped to the side. The court was surrounded by dispatched players from eliminated teams and other convicts in white cotton uniforms, lounging on the steps leading up to the library, sucking on ice cream bars or swigging cold Cokes.

"This is the championship. Winners get five-dollar commissary punch cards, runners up each get a pint of their choice."

"I'll have chocolate chip," Shooter taunted his opposing captain.

"Make Shooter's banana fudge," came Wade's retort, setting off a string of guffaws around the perimeter.

"Y'all know the rules," Barker continued. "Fifteen points, serve changes on loss of point, you don't have to serve to score. Rotation optional. Call it, Shooter."

"Heads."

Lt. Barker flipped a coin. "It's heads. Shooter serves. Let's have a good clean game here, boys."

"Yeah, squeaky clean," Nickie Green said, taking his position on the net in the front row.

The whistle blew again, Shooter tossed the ball high overhead and smashed it with a tight cupped palm as it fell. The ball screeched over the net, hit Cappy Saunders in the hands and shot out of bounds.

"That's one," Shooter smiled as the ball was

tossed back to him. He bounced it twice, flipped it up and smacked another one at Cappy, hitting him in the chest.

"Two."

"Time!" Wade said, motioning to his teammates to come close. "Look, these guys are going to kill us if we don't relax and focus on the ball. Pay attention!"

"One game and we're done, guys," Mitch Fonderlack shook his head like he did when the judge gave him twenty-five years for ten pounds of cocaine.

"We can't beat'em if we don't think we can," said Boggs the boxer.

Copper Coon smirked through the net. "You gonna play or hold knitting class?"

"Okay, guys," Wade said. "Grasshogs on three. One, two…"

"Grasshogs!" They clapped hands and took their positions, three in the front row, one in the middle, two in the back.

"Two zip, boys," Shooter mocked. "Here comes three." He tossed it low and did a quick stab, placing the ball in the open spot. Cappy made a valiant effort, plopped it up and Sam Green, the only black man in the game, tapped it over the net backhanded. But Nickie was there, set it high and Copper Coon smashed it back at Cappy's face, bloodying his nose.

"Time," Lt. Barker called. Cappy went to the sidelines for some tissues he twisted into plugs, stuck up his nostrils and scampered back on the court.

"Three!" Shooter served again and again, each ball misplayed by the Grasshogs in one way or another until the score rose to 11-2.

"Four more, Shooter," Buddy Sims said. "Let's send these chumps home."

Shooter grinned, lofted the ball and drew back his cupped hand.

"Whap!"

The dirty white ball dropped too quick and hit the net next to Nickie.

"Fuck me!" Nickie said, rolling the ball under the net back to Wade.

"Come on guys. Let's step up now." Wade feigned an overhand serve and came at it from below, lifting it past the third floor of the infirmary. It gained speed as it fell and Copper Coon stepped back to let it fall just hitting the line.

"In!" Cried a volunteer linesman attired in soft cotton whites.

"Yer momma!" Coon protested, staring at the spot where the ball landed.

"Hit the line, man," Buddy Sims said. "If you'd move your fat ass, I woulda got it."

"Fuck you!" Coon spat, taking a swing at Sims' head, but he dodged it easily.

"Three eleven," Wade said, bouncing the ball on the other side.

The players turned toward him as he faked the high

underhand and laid a scorcher over the center past Nickie Green. Sims darted out a forearm, but the ball had too much spin and careened out of bounds.

"Goddamnit, moron!" Shooter said. "Wake the fuck up!"

"Youse the moron," Sims shot back. "You served the net."

"Yeah, after eleven points. Let's see you get one."

"Four eleven," Wade announced, as the ball was rolled back to him. He smiled, tossed the ball up and came at it sidearmed so he could apply top spin. Nickie stuck up a hand as it cruised over the net and sent it high, Jim-Jam got set for the spike as Speedie Lane cupped his hands at his waist to give him the perfect set.

"Nickle bag of H if you miss it, Jam-Jam," Wade shouted.

Jim-Jam jumped with a mighty round house and met the ball at the top of its arc, but hit it too hard and it bounced on the macadam just past the line.

"Out!" shouted the linesman.

"Dammit, man!" Shooter was outraged. "Can't you guys do anything right?"

"It ain't me," Speedie said. "Set was perfect."

"Bullshit!" Jim-Jam countered, licking his lips, the thought of the heroin distorting his temperament.

"Set was good," Nickie added.

The favored team continued to argue as Wade held the ball and shared amused looks with guys on his side of the net.

"Play ball!' Lt. Barker shouted, blowing his whistle.

Wade tossed up another one and took a fake swing to see who jumped at the net, then tossed it up again and streaked it between Speedie and Jim-Jam. The ball dipped like a wounded duck and hit the court at Shooter's feet.

"Service ace!" taunted Denny Martin, staring down Jim-Jam who reached through a hole in the net and tried to tear Denny's lip. But the Marine was no stranger to dirty play, grabbed his hand and twisted hard, popping his wrist.

"Oww! Mutha fucka!" Jim-Jam charged at him under the net swinging his good arm. Denny caught it easily and kicked him in the groin. He went down, nearly unconscious with the pain. Lt. Barker ran over blowing his whistle.

"Out!" he yelled. "Both of you." He jerked his thumb toward the anonymity of the sidelines.

"Sure, boss," Denny said, easing off the court, winking at Wade and the others who nodded back. Taking out the opposing best spiker was a clever move.

Lt. Barker lifted Jim-Jam to his feet and helped him limp away. "No more of this shit," he said. "This is volleyball. It's a gentleman's game."

"Not in here it ain't," cracked Will Montrose from the sidelines, down six years for cattle rustling, a crime would have got him hanged a century before.

Barker glared at him and blew his whistle. "Keep it

clean, boys."

"Five eleven." Wade bounced the volleyball several times to bring his team's attention back into line, then lifted a deceptively shallow toss and sidearmed a fast topspin serve inches above the net. The blistering serve dove straight at Sims' face. He adroitly twisted to the side, scissored his fingers together and tried to set using his forearms, but the spin was too great and the ball whizzed by into the hedges, bringing cheers from those above hanging out the infirmary windows.

"Service ace," Lane Boggs taunted.

"Come on shit head," Shooter yelled. "Four more points and we ice these clowns." The other players around Shooter also added barbs and Sims shouted back.

At that moment, Wade had a brilliant realization

"Time L.T."

"Make it quick, Wade."

Wade motioned for his four remaining players to join into a huddle. "Look, we can beat these guys. They think they're the best."

"They are the best, Wade."

"I know. But that's their problem. They expect to win."

"They are undefeated, man."

"So what?"

"Four points and it's over."

"That's stinkin' thinkin'. All we need is 24 points and we win."

"How we goin' to do that?"

"By playing relaxed, having a good time. And heckling the shit out of them every time they screw up."

"Time." Barker blew his whistle and Wade's team took their positions.

"Six eleven," Wade announced loudly. "Coming at you again, Sims."

He bounced the ball then snuck an underhanded serve just over the tips of Sparky's fingers as he leapt, falling fast and smacking the pavement at Sims' feet.

"Haha," Boggs pointed at Sims and taunted. His teammates piled it on.

"Wheels are coming off."

"Gone on tilt."

"Stick a spork in him."

"Fuckin' clowns."

The taunts got everyone on the all-star team squabbling. As the game slipped away, they became more belligerent toward each other, destroying not only their collective cohesiveness, but made each player gun-shy about making a mistake. Before they knew it, the scrubs had won the game and had the momentum going into the championship.

And the Grasshogs didn't let up in the final. Wade's serves were delivered with precision, exploiting every weakness. His team heckled every mistake, reiterated every point.

To say losing in such a manner was psychologically

devastating to the all stars would be an understatement. Wade played every point like a master manipulator, serving fast and low to the angriest guy, looping a soft one over the head of a player still arguing over the last point, driving the ball with vengeance into the face of the player with reflexes diminished by mistakes.

"Okay, boys," Barker announced, glad his shift as referee was about over. "Fourteen to eleven. Game point." Wade tossed it high like he was going to jump and hit a top spin serve creasing the net and Shooter jumped to block it. But Wade faked the overhand smash and popped it lightly with a closed reverse fist. The ball arced over the net like a dove with sore feet and hit Shooter on the heel.

"Game, and match," announced Barker. "Grasshogs win."

The crowd of convicts gave a slight cheer and slapped Wade and the others on the back as the all-stars hung their heads and dispersed quietly after a parting string of profanity, muttering under their breath they should have won.

Shooter came up to Wade and offered his hand. "You got us."

Wade squeezed hard, feeling the warmth of a vanquished champion. "Thanks."

"How did you pull that off?"

"Your problem was you guys were too good," Wade said as he accepted the commissary punch card handed to him by the warden's bookkeeper.

"We should have won then."

"Too many chiefs and not enough Indians. Once you guys started blaming each other, I knew we had a chance."

Shooter thought back. "I can see that now."

"Complacency was your Achilles' heel."

"Next year I want to play on your team," Shooter said.

"We should be so lucky," Wade answered, holding up his card. "Buy you a pint."

"Sure. Thanks."

The two sportsmen got in the ice cream line at the edge of the prison yard surrounded by red brick walls forty feet high. And for a moment, they had transcended the dismal circumstances of their incarceration and found meaning in the sport they loved.

THE BOY WITH THE GOLDEN SHELL

"Those who don't believe in magic will never find it."
– Roald Dahl

Michael wandered the beach while his parents slept in the shade under a striped umbrella stuck in the sand. He walked the foamy edge of the surf where seaweed was pushed up by the waves. He bent to study and found little shrimp and crabs clinging to slippery leaves and shoots making up the floating nests. Sometimes he would find a colorful piece of plastic, or a broken lure, or a smooth brown seed. Once he found a glass ball that floated all the way from Portugal used by fisherman to hold up their nets.

Winter brought changing winds and man-o-wars navigated toward shore using their crimped purple bubbles like sails. Michael got tangled up in one once and came screaming out of the water. The lifeguard ran down, applied ammonia and gently pulled the sticky lines off welts around his waist and legs. He looked like he had been whipped.

Summers would bring tropical hurricanes when waves shoved the sand into mounds, and brutal winds scoured paint off cars. Morning light would reveal a yacht high-centered on the beach road, or wooden sections torn from piers, or oil drums loosened from passing tankers high up in back yards.

After a heavy wind was the best time to find coins. They would be lying on the sand, exposed and shiny. Pieces of glass would be visible too and jewelry – for whoever came first to pick them up.

One day a crowd of people gathered around something that looked like a big fish. Police sirens, screeching tires and men in blue came sliding over the sand in flat black shoes. Michael eased closer and saw it was a woman, white, puffy and still, her hair tangled in seaweed and her mouth open. There were little reddish half-moon pieces missing where fish had nibbled.

"She was drunk and fell off a cruise ship," his

father told him the next day, reading the paper over breakfast.

Michael loved the beach and, as it was a short walk from the back door of his parents' house, had immediate access. As long as he could remember he spent his afternoons, weekends and school breaks on the beach with friends. Or when friends weren't available, he would be there alone. He had many stories to tell about growing up and watching the changing seasons, the campouts and bonfires, things he found, and people he met. But there was one incident that would always color the rest.

It was a Sunday, the end of a long weekend. The sun was squashing down on the indigo waves, an onshore breeze bringing in the smell of the deep clean ocean.

There, at the waterline, something round caught the sun's light, emitting a golden glow. Michael's eyes were wide as he ran towards the object, hoping no one else had seen it and might beat him to the claim. But when he got there, he was all alone, only a solitary runner heading away down the beach towards the tall glass buildings where tourists stayed.

The object was partially buried in the sand. Michael dropped to his knees and dug it out with his hands. A wave came as he was working, and the backwash pulled him off the beach. When he gained his feet in the shallows, a golden shell was curled around his fingers.

Michael lifted the shell to his eyes and admired its beauty and design. It was an old shell with many concentric rings built by the creatures who had owned it and carried it on their backs as protection. But why was this shell empty and not a house for a conch or another soft mollusk? He shook the water and remaining sand out of the shell, and rinsed it clean and bright. Then he held the shell to his ear to hear the sea.

"Michael," came the voice from deep within the shell.

This startled him and he dropped the shell in the water. He started to leave, but stopped, went back and dove down in the surf. Michael didn't want to lose the mystery before he had solved it. The waves were rough and he felt around until he found the smooth curved surface of the shell and slid his fingers around into its mouth and brought it up. He climbed the weathered wooden steps to his house, rinsed off the salt water under the outdoor shower, then dried the shell and took it to his room.

He was still puzzled by what he thought the shell had said to him, but did not put the shell to his ear again that night. He set it on his bookshelf, did his homework and went to bed, not mentioning the shell to his parents at dinner.

*   *   *

The next day after school, Michael threw his backpack on his bed, put on his swim trunks and took the shell down to the beach. The thought of a talking shell was too spooky and he decided to return it to the sea where its rightful occupant would make use of it.

When he reached the water's edge, he cocked his arm like he would throw a football, stepped forward and launched the shell in a perfect spiraling arc. The pointed tip hit the shiny curl under a breaking wave and disappeared. Michael smiled, turned south and took a long jog to clear his head.

He ran fast and hard, barefooted on the soft sand down to the edge of the shiny buildings and back again. He dove into the surf to cool off and swam out past the shore break. On the calm water Michael flipped over on his back and stretched out to float spread-eagle. He squinted into the setting sun between his toes, its golden glow in his eyes. When his breathing slowed to normal, he rolled over and crawled his way back to shore with strong practiced strokes.

His mother waved from the back porch, signaling dinner, and Michael jogged out of the surf feeling fresh and alive. Then, his right foot came down on something curved and smooth. He looked down. It was the golden shell. Having worked out all the fear about a talking shell on his run, Michael was glad it had come back to him. He reached down and cut it out of the wet sand with his fingers. It was a beautiful shell and during his run he had regretted throwing it away. Now he had it again and would keep it on his bookshelf. He took it to the shower, cleaned it off and got ready for dinner.

That night, as he sat studying at his desk, his eyes drifted and fell upon the golden shell. He hesitated, not wanting to pick it up and hear it speak to him, yet curious if maybe he had imagined it to begin with. Never one to back down from fear, Michael reached over, grabbed the shell and brought it to his hear.

"Michael," the shell said.

He took a deep breath and felt his heart beat quicken. "Yes, this is Michael," he spoke into the shell as if it were a telephone.

"I want you to look out your window," the shell said.

Michael got up and looked out his window. The sun had been gone for an hour and the moon was full and large just above the calm ocean.

"I see the moon," he said to the shell.

"That is not the moon, Michael," said the shell.

"Sure it is," Michael laughed, figuring he had found a talking shell that was also stupid.

"Think, Michael," the shell said. "Think deeper into what you are seeing."

Michael paused and looked at the moon again, magnified by the thick atmosphere at the horizon. Its craters were visible as dark tones within the bright light creating the illusion of child's face. He thought of his science class. Then, it hit him.

"I see the moon only by the light reflected from its surface."

"Right, Michael. And where does that light come from?"

"The sun," Michael said reverently. He had been mistaken. This shell was a wise shell. It was his teacher.

"Good night, Michael," the shell said.

"Wait!" Michael said quickly.

But the shell did not answer.

*   *   *

The next day, Michael couldn't wait to get home from school and visit his magic shell. He picked it up from his book case and lifted it to his ear.

"Hi Michael," said the shell.

"Hi shell." That sounded strange. "What do you want me to call you?"

"Shell is fine," said the shell. "But my real name is Saoirse."

"Seer-sha?"

"Yes," said the shell. "That's who I was before I came to live inside this shell."

"You were a person once?" asked Michael.

"I was an Irish lass from Clonakilty, County Cork, in Northern Ireland."

"Ireland?"

"Aye."

"What happened so you got stuck inside a shell?"

"That's a story for another day," Saoirse said. "But

I am not trapped, not the way you mean."

"What do you eat?"

"I don't need to eat."

"Why not?"

"Because I don't exist in a realm which requires food."

"What do you look like?"

"I look like the shell you hold in your hand."

"A person can't look like a shell," Michael said, feeling confident.

"No, I don't look like a shell."

"Then why did you say so?" Maybe this shell wasn't much of a teacher after all, Michael thought. Maybe it was just a fluke about the sun's reflection off the moon.

"Because you needed an answer within the realm of your understanding to feel comfortable."

"Oh…" Michael paused. Then he said, "I don't need to feel comfortable. I want to know what is going on here!"

"Calm down, Michael." The shell said. "What is the most important thing to you in your life?"

That was better, Michael thought. A wise shell would be asking questions such as this. "Right now the most important thing is to find out why I am sitting here talking to a shell!"

"Why are you?" the shell asked.

"Because… because… I need to know."

"You need to know…"

Michael said quickly: "I need to know if you are for real or if I am going crazy."

"You are not going crazy, Michael," the shell said. "But other people will think you are crazy if you tell them you have a talking shell."

"Why?" Michael said. "I'll hand them the shell and they can hear it for themselves."

"I won't talk to them, Michael. Only you."

"Oh? You won't!"

"N'aye. Just you."

Michael then began to question himself. If he could hear the talking shell, but the shell would not talk to other people, then he best not tell anyone about it.

"That's right, Michael," said the shell.

"What's right?"

"What you were just thinking about not telling other people."

"What? You can hear my thoughts?"

"Yes. And you can hear mine."

Michael then realized the voice he thought was coming from the shell may not be coming from the shell at all. It may just be inside his head.

Just then his mother was at his bedroom door.

"Who are you talking to, dear?" she asked. Michael's mother was a pleasant well-proportioned woman with dark brown eyes and reddish brown hair she kept short due to the sub-tropical climate.

"Just thinking out loud, mother," he said.

Her eyes fell on what he was holding in his hands.

"What a beautiful shell," she said, coming close. "Where did you get it?"

"I found it on the beach."

"You didn't tell me you found a shell like this." She held out her hand and Michael slowly gave it up. She turned it over in her hands, admiring its perfect shape, its smooth golden texture.

"It's magnificent!" She started to raise it towards her head.

"Wait!" Michael cried, jumping up.

"Did you know," his mother continued, "if you put the shell to your ear you can hear the ocean." She did so and her eyes went out of focus as she listened. "Yes. Beautiful!" Then she handed the shell back.

"Thank you," Michael said, studying her face for anything out of the ordinary.

"That's a keeper," she said, pointing to the shell. "Oh, walk the dog for me, would you honey. I've got to do my nails. Your father's taking me out. Your dinner's in the microwave. Two minutes on high."

"Sure, mom," Michael said as she closed the door to his room.

Michael slowly raised the shell to his ear.

"See?" the shell said. "No one can hear me but you. They just hear the waves and the wind on the ocean."

Michael breathed a sigh of relief. "Our secret

then?"

"Our secret," Saoirse confirmed.

Michael put the shell back on his bookcase and hurried out to take Rollo, their Dalmatian, for its evening walk.

Rollo was a Red Dalmatian, a rare breed with reddish brown spots instead of black. He was a good runner and a good fisherman and would wade in the shallows and catch small fish. Once a school of pompano was swimming close to the shore and Rollo sprang and caught hold of a big one. The weight of the fish caused Rollo to tumble into the surf. He rolled over and over with the fish until they both were tired. When he brought it up and laid it at Michael's feet he fell down panting on the sand.

"Good boy, Rollo," Michael praised him. He cleaned the fish for dinner and it fed the whole family, including a nice piece of filet for the fisher dog.

Michael liked to walk Rollo near sunset when the world appeared coated in a golden hue. It seemed fresh and magical and reminded him of his golden shell. He wondered what it was good for beyond posing questions about sunlight reflecting off the moon. But maybe he was just imagining it all.

He picked up a stick from the seaweed all smooth and soft from its time in the ocean and tossed it ahead. Rollo ran after it, swept it up into his jaws and brought is back. Michael tossed it again and they worked their way down the beach toward the tall glass buildings where the rich people had penthouse condos or adults met each other for business or social.

A lifeguard was closing up his tower for the day, latching the shutters and locking the door to secure his floats and safety equipment.

"Hi Michael."

"Hey Jimmy."

"Rollo's looking sharp today."

"Always."

"Hey, I saw your mom before."

"Really? Where?"

"Bar by the pool."

"Okay… thanks."

"Take care." Jimmy locked up, shouldered his gear bag and waded the soft sand toward his car.

Michael thought it was strange Jimmy had seen his mother. She said she was going out with dad and they never went over here. He decided to take a look.

The golden hour was fading into darkness, held at bay by lights illuminating the pool area from high above and lower to provide moods. Michael crept up so his eyes were just above the concrete wall. Sure enough, his mother was sitting at the bar with a strange man. As Michael watched, the two of them became more animated and their faces looked like people on TV who were about ready to make out.

Then the man kissed his mother. Not just a peck, but a full-on passionate kiss. Her arms went around his neck and pulled him close.

Michael's face burned with tears. He tore himself away and started running toward home. Rollo loped
alongside, dashing ahead, then looping back around him in
quick ovals oblivious to the mental anguish of his best pal.
Michael climbed the wooden steps from the beach two
at a time and did a quick look around the house. His dad
wasn't there. Only the faint smell of his mother's perfume
tinted the air.

Michael ran to his room and buried his head in his
pillow and cried himself out. Then he thought he heard a
noise. He rolled over and tried to locate the source. It was
coming from the shell.

Michael threw his legs over the side of the bed and
went to the bookcase. The shell seemed to glow with a
golden light. He picked it up and pressed the hollow opening to his ear.

"How's it going Michael?"

"Horrible."

"What's the matter?"

"I just saw my mother kissing a strange man."

"That's not good."

"No. It sucks."

"Hate to tell you this, but your parents are getting
divorced."

"What?"

"Yep. Divorced. Sad but true."

"How would you know this?"

"How would I know sunlight reflects off the moon?"

"That was just a fluke."

"Was it now?"

There was a still silence as the words settled over him like autumn leaves.

"Okay," Michael gave up. "How do know?"

"You think life is all fun and games, Michael?"

"Why I…"

"It's a big bad world out there. You're still a babe in the woods. Babe on the beach is probably a better metaphor."

"Funny."

"Last guy who had me told me that?"

"What guy?"

"The guy after the one before and the one before that and the one…"

"How long have you been doing this?"

"Playing oracle with peoples' lives?"

"What's an oracle?"

"Someone who can see the future."

"But you are just a shell."

"Am I?"

"Unless I am imagining it all and I am talking to myself."

"Have you ever seen a psychiatrist?"

"Yes. Once when I hurt myself."

"What did he tell you?"

"That I needed to be more careful."

"He was right."

"My shell agrees with my psychiatrist. That's a good sign."

"I'd laugh but I'm a shell."

"Why are my parents getting divorced?"

"They are sick of each other."

"Is it anything I did?"

"Children always think that, but it's not true. You did nothing wrong. Breaking up is just part of life."

"I don't like this."

"Life is full of beautiful and tragic events, get used to it."

"So what do I do?"

"You deal with it."

"How?"

"Do you love your mom and dad?"

"Yes."

"Love them equally?"

"Yes."

"So how can you express this love during this difficult time?"

"Difficult for who?"

Michael sensed a presence and turned to find his father staring at him in the doorway.

"Who are you talking to, son?"

Michael blushed and tried to conceal the shell.

"No one."

"That looks like a great shell." He held out his hand. Michael put the shell into it. His dad turned it over and peered inside.

"It's a beauty all right. Where did you get it?"

"Found it on the beach."

"It's great living on the beach, isn't it son?"

"Are you and mom getting a divorce?"

The question froze his hand with the shell in mid-air.

"What makes you think that?"

"I just saw mom kissing another man."

"Where?"

"Bar by the pool in the glass building."

His father sighed, handed the shell back and sat next to Michael on the bed.

"Things don't always work out between people, son."

"But why? You and mom love each other." Tears streamed down his face.

His father took Michael in his arms.

"Yes, and you are the product of that love. We both love you very much."

Michael pulled away, his eyes red and accusatory. "We are a family! You said we would always be together."

"We will be together. Just not in the same house."

"What?"

"Your mother is moving out tomorrow."

"Oh no!"

"It's going to be all right, son. You'll see."

"No it won't. It will never be all right."

His father stood up and looked down at him. "Grow up, Michael. Face reality. No matter what you do you can't change it. Your mother and I will remain friends forever, but our love for each other just isn't like it used to be. We are still young enough to find partners we want to be with. You will understand some day. Hopefully some-day soon."

"I will never understand. You both have betrayed me."

"Maybe I should make an appointment for you to see Dr. Zeigler again."

"No! No shrinks."

Michael got up, grabbed his shell, and stormed out of the house to the beach. He trudged along in the sand, the rising moon sending daggers of light toward him re-flecting off the sea.

"My life is over," he muttered to himself.

The shell began to glow gold in his hand. He brought it to his ear.

"Your reaction is typical, Michael."

"What does that mean?"

"You have a right to be angry."

"I am angry."

"So what can you do about it?"

"I don't know. Be angry."

"You could stay angry, but does that really do anyone any good?"

"It's how I feel."

"You also have a mind. Do your feelings control your mind, or does your mind control your feelings?"

Michael had to think a moment before he answered.

"I guess my feelings control how I think."

"Can you reverse it? Can you cause your mind to override your feelings?"

"I don't know."

"Try it."

"How?"

"Say to yourself: 'Okay, Michael. Your parents are getting divorced. You can be upset about it and cry and moan. Or you can accept it and get on with your life.'"

"You sound like Dr. Zeigler."

"Do it."

So Michael did and he felt a strange sensation. He felt the heaviness of the emotions lift away and a new kind of peace settle over him.

"Wow."

"We all die, Michael. But few of us really live. To live fully we have to be able to control our emotions and get past any kind of disruption. It's part of growing up."

"A shrink in a shell. Hah!"

"That's the lesson for the day. Good luck."

"And good luck to you." Michael cocked back his arm and threw the shell as far as he could out into the waves. It disappeared in a patch of white foam inside a golden lance from the moon's reflection.

The next morning Michael got up with a new sense of responsibility. The anguish of the night before was gone, replaced with a calm strength that made him feel years older. He washed his face and went out to the breakfast room where his mother and father wore faces of guilt and frustration.

"Morning mom, dad." He went over and kissed his mom on the forehead, sat down and helped himself to juice and toast.

"Are you all right, son?"

"Never better. Slept like a baby."

His mother and father looked at one another in disbelief.

"I understand about the divorce. It's okay. We still all love each other. You gotta do what you gotta do."

"Why, Michael, that's very mature of you."

"Sure, mom. I want you and dad to be happy."

Rollo came up and nosed his way into Michael's lap. "Okay boy, let's go."

Rollo followed Michael from the table to the beach as his parents stared after him in disbelief.

Michael ran across the soft sand and explored the gentle surf on the wet sand. He waded out to his knees and nowhere could he find the golden shell.

Night Song

In our bed

    your feet kiss mine

    my thigh clamped tight

    arm cradles your back

    your head on my chest

I shift your ruby hair

    you sleep deeply

    murmuring sweet nothings

    in Maltese.

FALALA

"The heart has its reasons that reason knows nothing of."
– Blaise Pascal

Every morning Falala would rise before dawn, meditate and perform her ablutions in the outdoor salon Major Stands had built for her. It was a pleasant room overlooking a garden of jasmine backed by cinnamon trees inside a ring of bamboo. When the weather was proud, she would crank open the large windows so fragrance could drift in and quiet her senses while she bathed her mind in a silent mantra. The wordless sound had been given to her by a visiting seer who came once a year to the village and inducted those who had adequately prepared themselves. It took three years before the seer found her worthy, thus instilling a level of devotion she promised to keep inviolate as long as she lived.

Falala performed her daily ritual eagerly, cleansing first her mind, then her body. The Major wanted her clean in every way and spared no expense in constructing the magnificent rosewood tub. It was set on a rise so the breeze would enter the east windows with the first light, flow over her body and exit the room through windows designed to admit the setting sun. Falala was meticulous with the scented soap and soft brushes. She enjoyed the hot water and penetrating oils which kept her skin smooth as sable. Afterwards she would pose on the bamboo mat as Langeela combed her hair down past her waist with a hard brush made from whalebone.

"I love your hair, Falala," Langeela said this morning. "It reminds me of a horse's tail, but softer."

When Major Stands made his acquisition on her twelfth birthday, her hair was just above her shoulders. She was the youngest of sixteen children and the prettiest and fetched a sum which had kept her brothers and sisters fed and clothed for many years. He selected her for her beauty but also for the intelligence radiating through her emerald eyes. Cataracts had fogged his vision followed by glaucoma which closed down his sight, save the perception of night and day. What Stands knew recently of Falala came only from his memory and his ears.

"Do you know what tomorrow is?" Langeela asked

expectantly.

"No, love," Falala said to her best friend and confidant.

"Tomorrow is your birthday," she said joyously.

"My birthday?"

"Yes. Tomorrow you will be eighteen."

She shivered, remembering past birthdays, when she had received wonderful things. One year the Major had given her a gold necklace dotted with black pearls she would wear on summer evenings. Another year he surprised her with a dappled gray steed sporting a long white mane she would grip tightly as she rode bareback around the estate. There had been gifts of silken garments and clever toys and many sweet things to eat. But the eighteenth birthday was to be special, though she could not remember why.

"Eighteen," she repeated thoughtfully.

"Yes, my darling. It is what we have been waiting for all these many years."

"Oh?"

"Tomorrow, you will become a woman of legal age," she said with a touch of jealousy. Though Langeela had been well-rewarded during her two decades of service to the Major, she was not in line to become his heir.

Falala had never left the manicured pastures and fields surrounded by a high fence to keep in the wild game. Her every need was provided for, every whim catered to, every desire she knew of, fulfilled. She had never been allowed to venture into town, visit a friend, or return to the village of her birth. She had been completely severed from her past. Her life was that of a privileged captive.

In the mornings Falala studied history, literature, mathematics, biology, accounting, and in the afternoons athletics, riding and music. The Major's plan was for her to become the consummate woman in all ways. He took great care in selecting her tutors and instructed them on what subjects to teach and in what order. Being a consummate individual himself, he knew from experience what worked in the world and what knowledge was necessary to promote ripening of the body, mind and spirt.

Falala sat overlooking the garden, finishing her late lunch of quail eggs on sourdough toast with a side of blueberries and cream. Her saffron linen dress was cut above her knees and crocodile sandals bleached the color of driftwood adorned her manicured feet. She sipped the last of her ginger peach tea and watched the staccato interruption of a moving vehicle by cypress trees lining the perimeter road. The topless motorcar was red and shiny and carried a driver whose thick sandy hair was pushed back by the wind. She could not see the driver's face, nor would she have recognized him as it was his first visit to see his aging uncle since she had arrived.

Falala felt a strange tingle, rose from her seat and padded thoughtfully past the balustrades separating the broad flagstone terrace from the trimmed azalea hedges.

An orange butterfly landed on her shoulder as if to rest from a long journey before venturing onward.

"Hi, pretty one," she said, lifting her hand. The butterfly flapped once and glided to perch on her forefinger. She smiled at the gossamer creature, then pursed her lips and gently blew. The butterfly cocked its wings and took advantage of the breeze, lifting like a tiny kite toward the sky.

"Falala! Come here. I want you to meet someone," Major Stands called from the French doors of the mansion.

Next to him was the figure from the red sports car. Falala felt an abrupt surge in her chest as she locked eyes with the handsome stranger. It was like a key had opened a door, the door swinging wider and by the time she stood before him, a cloud of unsettling sensations had curled up inside her heart.

"Falala, this is my nephew, Brighton Stands. Brighton, Falala, my adopted daughter."

"Pleased to meet you," the young man said. When he took her hand, it was comfortable, like lying down on a beach of soft warm sand.

"And I you, sir. We rarely have visitors here," she said.

"Yes," the Major added. "In the tumultuous world today it's best we don't become too involved."

"Oh?" Brighton was curious. "You must travel then, sir?"

"The loss of my eyesight has curtailed many activities. And Falala has everything she could possibly need right here."

"Will you being staying with us?" she asked, steadying her voice.

"Just until tomorrow." His eyes fixed on hers. "My ship is in port and we sail with the tide."

"Brighton is captain," Maj. Stands added, breaking the tension. "Just like his father."

"That's impressive," Falala said, looking away.

"Quite boring following in his footsteps, but water flows downhill, does it not?"

"Brighton has always taken the easy way," Major Stands said with a touch of familial pride. "Wherever his looks didn't carry him, his considerable brain stepped in."

Falala didn't hear much of what next was said, though she nodded and smiled like she understood. She was mesmerized by the sight of this young man, the way he gestured, the clear merriment in his eyes, the cut of his chin, the crease in his trousers – everything! She felt like the butterfly she released earlier, having broken free of its chrysalis, spreading its wings, ready to be carried on the winds of fate.

"Falala!" They were looking at her. Major Stands' face was stern. "Are you there, girl?"

Brighton looked amused.

"Right here," she answered wanly.

"Pablo is here for your lesson."

The riding instructor had arrived at the edge of the terrace astride his black steed, the dapple steed alongside.

"Oh, do you ride?" Brighton asked.

"She does ride and beautifully. Run along now!"

Falala turned reluctantly and hurried off.

"Rides in a dress! Extraordinary," Brighton said. His eyes lingered on her perfect form as she leapt from the terrace, grabbed the reins, threw herself across its saddle-less back and took off in a gallop. "Wherever did you find her, uncle?"

"I bought her."

"Bought her?"

"Her family couldn't afford her and let her go knowing the opportunity. In this part of the world deals can be made. Would you like a drink?"

"Gin, if you have it."

Stands motioned, a manservant appeared.

"Two gin rickeys." He found the wrought iron table with his cane and the men sat down. The drinks arrived promptly.

"So, tell me, is the girl your… how should I say…"

"Do I sleep with her? Heavens no! I was sterile from the war and could have no children. I always wanted a daughter I could raise to become my heir and carry on the work here."

"I would think a son might be better equipped for that role, uncle."

"A son-in-law, yes," he winked conspiratorially.

"Someone competent to love Falala and protect my legacy, but without absolute access to the coffers."

"You old fox!"

"Checks and balances, my boy."

Brighton grinned and downed the rest of his drink. The manservant appeared at his shoulder with a fresh round.

"What about her? Her feelings? Her future?"

"Look around, son. I saved her from a life of unmentionable squalor and struggle. I have no progeny. She will inherit everything. She will become more, have more, than she could have possibly dreamed."

Brighton capsized his tumbler and motioned for another. "You're really quite mad, you know."

"Maybe. But have you seen her ride?"

Just then, out in the distance past the hedges, Falala appeared astride her mount. She rode in perfect unison, as if she and the horse were one, her long hair flowing, her face exhilarated with the vital passion of youth.

*   *   *

That evening they dressed for dinner, Major Stands in a traditional black tuxedo while the younger Brighton chose a blue brocade jacket with a shawl collar. The men stood sipping sloe gin fizzes in the parlor, where tall picture windows afforded a fine view of the lake. A pair of white swans cut fans of silver ripples between the pink and white lotus flowers perched among floating leaves, the sun sending shimmering lances of light through shoots of bamboo.

"You have a magnificent place here, uncle."

"Thank you. I was hoping you would visit today."

"A pleasure of unexpected refinement," he nodded toward the pianist.

Falala wore a lavender satin gown, impeccably tailored to her supple young form. She sat erect on the piano bench, her fingers dancing lightly over the keys, playing first Chopin's Sonata No.2 in B flat minor to warm up, followed by some lighter Scott Joplin which got the men smiling. She then demonstrated her virtuosity by attempting *Hammerklavier*, Beethoven's Sonata 29 in B flat major, with minor stumbles obfuscated by the spreading inebriation of her audience. Finally, she played Billy Joel's "Scenes from an Italian Restaurant," boldly singing the words. When she concluded, both men smiled with genuine applause.

"Bravo!" Brighton exclaimed.

Falala stood and bowed as if to a packed house at La Scala in Milano. Major Stands shuffled over, opened an arm and she slid against him, like a daughter to a loving father.

"I'm so proud of you," he said. A thin black velvet box appeared in his hand. "For you, Falala, in celebration of your birthday."

She pulled away and opened it, her eyes tearing as

she gazed upon the diamond necklace. "It's so beautiful."

"Like you, my precious," the Major oozed.

"Allow me," Brighton said, stepping in. He lifted the dazzling string of platinum encrusted jewels and draped it around her neck.

Falala glided to the full length mirror bordered in a wide frame layered with gold filigree. She touched the necklace so it caught the light and sent a prism of colors toward her benefactor he could not see.

"Thank you," she said, speaking from the heart.

"Happy birthday," Stands added as the butler rang the dinner bell. "Shall we?"

Falala took his arm and the three of them eased into the dining hall where a grand table was set with the finest silver and crystal. They took seats at one end, Major at the head.

The regal meal began with a service of pureed cauliflower soup with bacon crisps followed by a fresh garden salad of mixed greens drizzled with balsamic vinegar and honey. The first course was baked white fish with a delicious cream sauce whose ingredients defied analysis, except for the punctuating red bits of lobster.

"Delicious, uncle," Brighton said, enjoying sips of sparkling white wine. "I would guess halibut."

"And you would guess wrong, sea captain. Patagonian toothfish."

"Never heard of it." Brighton drained his glass and held it up for a refill. The server tipped the white napkin-wrapped bottle, filling to the brim.

"In 1977, a man named Lee Lantz was looking for a way to sell his ugly deep water fish to the American market. No one wanted to buy a product called Patagonian toothfish. He consulted some advertising men who devised the moniker 'Chilean Seabass' and it was a hit. He then won approval for the trade name which was expanded to include the Antarctic toothfish in 2013."

"Which one is this?" Brighton queried.

"I'm not sure and I doubt the chef is either. But what's in a name? It's the texture and flavor which count, yes?"

"Regardless, it's delicious!" Falala added, thoroughly enjoying herself, touching the necklace every once in a while to make sure it was still there.

"Sometimes at sea, we'll troll a line and bring in a swordfish or a blue marlin," Brighton offered. "Ships' cooks are best in the world and our guy can cook the same fish a different way for days and you'd never know it."

"Never know what?" Falala asked.

"What?" Brighten looked puzzled.

"She's challenging your diction, son."

"Diction?"

"The choice and use of words and phrases one employs in speech or writing," the Major said, amused.

"Our cook cooks a fish so many different ways we can't tell it's the same fish?" Brighton was getting flustered.

"I knew that was what you meant," Falala added, "but literally what you said meant something else."

Brighton looked perturbed. "And what was that, Fa-la-la?"

She shook her head, not wanting to embarrass him further.

"It's nothing, Brighton. Forget it." Major said curtly.

"No, I'm not going to forget. I said what I mean and I mean what I said."

"That's the same thing," Falala laughed, shaming him with her eyes.

"What's the same – "

"Forget it!"

Brighton fumed. "I don't see what –"

"Drop it." Stands added emphasis by slapping the granite table. "As bright as you are, you can't win an intellectual argument with my protégé." The Major smiled.

Brighton quickly consumed what was left of the sparkling wine.

The servers appeared, dishes were cleared and the table whisked in preparation for the next course after delivering a lime sherbet intermezzo. The butler switched glasses like a sommelier and filled them halfway with a robust Argentinian Malbec.

Next, plates of medium-rare prime rib arrived, garnished with broasted new potatoes and asparagus spears. The trio ate in silence for a few moments, not wanting words to intrude on the glorious gastronomic experience. Finally, when not a morsel was left standing, Brighton pushed back from the table and stood up.

"You're killing me with this meal, uncle. I've got to walk a bit to wake up."

"Come back for dessert," the Major called as his nephew went out the side door to the terrace.

Again the dinner implements were removed and replaced with fresh glasses, a silver pitcher of iced water, demitasse cups and a square plate overladen with petit fours. Falala set her napkin on the tablecloth and stood up as the waiter hurried to pull out her chair.

"Be right back," she smiled.

The Major's ears followed her footsteps as she moved across the marble floor on the way to the loo, every inch a women inside her satin dress. He pulled a pipe from his jacket pocket, and gently tamped a measure of fresh McConnell's Scottish Cake into the briar wood bowl. He ignited the mixture with an antique gold lighter he had won from an American novelist in a game of gin rummy; they had shared a cabin on a tramp steamer years before he made his first fortune.

Major Stands puffed on the bowl, enjoying how grand his life was at the moment. He now had everything he had ever wanted within his immediate surrounds. Whoever said you couldn't have your cake and eat it too was not aware of the life skills possessed by Major Bartholomew Winston Stands, master of all he surveyed.

Tonight, the final chapter of his long and tumultuous life would be written.

*   *   *

Falala rinsed her hands in the golden wash basin and dried them on a scented towel. She gazed at herself in the mirror, sliding a delicate finger under the diamond necklace and lifting it once again to see it sparkle. She smiled and breathed deeply, relishing her good luck. She had used her opportunity wisely, had learned many things at the estate and had prepared herself for what she knew must eventually happen. She applied fresh lipstick, ran her hands down her sides to smooth her dress, and pushed open the lavatory door, almost hitting Brighton.

"Oh?" she said, startled.

Brighton's lips parted into his best winning smile as he cocked an eyebrow – a look which most always resulted in getting his way with a barmaid, a cabin girl, a wife or daughter in passage on his ship. He said nothing and slowly moved in, his eyes boring into her, dissolving her will. His hands reached her waist and pulled her tight up against him. He pressed his lips to hers and sought full entrance with his tongue. He felt her breath come heavy and her legs go weak. His hands sought to discover more of her when she suddenly tensed, grabbed his hands and pushed them over his head against the door, her face inches from his.

"Oooh! I love it when the girl takes charge," Brighton mocked, his essence straining inside his tight trousers.

"Not here," Falala said. "Two a.m. My bedroom." She then kissed him quickly, raised her knee to acknowledge his groin, then released him and walked calmly away.

*   *   *

"Coffee, my dear?" the Major asked as Falala returned to the table.

"Allow me." Instead of accepting the chair the butler pulled back for her, she grasped the silver service and poured her surrogate father a cup, then herself.

Brighton eased up adjusting his tie and sat down.

"Coffee?" she asked with a conspiratorial wink.

"Yes, please." Brighton steadied himself as Falala filled his cup.

"Have a good walk?" the Major asked, trying to assimilate the subtle change in his voice.

"Quite nice. The air here is so pleasant. Is it like this always?"

"We do have our rainy season, but it's most often as you experience it today, though we do expect a storm later tonight."

"Should I look the world over, I doubt I would find a more lovely or congenial spot. You are blessed, uncle."

His eyes drifted toward Falala, but found no confirmation of her earlier promise.

The Major puffed his pipe and took a sip from the demitasse cup with his initials in gold. "It didn't happen by accident, my boy. A long life of hard work and right decisions. And a little luck."

"Yes, luck," Brighton continued. "My father said you made your fortune in lumber. Right place at the right time sort of thing."

"I arrived in this country broke, yet with a burning desire I could be something. My first week I was hired by a man with vast land holdings that were draining his other resources. The land was a nuisance to him and he did not know what he possessed. I surveyed the land and found it rich in exotic hardwoods. I had a connection in the States looking for a large quantity of ebony, bubinga and cocobolo for a decorator doing a hotel in Dallas. I put the deal together."

"So, you made your money in the middle?"

"That's the best way. I managed all the transactions, the logging crews, transportation and contracts. Five years later the land we sit on today was cleared and I had millions in the bank."

"You gained this property as part of the deal?"

"After the timber was gone, it seemed worthless to the owner. I bought it for a song."

"Like Rockefeller," Falala interjected. "He saw drillers hitting dry holes and going broke on the resources side, and the demand for refined gasoline products on the supply side. He didn't gamble in drilling, but built a refinery and became the middle man. Every transaction turned a profit."

Brighton was stunned. "My word. Your book learning is extraordinary! I wonder how you are on the experience side?"

Falala knew what he was up to, but she didn't mind.

"Enough of this," the Major interrupted. "I want to hear about you, Brighton."

"I plan to make senior captain and command my own boat, hopefully as part owner. That's where the real money can be made. I have the credentials, just need to find an investor."

"Perhaps luck has finally come your way. How much?"

Brighton had come all the way to this remote outpost, hoping his uncle might have loosened his purse strings since his last visit. He found himself rewarded with a stellar opportunity. *I better not blow it!*

"I've located a suitable ship with a motivated seller. He's lost interest in the cargo business which has been hemorrhaging money."

"That's it! The best time to buy is when the other fellow is on the ropes. How much?"

"I have to perform a due diligence, but my best guess would be a million two." Brighton drained his coffee and bit his fingernails in anticipation, watching his uncle's brow furl in contemplation. He did not want to seem too eager and held his peace.

"You go to that man and tell him you have a possible investor who wants to see his books. Cavendish will go with you. Right, Horace?"

Horace Cavendish, Major Stands' lawyer of forty-seven years, was recognized by the sound of his black rubber-soled Gucci loafers on the marble floor.

"Why, yes," Cavendish said. "Hello all."

"Meet my nephew, Brighton."

Brighton stood and shook his hand. "Nice to meet you."

"And, of course, you know Falala."

"I do indeed." They exchanged nods.

"Did you bring the papers?"

Cavendish tapped his black leather briefcase.

"Splendid. Let's all go into my study. An aging bottle of Boulard Calvados has been waiting for this special occasion."

The study was masculine in every detail, from the deep mahogany wainscoting to the vintage oxblood Chesterfield sofas and arm chairs. The Major positioned himself behind the massive walnut desk, his pipe tobacco adding a rich aroma to the atmosphere.

Cavendish opened his case and withdrew several sets of prepared documents and checked his watch.

"Twelve ten."

"You are now eighteen, my dear," the Major

grinned.

"Falala," Cavendish said, offering a gold pen which cost as much as a small automobile, "once these papers are signed you become the Major's sole heir, owning legal rights and privileges to all his holdings, transferrable immediately upon his death."

Falala, sitting comfortably on the old man's lap, stroked his hair and looked into his sightless eyes. "Are you sure you want to do this?"

"Yes, my love. It has been my promise from the day we met."

"What about Brighton?"

"He will have his investment in the ship or whatever he desires up to two million. But that will come much sooner. I don't plan on dying tonight!" He laughed.

"Oh, you are the most wonderful man!" She hugged his head and kissed him on the forehead.

Cavendish and Brighton looked at one another, trying to plummet the depths of each other's understanding about the relationship dynamics on display before them.

"The pen!" The Major held out his hand. As was their practiced custom, Cavendish gently guided his signature by holding his wrist.

"Right there."

Stands pressed the stylus to the page and scrawled his name as his lawyer turned the pages.

"There... There... And there. All done."

"Tell them what else, Cavendish."

"The Major has decreed should either of you perish before the other, God forbid, the bequest shall transfer."

"Does that mean –"

"Yes, Brighton. You two are to be my sole heirs except for stipends left for my help."

"Quite generous stipends," the lawyer added.

"And it is no accident this has occurred on this day both of you are here. I wanted you too to meet and possibly…"

"Possibly what, uncle?"

The Major sat up straight. "Form a proper union. Produce heirs of your own."

Brighton and Falala looked at one another with new eyes.

"No hurry," the Major inserted. "Take your time. I know I sprung this on you. I am an old man of 92 years who can't see. I want to place my life's efforts in competent hands so they won't be squandered."

An awkward silence fell over the room.

"Hooray!" The Major exclaimed with uncharacteristic zeal. "The Calvados. Brighton, would you do the honors, son?"

Brighton found the dusty bottle on the bar, brushed it off and turned four glasses upright on the desk, filling them halfway with the rich golden liquid. He passed the vessels around, and touching his uncle's glass first, proposed a toast.

"To my uncle and his ingénue, the magnificent

Falala."

They drank.

"To Falala!" the Major was quick to follow. "The shepherd to be."

They drank again, their senses invigorated by the throaty sting of the apple brandy.

Falala raised her glass. "And to Major Bartholomew Winston Stands, the man who makes it all possible."

"Here, here!" Brighton added, the evening's mixture of gin, wine and now Calvados beginning to rend a tear in his sensibilities.

The aged benefactor was also was beginning to fade. He rose unsteadily to his feet. "What an evening! Good night all."

He reached for Falala and gave her a hug, whispering into her ear: "I know you will do the right thing."

"Always."

The Major caned his way around the desk to the door and tapped across the marble floor to the elevator.

"That does it for me," Cavendish said, clicking shut his briefcase. "You both are very fortunate. I hope you will cherish and respect what Major Stands has done for you."

"But of course!" Brighton effused. "He's the best!"

Falala raised an eyebrow, then bowed her head. "I am also very grateful for all *you* have done."

When she met his glance the lawyer saw something new behind her eyes, a kind of power and intelligence that had lain dormant but was ready to burst forth.

"Goodnight," Cavendish said. "It might be a good idea if you two get to know one another." Rubber soles squeaked his departure down the long hallway as a distant clap of thunder set the moment on edge.

Brighton assessed the emptiness of his glass and reached for the bottle. "Have another?"

"No thanks. Think I'll turn in." She stood to leave, but he blocked her way.

"The servants will see us. My room. Two a.m." Her lips brushed across his with a promise of sweet anticipation.

*   *   *

The rains came in heavy clumps hitting the roof like a torrent of fat toads. From Falala's bedroom on the third floor, she could see the gardens flooding and the bamboo shaking in the moonlight as if tugged by a giant hand. She stood at the French doors and watched water puddle on the balcony and gravity pull it down through gaps in the balustrades to the terrace below. The heavy rain continued until 2 a.m. when it lessened to a sprinkle, leaving the air cool and humid and the glazed tile balcony slippery.

A soft knock at the opening door. Brighton entered slowly, feeling his way through the room. A flash of lightning illuminated his desire, standing naked under a sheer negligee on the balcony. She was looking at him, not moving, wanting him to come to her. A breeze lifted the thin fabric and he moved faster, hitting the slippery tile with his leather soles, sliding toward her, reaching for her.

She ducked under him and felt him land across her back. She stood up, her powerful legs pushing to aid the momentum as he continued over the railing, grasping for her, hands sliding across her muscled torso, fingers curling around the soft silk, falling. Falala was pulled with him, her hands hitting the balustrade and bracing as he ripped the gown away from her, leaving her naked.

Lighting flashed and their eyes met in stunned surprise before his back hit the planter, breaking him in two. Thunder rolled down the valley beyond as rain lashed down with the vengeance of a broken promise.

In his room, Major Bartholomew Winston Stands smiled as he took his last breath, knowing his life's work was done, safe in the hands of the two young people he had brought together to protect his legacy. It was now up to God to sanctify their union.

*   *   *

Morning sunlight illuminated the dual tragedy. The house of Stands was in chaotic overdrive. Two bodies. Police inquiries. Matters of property. A last will and testament barely hours old.

Falala remained secluded in her quarters comforted by Langeela while Cavendish handled the details with the authorities. At a certain point they came to Falala for questioning.

"The Major made a fresh will last night making you the primary heir," stated the Investigator.

"He was very generous."

"His nephew, Brighton, was also included. Now that he is departed, everything passes to you."

"I hope to do the Major's wishes honor."

"How long had you known Brighton?"

"He only arrived yesterday."

"Yet he came to your bedroom last night?"

"Yes. It was a shock. The whole thing is a shock."

"And you stated he slipped on the tile and fell over the balcony."

"I tried to grab him but he was too heavy."

"What was he doing there? In your bedroom?"

"I don't know. I was watching the storm and he just appeared."

"Did you have plans? Did you invite him?"

"No! We just met."

Cavendish intervened. "It's clearly an accident. I think she has been through enough."

"Strange how her benefactor and his nephew died within minutes of each other," the Inspector continued.

"Life is strange," Cavendish answered.

"A coincidence that only hours before a new will was signed bequeathing a vast fortune to someone who is neither related by blood or by legal standing."

"Coincidences happen."

"I don't believe in coincidences."

"You are a cynical man, Inspector."

"Who is Falala to you, Mr. Cavendish?"

"Only my charge, my client if you will. I have been the Major's lawyer since he took possession of this property, almost five decades ago. Now it is my job to carry out the Major's final orders."

The Inspector pulled at his mustache and closed his notebook. "That's all for now. Sorry about your loss, miss. Good day."

And so the legal matter ended.

The bodies of the uncle and nephew were buried together under the last remaining bubinga tree overlooking the residence compound from a hill in the corner of the property. Falala was seen to shed an occasional tear, but otherwise took charge of running the household, a role the Major prepared her for through the many years of tutelage.

Cavendish facilitated running the paperwork through the courts, helped manage the Major's ongoing enterprises and was kept on a generous retainer. Langeela was moved into Falala's quarters when she took up residence in the main house after a thorough redecorating. The household staff was given a modest raise and allowed to keep their jobs.

Then, the migration began.

Falala returned to the village of her birth with a

truckload of clothes and gifts for her brothers and sisters. They welcomed her like a long lost hero, a moment she had waited for from the day she left some six years before. After the reunion she gathered all those who wished to join her and installed them in the mansion.

The Major's resources were vast and Falala proved an able steward. Income increased from business and allowed Falala to exercise her final childhood wish. The land the Major had raped for profit then bought for a pittance was to be returned to its natural state. Seedlings of teak, cocobolo, bubinga and other hardwoods were obtained and planted by her brothers and sisters, so one day the forest of her ancestry would cover the land and return it to the splendid condition of *her* forefathers.

THE DONOR

*"One for whom the pebble has value must be surrounded
by treasures wherever he goes."*
– Par Lagerkvist

Fasil Babba swept the streets in front of the palace with a sisal broom he made himself. Like every other day of his adult life, Fasil had risen before dawn and, while his wife and four sons slept, ate quietly in the tiny alcove by the wood stove. He brewed a small pot of Turkish coffee he sweetened with Geimer, a thick cream made from buffalo milk Aisha had churned the night before.
He tore hunks from an oval loaf of samoon or maybe flat pieces from a sheaf of khai. Sometimes there was honey or date molasses, or libna, yogurt with olive oil, to dip the

bread in. Fasil ate until he felt a fullness. It would have to sustain him all day.

When Fasil reached the streets, his legs were limber from the three kilometers' walk. Light was beginning to silver the cobblestones while the gas lights overhead crackled with a quiet intensity. He began at the far corner, enjoying the warmth spreading through the muscles of his arms and torso. The tips of the broom whistled as they whisked away dirt and refuse from the previous days' encounters.

Sometimes there would be things of value among the leaves and food wrappers – coins, silver charms or small articles of clothing. Once Fasil found a 10,000 riyal note tucked inside a sock dropped by a palace visitor that had washed into the gutter after a rain. His heart beat wildly as he fingered the bill, glancing around cautiously. Finding no eyes upon him, he ever so carefully folded it in his palm and tucked it away behind his testicles as he bent down to adjust the bindings of his broom.

Fasil could barely contain himself as he completed his rounds that day. His mind raced with thoughts of what he could do with such a sum. Aisha would have that dress in the store window she passed every day on her trip to the square to obtain water. His sons would have new clothes and even a second pair of shoes. He would buy a spring goat and host a feast for all his cousins and in-laws in the larger flat he would lease from Zubair, the landlord. He would enjoy the look on the bearded face of the man who took great pleasure in evicting those who could not pay. Now Fasil could pay and afford a nice place that would elevate himself and his family.

But wait! How could a lowly street sweeper possibly afford such splendor, such grandeur, on his pittance of a salary? He would be noticed and reported. The owner of the note would come forward and demand reimbursement, or worse – say Fasil had stolen it. The Sultan's guards would come for him. He would be made to confess many crimes he had not committed before the sword finally separated him from his head. His family would be outcast and suffer the penury of shame.

No, Fasil did not buy the dress, or the shoes or the spring goat. He did not contact Zubair about the larger flat. Instead he secretly plastered the note inside a mud brick behind the palett of his marital bed. He told Aisha about their new fortune, but only after weeks of prodding, as she could detect within him a mischievous humor for which no explanation could be found inside their circumstances. She trembled uncontrollably and was unable to sleep for three days. He made her swear an oath: the money would only be used if something happened to him. She would say it was his savings, an accrual from twenty years of service to the Sultan for keeping the streets clean. Until that day, the note would remain their secret.

"What could happen to me?" Fasil exclaimed into the dawn air. The sound of his words startled him, and he looked around to see if anyone had been witness to the mad street sweeper who shouted aloud to himself.

There was no one. Only the sound of the morning birds and approaching hooves on the stone streets.

He brushed the dirt from the mortar joints, his arms firm and his legs sturdy. His strong heart pumped oxygen to his muscles all day, regardless of the exertions required by his job. Dr. Hashid told him during his annual physical he had the heart of a man 25-years-old, though he was 36. His father worked hard all his life and had lived to seventy-four years. His mother also worked as a seamstress until she was eighty-eight. His grandmother had been the oldest woman in the city, passing to the paradise of Jannah at 99. Hard work, simple food and clean living were real attributes he could be proud of, despite his lack of material possessions.

Fasil never worried about getting sick. The Sultan provided excellent medical care for all in his employ. How else could a street sweeper afford four children? Every birth had been paid for and there had been a stipend to help with expenses. He had been a loyal worker for sixteen years, sweeping the Sultan's streets from dawn until midafternoon six days a week.

At home, Fasil taught his sons mathematics so they could become engineers. They would win scholarships, go to college in America, and one day design bridges and skyscrapers. The sweat of his brow and the strain of his back would pass through his sons into highways, carrying people from city to city. His efforts would be reborn into buildings, providing shelter and comfort for many people. The mustard seed was tiny, but oh how vast the tree!

As the sun rose to light the palace of Istana Nurul, the streets resounded with the bleating of goats and the cackle of arriving shopkeepers. A donkey-drawn lorry clomped up from an outer village, creaking under its load of burlap bags tight with rice. Rug weavers and basket makers assembled their displays around the fountain, pulsating plumes of water falling melodiously in the windless dawn. White-shrouded women filled water into earthenware vessels for the day's cooking and ablutions.

"Morning, Fasil," waved Shanu Merka, the ironmonger, as he drove past, his old truck barking fumes tinted with motor oil and anti-freeze.

"When are you going to fix that head gasket?" Fasil chided. "Your stinking exhaust despoils our pristine air."

"A strange comment from one who has never owned a car," Merka replied.

"I prefer my legs to that stink pot!" Fasil smiled.

"Our air has not been pristine for decades, Fasil, ever since the British came with their pumps and refineries."

"You should thank Allah for the British, Shanu. Without petroleum our country would still be in the Middle Ages."

"Hah! And we are much better for it! I forgot: Our wives wear jeweled gowns and dine on roasted squab. Our sons drive Ferraris."

"You must have dreamt you were the Sultan," Fasil added, his sweeping rhythm uninterrupted by the banter.

"Soon," Merka urged, as his truck smoked along. "When we receive 'The Great Distribution'."

"Your ass in a pig's eye," Fasil concluded the daily ritual, as Merka's truck disappeared down a side street where racks of fresh produce were set for purchase.

The Great Distribution was the fabled event promised to the people by the Sultan's late father forty years ago, when the desert was found floating on a sea of sweet crude oil. To share in the revenues was to be the birthright of every citizen once the initial expenses of building the city's infrastructure had been repaid. The Sultan's economists decided the next year would be the one. Then the next year. Then the next.

Fasil contemplated these things as leaves danced before the tips of his broom, making little leaps into mounds lifted by his wide-mouthed shovel into the rolling bin. He would occasionally stop and look at the street behind him, how the true color and texture of the stones were liberated from the daily dust because of his hand. He smiled, enjoying his work. He was a great street sweeper, the best in all the city. He did the Sultan honor with every arc of his broom.

As Fasil approached the palace gates, he heard the familiar noise of the motor engaging the chain as it pulled the heavy metal wings open. He marveled at the precision of the movement, the beauty of their design, ornately rendered in brass, the Sultan's family crest in bold colors and gold leaf. One day his son may create such a gate. He paused sweeping and stood back, anticipating the approach of the Rolls limousine which invariably followed.

The shiny vehicle stuck its nose through the gates, the flying goddess magnificently polished by the Sultan's garage man. His vehicle would never damage the air like the truck of ironmonger Merka! Fasil stood erect and adjusting his clothing, wanting to present his best self as the car passed by. He never knew if the Sultan himself might be inside behind the tinted windows.

The black Rolls Royce exited halfway through the gates. Then stopped. For a long moment there was no movement. Then a door opened and the Sultan's bodyguard stepped out. He was a huge man, long mustache, dark piercing eyes beneath a perfectly shaved head. His eyes rested upon Fasil as he closed the distance between them with three long strides.

"Are you Fasil Babba?"

"Yes. I am Fasil." Never before had he spoken to one so high. His legs began to tremble. He wondered what he had done.

"Come with me," the huge man said, motioning to the open car door.

Fasil looked around, not knowing where to place his broom.

"Leave it there," the guard spoke, his voice booming like a canon.

Fasil gently set his broom against the pushcart and brushed the specs of dust off his thick cotton kurta. He cautiously followed, but could not bring himself to step into the luxurious interior of the car.

The big man smiled. "I am Atar, the Sultan's manservant. Don't be afraid."

But Fasil was afraid as he stepped inside the Rolls Royce, smelled the soft plush leather of the seats, and heard the security boasted by the sound of the door closing, sealing him inside.

Atar nodded. The driver spun the car in a circle outside the gates and headed back toward the palace, looming large and formidable in the distance. They rode in silence, facing forward, no sounds except the majestic hum of the engine.

Without moving his head, Fasil swiveled his eyeballs to absorb everything sliding past him: the manicured gardens, the field of polo with riders in bright costumes, the beautiful women in gorgeous saris. Never before had Fasil been inside the palace gates. The rumors were exceeded by the grandeur glimpsed by his eyes.

What had he done to deserve such a tribute? His mind raced back. He had given his best for sixteen years, sweeping the streets of the palace to make them shine, to the best of his ability. Maybe he would receive some kind of bonus? Some kind of reward? Maybe the Great Distribution had finally come through and this was his day to receive his due? He smiled and allowed himself a moment to enjoy the promise about to be fulfilled.

But wait? What if it were not the Great Distribution, but something else? A cold sweat began to emanate on top of his nose where it always started when he was afraid. The ten thousand riyal note! It had been reported and now he was being taken in for questioning. That had to be it!

Fasil dared to swivel his head and look at the man next him. Hands big as pork loins could surely snap his neck easy as he could a sisal broom handle. Why else would he be transported in such luxury? To set him up. To lull him into a false sense of security. They would be able to tell immediately from the look in his eyes, the change in his breathing when they confronted him with the question. He was an honest man and could not conceal the truth.

But was he? Oh, why had he not presented the note when he found it? He would then have been revered as a truly honest man and maybe given a reward. Now his life was over. His family would be outcast. Atar's enormous bald head turned to face him and in his eyes Fasil saw nothing but doom.

He managed a weak smile and turned away quickly. His mind sped back again, combing memories for possibilities which could have led to his detection. Maybe Aisha had dropped a hint at the fountain, boasted of their bright future? Maybe she had told one of his sons who had confided in a jealous friend? Maybe someone had seen him after all pick up the note?

Or, maybe they did not know, and it was up to him to withstand the rigors of questioning. Fasil calmed his breathing and steeled himself for what lay ahead, as the Rolls Royce stopped in front of palace.

*   *   *

Fasil sat on a blue velvet settee in the largest room he had ever seen. He guessed the walls were alabaster and the floor veined marble from an Italian quarry he had read about once in a book. Sides of the towering windows were inlaid with mosaics depicting the history of the ruling family, and brocade cushions allowed seated comfort on the sills.

Lighting in the recessed ceiling illuminated a mural, similar to what Fasil had seen in a photo of the Sistine Chapel, although it featured the royal family. The room was divided from other rooms by open pillars, each room arranged in seating areas with upholstered chairs and couches. He guessed a hundred people could fit easily into the room without touching one another.

"Fasil Babba?" a recognizable voice said, approaching.

He turned toward the voice. It was his doctor. He stood up.

"Dr. Hashid?" Fasil exclaimed, his thoughts jetting a million miles away from the lost riyal note. Had something happened to Aisha? One of his sons? "What is the matter?"

Dr. Hashid put his hand gently on Fasil's shoulder. "Do not be concerned."

"Is it Aisha? Is she pregnant again!"

"No no no," Hashid smiled. "You have enough sons. For both of us!"

"What then?" Fasil was puzzled.

Dr. Hashid motioned and they sat on the settee.

"Someone wants to talk to you. He will be here in a moment. Before you respond, I want you to listen to everything he has to say."

"But… am I…"

"Shush," his physician said. "I can tell you no more."

They remained seated in the longest silence of Fasil's life. People came and went out of the rooms. Some would glance in his direction, then look away. Some would smile. Others would not. Finally, footsteps on the marble floor grew louder as an elegant thin man of regal bearing approached. His aquiline face might belong to a prince or a grand inquisitor. Dr. Hashid stood and Fasil hopped up after him.

"I am Rasha Lumpour," the man said. "I represent the Sultan in all matters personal and confidential."

"Yes, I have it," Fasil wanted to blurt out, as he jumped to his feet. "I have the ten thousand riyal note. I did not spend it, but kept it safe."

But he did not speak, he held himself back as his

doctor had advised. Instead, he simply smiled and nodded.

"Please, let us sit down." Rasha sat on the grand hassock across from the blue velvet settee. "Dr. Hashid has told us all about you. You are a man dedicated to serving the Sultan, and have been a loyal employee for many years. The Sultan wishes me to convey how grateful he is for the condition of the streets around the palace."

Fasil could barely conceal his sigh of relief. "It is my work," he said.

"And a fine job you do," Rasha added. "Dr. Hashid has also told us of your family and their history. Particularly their medical history. Your grandmother was once the oldest woman in the city, is that correct?"

"Yes. Antoowa Jagil. There is a plaque by the fountain in the square which bears her name."

"And you, Fasil. Strong as a water buffalo! Sweeping streets is the ultimate aerobic exercise, is it not?"

"Ah-ro-bik? I am not familiar with that term," Fasil confessed.

"It's a method of maintaining good health, characterized by low cholesterol and triglycerides, a strong even heartbeat and open arteries."

"Oh."

"Dr. Hashid says you have a strong heart, the strongest one he has ever seen."

Fasil looked at Dr. Hashid who replied. "That is correct."

"Your exercise and plain diet, though unglamorous,

is perfect for maintaining a healthy body, and a healthy heart."

Fasil was beginning to wonder what was going on. No mention of the note. The man was talking to him like a friend about the food and work of a peasant. Then there was a pause of silence while the men just looked at one another.

Finally, Fasil spoke: "Is this about the Great Disbursement?"

Rasha smiled at Hashid. "It's better than that. But first, there is someone who would like to meet you."

The Sultan had been standing, unnoticed, off to the side under a Corinthian column draped in orchid vines. He plucked a purple flower and spun it in his fingertips as he approached. His dashiki was spun of the finest white silk with a high collar and sleeves banded in gold thread.

Fasil could not believe his eyes. He had only seen the Sultan in photos and on the television his brother had won in the lottery. He looked above the Sultan's perfect teeth, surrounded by his perfectly manicured goatee, into his eyes. They shone like polished onyx and seemed to hold all the answers to life's greatest mysteries.

Fasil was overcome with emotion, slipped out of his seat onto his knees. He bowed his head, just as the Sultan reached him.

Then the strangest thing happened. The Sultan got down on his knees in front of Fasil Babba and gently lifted his head by the chin.

"It is I who should be bowing to you," the Sultan said.

Fasil's eyes could not hold back the torrent of tears that burst forth. He covered his hands, at once astonished and ashamed. He felt a soft cloth being pressed into his hands. He took it and dried his eyes. Arms lifted him to his feet and when he recovered himself, he was sitting between Rasha and Dr. Hasid with the Sultan sitting across from him.

The Sultan smiled, bemused, twirling the orchid. He tilted his head and spoke frankly, as if to a friend, an equal.

"So, what do think of our palace?"

Fasil was dumbfounded. It was like a dream. He had no idea how to behave. Whatever gods there were seemed to be with him and he felt his spirit rise above fear into a kind of calm elation. When he spoke it was with the utmost confidence.

"The palace is magnificent."

"Yes it is," the Sultan continued. "It was built by the people for my great grandfather out of the love and honor they had for him. It is the finest edifice in our country."

"He must have been a great man," Fasil said, as if an angel had lifted the load of his concerns and given him the temperament of a saint.

"He was," the Sultan said causally. "Though not everyone thought so. Did you know there were over 47 attempts at his life?"

Fasil pursed up his chin as if he were a scholar, hearing for the first time a little known fact that had escaped his serious study. "I did not know that."

"Yes," the Sultan said. "Those so foolish quickly learned the errors of their ways by means most unpleasant."

Fasil's heart sank. He did know about the riyal note. What a clever man the Sultan was to toy with him like this. He was a mouse in the lair of a lion, soon to be a morsel bitten and discarded. Oh, lord or lords tell me this is a bad dream from which I will awaken!

"However," the Sultan continued. "This is not a matter for us to discuss." He paused, looked at each of the men in turn then set his eyes on Fasil. "How would you like to live here?"

Fasil gasped. He felt the blood drain from his face and rush toward his knees. Then he took a deep breath and gathered himself. Perhaps he had earned a special assignment!

"You wish me to sweep the floors in the palace?"

The Sultan smiled wryly, looked up at the ceiling and had a belly laugh that resounded off the walls. He stood up, took Fasil by the hand and said: "They will explain it to you. I hope you will accept." He then handed Fasil the purple orchid, turned gracefully and floated away.

Fasil starred in disbelief, watching as two dark-haired ladies in bright yellow saris came up to fill the Sultan's arms.

"So," Rasha said. "Would you like to see your quarters?"

The next hour or so Fasil was in a daze. He was led over the marble floors through many rooms filled with people who seemed to have nothing to do but stand around and look beautiful. They took him outside to glimpse the clipped hedges of the conundrum and past the wading pools filled with lily pads and lotus flowers big as dinner plates. Finally, they arrived at a bungalow set at the far end of the palace near the garage housing the Sultan's collection of amazing automobiles.

"This is it," Rasha said, opening large double French doors into a room overlooking a courtyard. The apartment had six bedrooms and six bathrooms, each one decorated in a different color. There was a spacious open kitchen with modern appliances, a large living room and a separate study with a big screen TV and shelves of books running floor to ceiling.

Fasil pinched himself until the pain was so severe he knew he was not dreaming.

"May I use the bathroom?"

"Of course, Fasil. Make yourself at home."

The fixtures were new and sparkling clean. He could imagine how Aisha and his sons would marvel at these surroundings. One day a lowly street sweeper, the next day the Sultan's private sweeper of the palace! Such rewards were promised to those with a pure heart, and for once all doubt was removed from Fasil's sense of piety. He could not believe the power of the flush, the subsequent coolness of the water as he washed his hands, then dried them on a towel sweetened with jasmine.

When he returned to the living room, Rasha and Dr. Hashid looked up at him, their faces lined with serious import.

"Sit with us, Fasil," Dr. Hashid said.

Fasil sank into the plush cushions of the leather armchair. "I'm listening," he said. Whatever was going to happen next was his destiny.

Dr. Hashid spoke first. "The Sultan has a bad heart. He could die any day from a heart attack. Then again, he might live forty years and never have a problem. A lot of it depends on his diet, his exercise regimen, and curtailing his vices."

"The Sultan is a man with big appetites," Rasha broke in. "He likes to drive fast cars. His race horses win against the best in the world. He likes good food and drink. And he has an eye for the ladies."

Fasil shook his head. "What the Sultan does is his business. The Sultan wants me to work in the palace. I will be the best sweeper inside as I was on the outside."

Rasha sighed and exchanged a glance with Dr. Hashid.

"He wants your heart, Fasil," Dr. Hasid said. "Not now, not today, but sometime in the future."

"My heart?" Fasil did not understand.

"That's the deal," Rasha continued. "You and your family live here. All of your needs will be taken care of for the rest of your lives. Your children will receive the best education money can buy. They will be able to go as far as their talents will carry them. Your wife will be honored and respected. She will have the finest things money can buy. Your line will go on and be supported by the royal family."

"Live here? My family? In the palace?"

"Yes," Dr. Hashid interrupted. "You will live like a prince until the day you make the ultimate sacrifice."

Rasha started to pace and lit up a thin black Turkish cigarette ignited by a gold lighter from his vest pocket. "You will travel with the Sultan in his private plane. You will see things few ever get the chance to experience. Your life will be a magical dream."

Fasil felt like the wind had just been knocked out of him. His head spun in a hundred directions at once. Then he slumped back against the fine black leather of the Sultan's armchair and started to weep.

*   *   *

When Fasil entered the small mud hut of his domain, his eyes met those of his wife and his four sons. He had never seen such worry in their faces as they stood watching him approach. Aisha rushed into his arms.

"Are you all right, Fasil?" She felt to make sure his limbs were all there and not broken.

"Never better, my love," Fasil said with an uncharacteristic calmness. He had the answer to their prayers, hopes and dreams. But he knew he must reveal it slowly to prevent hysteria.

"Are you in trouble?" Her face revealed her concern about their secret cache.

"No trouble."

"We heard you were taken by the Sultan's guards," said Nedar, his oldest son, tall and lean like a willow, possessed of a nimble mind to match.

"Taken, no," his father said, enjoying his family's undivided attention. It had been a long time since he had them all together focused on one thing. "I was *invited* to the palace."

"The palace!" exclaimed Sansur, his middle son, whose broad smile and cheerful disposition could assuage an argument or seduce a young maiden with equal charm.

"You've been inside the palace?"

"Inside, outside, all through the palace and the gardens. A spectacular place indeed!"

His sons looked at one another. Langoon, the second brother, a cynical student with an acerbic wit, studied his father and bent close to smell his breath.

"No, I have not been into the honey wine, Langoon. Come, sit, and I will tell all of you what transpired on this miraculous day."

They sat and Fasil recalled his experience, remaining true to the circumstances, all but the last. When he finished, Aisha rose to make tea while his boys stared at him with profound respect. Finally, Mamoosh, the youngest son who spoke with a lisp, ventured to ask him what his job with the Sultan would be.

Fasil, not wanting to reveal the dangerous truth, said simply: "The Sultan has chosen me for a special assignment. My many years of hard work and dedicated service will be rewarded. And all of you will benefit along with me."

"What does that mean, dear?" Aisha said breathlessly, setting the chipped porcelain tea service down on the small wooden table.

"It means…" Fasil paused, grasped the teapot and began to pour a cup for each of them, handing one to Aisha first. "…that we all will be moving into the palace. The Sultan has given us a special bungalow with six bedrooms."

The cup fell from Aisha's hand. Langoon caught her limp body before her head reached the dirt floor.

*   *   *

Moving day. A shiny new truck stood outside Fasil's hut. The driver was at the tailgate as the family's meager possessions were passed to him by the four sons. Fasil and Aisha watched and chatted with the neighbors who observed the procession with amazement.

"What is it like?" Sasha, the fishmonger's wife, asked, her tight lips compressing hidden envy.

"As you might imagine," Fasil said, confidence building in his new role. "The palace is finest in the world, second only to the Taj Mahal."

"You have met the Sultan?" asked Benoth, who was up before dawn every day bringing fresh fruit into town from the orchards.

Fasil smiled. "Yes, I have met the Sultan. A wise and generous man. Youthful in appearance and temperate in all things."

His cadre of neighbors was too astonished to speak. Fasil added: "Except in matters of the heart. Then the Sultan is quite, how shall I say… adventurous."

Jaleela, the ripening daughter of Shanu Merka, the ironmonger, became flushed and started to swoon. Nedar, who had watched her develop since grade school, rushed to her side and steadied her with a hand wide and strong as a dinner skillet. She fell against him, her bright brown eyes rolling upward to meet his. Not good enough as the son of a street sweeper, Nedar now may have progressed out of her reach.

"May I visit you in the palace?" she asked.

Nedar's lips parted in an alluring smile. "We shall see what the future holds."

The other sons stood idle next to the truck, all the possessions loaded.

"Let us go," said the driver, a burly man with a full beard who carried a dagger inside his wide black belt.

Mamoosh assisted Aisha into the cab and the boys clambered aboard where they could. Fasil started to join his wife, when he suddenly remembered something and ran back into the hut. Everyone waited, the suspense thickening like lamb porridge over a wood stove. In a moment Fasil appeared with a mud brick.

Zubair, the landlord, who had just approached the commotion, came up to him, put his hand on the brick.

"I'll have that," he said.

"No," Fasil said, tucking the brick under his arm.

"The brick is part of your apartment, Zubair insisted. "I must then deduct its value from your deposit."

"Keep the *entire* deposit," Fasil stated boldly. "I don't need it."

"You don't need the deposit?" Zubair said, incredulous. "Who does not need their deposit?"

"Someone who is moving to the palace," Fasil said with finality.

"The palace?" Zubair exclaimed, his brow furled into rivulets like a spring field ready for planting. Then he broke out into wild laughter. "The palace! A street sweeper moving to the palace!" He slapped his knee. "You have finally gone mad, Fasil. All those strokes with the broom have swept away your mind."

"It's true," Shanu Merka, the ironmonger, said. "He is to be the Sultan's special assistant."

Zubair's mouth hung wide open, like a hippopot-
amus ready for a tooth cleaning. He raised his hand to
speak, but Fasil had already climbed aboard the truck,
now motoring away from the neighborhood to which he
would never return.

*   *   *

Living in the palace was not as easy as it might
have seemed. The transition was overwhelming to the
family of a lowly street sweeper who once had to watch
every riyal like it was their last.

First, there was the food. Everything they ever
imagined was available in whatever quantity they wanted. Roasted goat with rosemary, sliced thick with pink
centers nested in a bed of couscous, was Fasil's favorite.
Aisha preferred roasted chicken with tamarind and stewed
squash. Each of the four sons had their own favorite, from
squab to ocean perch to even eye of beef steak.

Before long, the new clothes they been given when
they entered the palace grew too tight and had to be exchanged. Their old clothes had been taken from them and
burned along with most all of their possessions which
never left the truck.

Only the one mud brick remained to remind them
of their past life outside the palace, the 10,000 riyal note
tucked inside. Fasil kept it on a shelf in his room, stating
to the housecleaners it was to remind him of his humble

origins so he could be eternally grateful. Thus it remained, hidden in plain sight.

During the day the boys attended classes, led by the best educators in the land. The three oldest boys, Nedar, Sansur and Langoon, were of preparatory age and were given math, science and technology courses requisite to becoming engineers. Mamoosh, the youngest, was assigned to a tutor, a linguistic expert, and within a month his lisp had all but disappeared.

Aisha was given a handmaiden to look after her clothing and physical person. The luxury of having someone dress and adorn her brought tears to her eyes as she bowed her head in shameful innocence. Finally, one day, when Aisha was finishing her bath, Mya Poura, the handmaiden, enquired as to her consternation.

"I do not feel worthy," she confessed.

"But why?" Mya asked.

"I have done nothing to deserve this treatment, this kindness," she said bashfully.

Mya wrapped a thick towel around her shoulders and continued to rub dry her hair. "What did the Sultan do to deserve his station in life?" she asked.

After a pause, Aisha said: "He is of the royal family."

"Right," Mya said, drawing a silver comb through Aisha's long black hair. "He was born into it. He was lucky."

Aisha was astonished. "He was very lucky."

"Yes," Mya continued. "We are lucky to be here to share in his luck."

"I guess we are," Aisha said, awakened from guilt into cheerfulness.

"Right. So, we enjoy it. As long as it lasts." Mya finished combing and began to braid.

"As long as it lasts," Aisha repeated, her eyebrows curled like caterpillars deciding where to place their cocoons.

"Life doesn't go on forever," Mya said. "One day we must meet our maker."

"Yes. It is inevitable."

Mya did not explore the topic further. Did not reveal that she knew about what Fasil had promised in exchange for his family's future.

"There you are," Mya said, placing a silver clasp at the end of the braid that hung thick as an eel's tail. She held a mirror for Aisha to see.

"Beautiful," proclaimed Aisha. "How can I ever thank you for what you do for me every day."

"You could offer me a cup of jasmine tea," Mya said, picking up her tools and stowing them neatly in the scrimshaw hamper carved from the tusk of an Asian elephant.

*   *   *

Since moving to the palace, Fasil felt like he had stepped inside a whirlwind. Every moment of every day was spent in preparation for serving as the Sultan's special assistant. His real purpose was supposed to be a carefully guarded secret, but over time it began to leak out. There were furtive whispers among the palace staff every time Fasil rounded a corner or stepped into a limousine with the Sultan.

Whenever the Sultan left town, Fasil went with him, especially on his private Boeing 777. Fasil trembled as the Rolls Royce carried him to the runaway, as he climbed the stairs leading to the luxurious cabin.

"Never in my imagination have I seen such a plane," Fasil said to Rasha who also accompanied the Sultan everywhere.

"Take your time and explore," Rasha said. "This plane is remarkable in many ways."

Fasil entered the spacious main cabin with leather couches and plush chairs that tilted horizontal for sleeping. The plane had extra-large windows for viewing the world from 40,000 feet. He saw flashes of red and blue light coming from the walls and moved closer, finding rubies and blue sapphires glued in random patterns mixed with diamonds and emeralds.

"The stones alone are a sultan's fortune."

"Yes, Fasil. They are the pleasure of his ladies."

Fasil saw a burned out place in the carpet near the partition wall. "Oh no, what happened here?" Then he saw the charcoal brazier and could smell the odor of roasted goat.

To the side was a stainless steel door with a window. Fasil peered in but it was dark and nothing could be seen.

"Let me show you," Rasha said, moving past Fasil and unlocking door. He flicked on a light and the realities of what Fasil had agreed to do shot through him like a lightning bolt.

In the center of the room under the large light was a padded table where a man would lie to have an operation. Another similar table was bolted to the floor next to it where the donor would perform his final act of service. The back wall was replete with state-of-the-art machines to measure oxygen flow, brain waves and heart rate.

"Yes, Fasil. The Sultan must be prepared wherever he travels."

"I see," Fasil said bravely. "There are worse places to die than inside a luxurious airplane."

Rasha laughed. "Your positive attitude is admirable."

Others began to board the plane – the flight attendants, several of the Sultan's mistresses, Dr. Rashid. The pilots had begun their preflight routine and the sound of engines warming up added a soothing undertone to the atmosphere.

Fasil glanced out the window as the Sultan's majestic Bentley pulled up to the gangway. Atar got out from behind the wheel, opened the rear door. The Sultan climbed the stairs as Atar parked the car in the hangar.

Fasil's heart beat wildly. What was he supposed to do? Where would he sit?

"Sit here," Rasha said. "His majesty wants to talk with you."

Fasil trembled as he slid into the seat facing the oversized leather chair next to a wall encrusted with jewels. The entourage found seats near the back of the plane.

"Fasil," the Sultan said warmly, plopping down across from him. "How is your heart today?" He then bellowed a laugh that infected the cabin.

"My heart is fine," Fasil said, looking around at the smiling faces of everyone.

"They all love you, Fasil. Do not be afraid. Have you ever been to the Maldives?"

"Maldives?"

"Of course not. It is a fabulous spot. An island surrounded by crystal blue waters with cottages built on stilts."

A gorgeous dark-haired flight attendant arrived with two flutes of champagne on a silver tray. When she leaned over to offer them to the Sultan, her cleavage caused Fasil to blush and look away.

"Thank you, my dear." The Sultan took the two glasses, handed one to Fasil and held his up for a toast. "To a long life."

Fasil had never had champagne before, but managed to clink the Sultan's glass. He found the bubbles strangely refreshing.

"So, how are you adjusting to the splendid existence?"

"I live in a constant state of wonder and amazement," Fasil said.

"Haha. That's good. Wouldn't want you to become complacent." He held out his empty glass and it was immediately refilled. "One more for you too."

Fasil held up his glass and the golden liquid flowed from the mouth of the green bottle.

"Thank you."

"My pleasure," said the girl with the most perfect figure Fasil had ever seen. "Better buckle up."

She showed him how to fasten his seat belt as the engines began to pull the jet away from the hanger. He then began to regale him with stories of his life and exploits around the world until Fasil, weary from the excitement and champagne, fell asleep.

The Sultan smiled, kissed his new friend on the forehead and retired to the spacious cabin in the back where three playmates were waiting to exercise his appetites.

*   *   *

The "splendid existence," as the Sultan was fond of calling life for those who lived with him in the palace, was beginning to cause problems for Fasil's offspring. When one is poor, daily survival keeps one sharp and humble.

When one suddenly has all the constraints of poverty removed and becomes elevated not by merit but by luck, a void develops in the progressive competence of one's self worth. A veneer of lassitude clouds the perceptions and disconnects one from visceral survival impulses. Even though Fasil's wife and sons were as honest and honorable as they could be, the exigencies of their new environment gave them a prestige that was hard not to exploit.

One day Nedar arranged for a chauffeur to drive him to his old neighborhood. Through the window of the Rolls Royce the squalor of his former dwelling was astonishing. He could not imagine living in such a place though he had for most of his life. Even more astounding were his memories of being happy in such a place. His family was loving and close and they found ways to laugh at the smallest gifts and be grateful. Now he felt spoiled by luxury and ashamed he had such a negative reaction to his life as it once had been.

"Nedar," cried a voice from the street. "Is that you, Nedar?"

He rolled down the window as this beautiful girl came up to the car. He told his driver to pull over and stop.

It was Jaleela, daughter of Shanu Merka, the ironmonger, all grown up.

"Jaleela?"

"Yes, Nedar." She came to the window and leaned in. She smelled wonderful and fresh. Her smile was wide and sincere. Her dark almond eyes were swallowing him whole. His youthful infatuation rose to the forefront of his senses.

"Would you like to take a ride?"

"I don't know. Where would we go?"

"We can go anywhere."

"I would like to go to the metro and get an ice cream."

"We can do that." He opened the door for her and she slid in next to him in the back seat.

"Can we put the top down?" Nedar asked and the driver complied.

"The metro sir?"

"Please."

The big car pulled away and started to veer toward the highway.

"I'd like to drive this way," Jaleela pointed ahead where their route would take them past the shops and all the people they knew.

"Sir?" the driver exchanged a glance with Nedar in the rear view mirror.

"Yes, do as she suggests."

Jaleela giggled and slid next to Nedar and took his hand so everyone could see them. She smiled and raised her chin and sniffed the air like it was filled with the fragrance of gardenias.

*   *   *

The season of feasts was upon them. Those in the palace were expected to attend many functions looking their best. Aisha was getting her nails done.

"I need to ask you something, Mya."

"Anything, my dear." The two of them had become best friends with only one piece of information yet to be discussed.

"When I walk through the palace and on the grounds, everyone is so nice."

"Everyone is nice to everyone here."

"More than nice, I mean. Too nice."

"You have a problem with that?" Mya smiled. "Other hand."

Aisha lifted her other hand out of the bowl of warm lemon water. Mya dried it with a towel and began to address her nails like a sculptor.

"I'm a good person, but something else is going on and everyone seems to know what it is but me."

Mya paused and took a deep breath. "I knew this day would come."

"You must tell me."

Mya held her hand tenderly, looked lovingly into her eyes. "It's Fasil."

"Is something wrong?" Aisha's reaction was to pull her hand away, but Mya held it.

"I will tell you. But you must promise not to change anything you are doing."

"What would I change?"

"You must not change the way you behave to Fasil, your family or anyone in the palace."

"Why would I do that?"

"Believe me, this is serious."

"Did Fasil do something wrong?"

"No, my dear. Fasil is a hero to everyone in the palace."

"A hero?" Aisha started to relax.

And then Mya explained how Fasil had agreed to donate his heart should the Sultan ever need it in exchange for the blessings provided to his family.

*   *   *

Fasil was buttoning his formal tunic when Aisha burst into the room. He smiled into the mirror until he saw tears streaming down her face. He turned and took her into his arms.

"How could you, Fasil?" She was limp as a willow, shivering.

"What is it, my love?" Fasil's mind raced back through his memory for an incident responsible for such a reaction. There was the lady, one of the Sultan's mistresses, who had come to him in the night at the bungalow in the Maldives.

"I didn't do anything with her, I swear."

"What?" Aisha pulled away and looked him in the eyes.

"I told her about you and made her go away."

"What are you talking about?"

"What?" Fasil realized this was not the object of her concern and blushed foolishly.

"Your heart, Fasil. For the Sultan."

Fasil breathed a sigh of relief. "Oh that."

"Oh that!" She began to hammer his chest with her fists. "How could you?"

He caught her hands and pulled her gently to sit down with him on the bed.

"For you," he said. "And the children."

"You will not be there, Fasil. Where will the children and I be then?"

"You will be taken care of for the rest of your life. Our children are getting the best education, will have good jobs and maintain the lifestyle. This is a good thing. Something I never could have provided on a street sweeper's salary."

"But you will be dead," she cried.

"Yes, my love. Every man dies, but few really live. The trade is worth it. I have come to terms with it and now you must."

Her tears had turned to sniffles and he handed her a tissue.

"I would rather live with you in that hut than lose you."

"Don't be foolish. We have lived more in the last two years than we would have lived in a hundred lifetimes at our former level. Besides, the Sultan is healthy as a horse. He eats and drinks like a king and woman flow in and out of his bedroom."

Aisha's expression changed. She furled her brow as her eyes bore into him. "What lady in the Maldives?"

Fasil gasped and was preparing to fend off the grilling when there was a knock at the door.

"You must come quickly," Rasha said. "There is a man at the gate with his daughter and he is very angry."

He led them through the palace to where a car was waiting. Fasil and Aisha road anxiously in the back wondering what the problem could be.

Fasil recognized them first. "It is Shanu Merka, the ironmonger."

"With his daughter."

"Look what your son has done" Shanu said, pointing to Jaleela's swollen belly.

"Which son?"

"Nedar, the philanderer."

"Be careful with your language, Shanu," Fasil warned.

"When did this happen?" Aisha asked.

"Three months ago. Nedar drove into town in a big car and took Jaleela to get ice cream."

"Ice cream?"

"Everyone saw them," Shanu continued. "Driving in the back of that convertible like little love birds."

"Is that right, dear?" Aisha asked.

"Tell them," Shanu told his daughter.

Jaleela looked at them with sad accusing eyes. "We had ice cream. And then we drove around a while out by the reservoir. Nedar had a blanket and we took a walk."

"They took more than a walk," Shanu said.

Aisha looked at Fasil. "Did Nadar ever say anything to you about this?"

"No, nothing."

"Now Jaleela is pregnant," Shanu groaned. "I am disgraced. Our family is disgraced."

Rasha had been listening in the background and stepped forward. "Not to worry. I can arrange to have this taken care of."

"Taken care of?" Shanu looked as his daughter. She shook her head. "No. Jaleela is going to have his baby. They must be married immediately."

"Married?" Fasil quizzed.

"Yes," Shanu insisted. "It is the only solution. To save face."

"I think we need to bring Nedar into the conversation."

Shanu smiled ingratiatingly. "Fasil, we have been friends what, forty-five years? We were boys together. Grew up together. It makes sensed that Nedar marries from his own kind, his own neighborhood."

"I don't know." Fasil and Aisha shared a glance.

"Look at Jaleela, how pretty she is. Every boy in town is after her. But she only has eyes for your Nedar."

He nudged her.

"I love Nedar," she said. "And he loves me. Our baby is the proof."

"If I may intrude," Rasha said taking control of the situation. "We should bring this lovely young lady to see Dr. Hashid. She deserves the best of care."

"Yes yes, the best of care for Jaleela," Shanu added, looking over their heads towards the palace. He was starting to sweat and did not notice his tongue had appeared and was licking his lips.

"Give me your address and we will send a car for her tomorrow."

"Why not today? We are here today."

"Dr. Hashid is busy today. Tomorrow. Shall we say ten o'clock?"

Shanu and Jaleela looked at one another and found agreement.

"Ten o'clock then." Shanu offered his hand to Rasha who ignored it, but he moved it swiftly toward Fasil.

"Good to see you my old friend."

Fasil accepted his hand. "If only circumstances were less… surprising."

They watched the ironmonger and his daughter walk back to their car which sputtered when the engine started, discharging a cloud of oil and antifreeze.

"This kind of thing has happened before," Rasha told them as they got back into the Rolls.

"If Nedar is responsible it is only right that he mar-ry her."

"Dr. Hashid will find that out tomorrow with a DNA test."

Aisha nodded silently, her mind trying to process her husband as a heart donor and now her son as a father. The gods are working overtime.

The next day the DNA test came back negative. Nedar was not the father. He received a stern warning from his father and counseling from Rasha about the perils of being a person of means and associating with those who want what you have and will do anything to get it.

Shanu and Jaleela were provided with free medical care and a generous one-time stipend with the condition they never bother Nedar or his family again.

*   *   *

A year went by. Then two. Three. Then one night about 2 a.m. they came to rouse Fasil from his sleep.

"The Sultan needs you."

Fasil rose quietly, knowing this day would come. He got dressed, kissed his wife lightly on the forehead so as not to wake her and went with Rasha. Though he had seen the compact traveling facility on the Sultan's jet, he had never been to the world-class operating theater deep within the palace.

His legs started to shake when he was greeted by the bright lights and team of medical professionals dressed in turquoise scrubs. The room was large and spacious with every imaginable piece of medical diagnostic and surgical equipment requisite to maintaining the life of the patient before, during and after surgery.

The Sultan was lying on a padded gurney, his legs flat and his torso elevated. Wires ran from his barrel chest to machines where his heartbeat was registered by bouncing lines. He was wide awake and greeted Fasil warmly.

"Come in my loyal friend."

Fasil entered slowly in a daze, his mind attempting to grasp what his eyes and ears were telling him.

Dr. Hashid at once put his concerns to rest. "His majesty has had a mild heart attack but is stable now."

"Does that mean…"

"Yes, Fasil, Everything is fine. You may return to your bungalow."

Fasil raised and steepled his hands before his chest and bowed over them as Rasha took him by the arm and led him away.

Lights were on and his wife and sons were awake, huddled together on Aisha's bed. She gasped when he entered as if seeing a ghost.

"Fasil!"

He went to her and took her in his arms and let her cry herself out as he answered his sons' questions. "It is not my time," he said. "Maybe one day, but not today."

"Allah be praised."

"And peace be upon you."

The family spent the day together, grateful for their lives and the many blessings Fasil had brought to them.

*   *   *

The years went by. Nedar had graduated university with a degree in engineering and was working for an American company in the biotech department while writing his doctoral dissertation. Sansur had opted for a career in the arts and was assistant curator at the palace museum, his degree in art history a good platform for assessing works for purchase. Langoon had decided to become a doctor and was in his second year of medical school. Mamoosh was on the debate team in his senior year at high school, having turned his speech impediment into the powerful voice of an orator.

Aisha worked part time as a volunteer to assist poor people of the kingdom enlist for social services. Keeping busy was the best way to soften the omnipresent possibility Fasil could be sacrificed at any moment. It was like living near a volcano whose eruption was forecast in the foreseeable future.

Fasil continued to remain within easy reach of the Sultan, his doctors and the closest operating theater. When the Sultan left the city for business or pleasure, Fasil accompanied him on his jet, sitting in the special seat near the back reserved for him. Fasil had become accustomed to travel and became adept at using the recording features on his smart phone to capture sights and sounds from all the incredible places in the world he had visited. He shared these with his family after every trip.

"Do you see now why I am the Sultan's donor?" Fasil said after a round of images was shared with his family after dinner. "How else could I have experienced all the wonderful places and things?"

"Or how else could we have afforded our education and attained careers beyond our dreams?" Nadar added.

"You have truly blessed us, Fasil," Aisha said.

"Yes father."

"You are our hero."

"You all are my heroes," Fasil smiled. "You have blossomed like desert flowers graced with spring rains."

The scare of that night when Fasil was called still lingered in their minds. But over time his death became accepted as inevitable. Grief handled by small doses in advance lessens its impact.

"Every day of life is a day to be celebrated," the youngest son spoke up.

"You are wise beyond your years, Mamoosh." Fasil then opened his arms and his sons moved into them like baby owls under their father's wings.

Life has its ironies, and just at the moment of greatest closeness, the family heard a knock at the door. Somehow they knew this was the time.

Rasha stood there, his face grave.

His boys fell away and Aisha rushed into Fasil's

arms. She hugged him like a palm tree in a hurricane and started to weep.

"Tears of joy, my love," Fasil stroked her hair. "How lucky we are to have had something so hard to let go of."

"We must go, Fasil," Rasha urged.

Fasil kissed Aisha for the last time, nodded to his sons and they pulled her away and gave her comfort.

The walk through the palace to the operating theater was the longest walk of Fasil's life. Even the half day it took to sweep the front section of the palace seemed shorter.

The operating room was full of turquoise scrubs and covered mouths. Everyone was busy in their preparations.

"In here."

Fasil was escorted behind a curtain. He was assisted out of his clothes, sprayed with an antiseptic mist and wiped down. A turquoise scrub was placed around him with a tie at the neck. It opened in the front.

The padded table next to the open table where the Sultan would receive his heart was prepared for Fasil to lie down. Straps went around his ankles and his arms were brought out and strapped down in the position of a cross.

"You will feel a little prick and then nothing," the anesthetist said, inserting a needle in a forearm vein.

"Thank you for your service," Dr. Hashid's voice was recognizable behind the mask.

"It is my pleasure," Fasil said before the drugs interrupted his prayers and obliterated his conscious mind.

*   *   *

Fasil woke up in a cheerful white room illuminated by sunlight streaming through a window. He was in a soft bed with clean sheets. The air smelled sweet like jasmine and flowers were set everywhere in colored vases. Faint music emanated from everywhere.

"I must be in heaven," Fasil whispered to himself, wondering if his ears could hear his voice.

He wiggled his fingers and found his arms were at his sides. He pulled them over his thighs and flexed the place in his arms where the needles had been inserted. His breathing quickened as he raised his hands to feel the wound in his chest. It would be long ridge running from the top of his sternum to his diaphragm.

Nothing.

No ridge.

No stitches.

His chest was smooth as it was when he entered the operating room.

What was going on?

Fasil tried to sit up but felt a sharp pain in his abdomen and lay back down. He lowered his hands to the spot and found a small bandage taped over a wound.

The door opened and Dr. Hashid entered, his face a

mixture of joy and sorrow.

"How are you feeling?"

"I don't know," Fasil said. "My heart is beating in my chest but I have a wound in my lower abdomen."

"The Sultan is dead, Fasil."

"What?"

"He crashed his Ferrari and there was no way to save him in time."

"But… my wound."

"His mistress was also injured, but not as bad. She was thrown from the car and punctured a kidney."

Dr. Hashid allowed a moment for his words to sink in.

"The Sultan's mistress has my kidney?"

"Yes."

"The Sultan didn't need my heart?"

"His head went through the windshield. He had too much brain damage to survive. Your debt has been paid in full."

Fasil laughed quietly to himself as Dr. Hashid left the room. Then he broke down and wept tears of joy.

*　　*　　*

Fasil moved his family out of the palace into a nice home provided for him on the coast. All bills were paid. In his will the Sultan left instructions for their every need to be taken care of as long as they lived. Funds were also put in trust to ensure Fasil's children's children would receive the same treatment. The house was put in their name and was a valuable family asset, never to be sold, only transferable to family members.

Aisha was excited and grateful to have Fasil home, his obligation removed forever. They would walk on the beach, find shells, swim in the ocean and celebrate each glorious sunset. Fasil found volunteer work and Aisha maintained her position helping the underprivileged. The boys continued with their work and their studies, coming by every weekend for a family dinner.

"We are truly blessed," was a phrase often uttered by everyone in Fasil's family.

One morning, Fasil noticed a young man sweeping the street in front of his house. The next morning he was there again.

And the next.

Fasil observed through the window his strokes with the broom and shook his head. He opened the door and walked out in the street.

"Excuse me."

"Yes sir."

Fasil stuck out his hand and the boy gave him the broom.

"I have been watching you. You waste too many strokes. You need to sweep this way and then this way."

Fasil demonstrated the technique he had developed during the many years sweeping the front of the palace.

"How do you know this?" the boy asked.

"Try it." Fasil handed the broom back.

The boy mimicked Fasil's strokes and looked up with appreciation.

"Do it like that and you will save ten minutes every hour."

"Then I will become a great street sweeper," the boy said. "But I will never have a fine house like you."

"If you work hard and stay an honest man, the gods will bless you." Fasil winked at the boy and went back into his house

"Thank you." the boy called after him.

The next morning Fasil watched as the boy employed the strokes he had demonstrated, finishing his work in record time. He stood back in the shadows as the boy lingered in front of Fasil's house, hoping his teacher would again appear.

That night, when the town slept, Fasil rose before the first bird. He took the mud brick down from the bookcase, carried it to the sink and broke it open. He pulled out the 10,000 riyal note, dusted it off and tucked it inside an old sock.

Fasil crept out the front door just as the sun was beginning to enliven the horizon. He looked around, then walked out to the curb and dropped the sock in the gutter where the young street sweeper would find it.

ACKNOWLEDGEMENTS

Special thanks to all the people I have known whose lives have inspired these stories, all or in part. Without other people there would be no stories except for one man alone in the wilderness (unless you are Jack London!).

My appreciation to my fellow scribes in the Eagle Creek writer's group in Lexington who have listened to some of these stories read aloud and made comments. My stories are stronger and clearer thanks to you.

And to Jennifer Barricklow for her excellent proofreading. She caught many more errors than my tired old eyes could percieve.

THE AUTHOR

Dax Xenos is the pen name of the author who has made a career creating psychological and criminal justice-related educational documentaries seen by millions of people around the world in colleges, universities, institutions and government, including: *American Law: How It Works; Civil Court Process and Procedure; Cognitive Psychology; Criminal Court Process and Procedure; Culture Identity Behavior; Employee Theft; History of of World Criminal Justice; How to Tell if Someone Is Lying; Identifying the Violet At-Risk Student; Interpreting Nonverbal Communication; Loan Fraud; Money Laundering; Psychology of Criminal Behavior; Psychology, Criminality & Incarceration in America; Psychometrics I: Personality & Forensic Assessment; Psychometrics II: Intelligence & Ability Assessment; Religion Politics and Law; Robbery: The Aftermath; Teen Violence; Terrorism: Weapon of Fear; The Belli Tapes: Winning At Trial; The Extortion Set; The History of Sociology, and many others.*

He holds a PhD in psychology and was a licensed general contractor in Florida. He learned about incarceration first-hand in a Texas prison where, as an inmate, he worked in the new construction office before becoming editor of the prison newspaper. His many publications and awards include a PEN fiction award for his short story, "Death of a Duke."

www.daxxenosbooks.com

www.ingramcontent.com/pod-product-compliance
Lightning Source LLC
Chambersburg PA
CBHW051242270626
47162CB00001BA/253